**Her brain**

Somehow her feet wouldn't budge, trapped in the incredible presence that was Ty Hawthorne. The sun-kissed complexion, the short dirty blonde hair, a perpetual five o'clock shadow that framed his chiseled smile. No picture in a magazine did justice to the real thing, and his proximity crippled her best intentions. Finally she managed to step back, picking up her jacket and purse from the coffee table.

"Don't leave."

"Get out of my way."

"Gracie, please." He jumped into her path, his rippled bare chest peeking out at eye level from under his black leather jacket. "Please, not like this."

He touched her face. He traced the line of her jaw. Strong but gentle. Her skin tingled like it had a memory all its own. "I really have to get home," she stammered, hating the obvious tremble in her voice. "I have a million things to do."

"Look, I'm sorry for being late, and for how I look. Manny's finding me a shirt."

"Who's Manny?"

"He's my assistant."

"Oh."

"I know you were counting on me, and I should have been here. I let you down and I'm sorry." He ran his fingers through her hair. Her breath hitched in response. His words were exactly what she wanted to hear.

Five years too late.

# Take Two

by

Danielle Bronson

This is a work of fiction. Names, characters, places, and incidents are either the product of the author's imagination or are used fictitiously, and any resemblance to actual persons living or dead, business establishments, events, or locales, is entirely coincidental.

**Take Two**


Contact Information: info@thewildrosepress.com

Cover Art by *Kim Mendoza*

The Wild Rose Press
PO Box 706
Adams Basin, NY 14410-0706
Visit us at www.thewildrosepress.com

Publishing History
First Champagne Rose Edition, 2009
Print ISBN 1-60154-449-9

Published in the United States of America

## Dedication

To Kara: no one watches TV like we do!

## Chapter One

Blood. So much blood.

Fog swirled like an angry storm in front of Ty's eyes, stinging his throat and filling his chest. A long corridor stretched out in front of him but he couldn't see the walls. Blood dripped from his fingers.

Her blood.

"Grace. I'm here! Just hold on, I'm coming!"

Panic distorted his vision. His instinct propelled him; like running through water, his legs couldn't keep up.

"Grace! Grace, answer me. Where are you?"

Finally, the fog thinned. It swirled and molded. He made out a figure in the distance. An angel? A ghost? He blinked once, twice.

Then he saw her.

And the baby in her arms.

Her face was expressionless and pale as her gown. Her long red hair fell in breast length tangles. Her sea green eyes stared blankly through him.

"I'm here now," he whispered. "It's okay. Let me have the baby."

When she took a step forward, a staircase appeared. Steep and infinite, and somehow he knew what waited at the bottom. Her foot emerged from under her gown and hovered over the top step.

"Grace, no!"

The child fussed in her grip. Little fingers, little toes swam in the fabric. He moved toward her, one hand outstretched, the other with his fingers curled in invitation. She didn't take it. Instead she stepped back and fell, fading into the billowing fog.

"Grace! Grace!"

****

Ty Hawthorne bolted straight up, knocking his pillows from the bed. The sheets stuck to him like cellophane, and his body quaked with chills. Wide-awake now, but he still saw her. Smelled her scent of spring and spice and felt her skin on the pads of his fingers. This time he had almost reached her. Almost saw his child's face.

Almost.

The first time it happened, he thought he'd died. It was a strangely satisfying feeling to know he got exactly what he deserved. Unfortunately, he still existed. Even his dreams didn't spare him torment.

The white waves of the textured ceiling taunted his eyes, and the space around him, that had come to a stop, now spun like a carnival ride. A nightmare was one thing, but the added bonus of a killer hangover struck a nasty one-two punch.

Just another wild night in the Big Apple.

Or was it Toronto? Definitely not Chicago.

He could remember pages of script in one pass, but his location slipped his mind. He sat up, and his stomach protested the sudden move. The curtains, mercifully drawn tight, let in just enough light to show that last night had been eventful. The room looked like it awaited a claims adjuster. Broken wineglasses on the floor, boxers hanging on a lampshade, a bra dangling from the bedpost. His insides lurched when he took a breath. Stale wine mixed with even staler sex.

"Well, well, well, so Ty Hawthorne is an early riser," a woman purred from somewhere under the sea of rumpled linens beside him. "I thought after last night you'd sleep in."

Wonderful. He wasn't alone.

"You a morning person, baby?" the voice asked. "'Cause I was just thinking how we could spend the time." Straw-blonde hair peeked out from the satin sheets, and her chipped, red nails clutched the pillow beside him. Her accent sounded Brooklyn. He must be in New York.

"I'm pretty wiped out." His words sounded as ragged as he felt. "I can see why. It looks like Beirut in here." He brushed an over-processed strand of hair from his mystery companion's raccoon eyes. "Did you sleep well?"

"Sure, what I got of it," she cooed. "Anybody else who flew in from Italy would have had jet lag. You've got pretty good stamina."

Italy! That was it. He remembered filming a movie in Milan and flying back to the States last night. Or was it the day before? Were they stewardesses? No, wait.

And then suddenly it didn't matter. He was distracted by a hand that snaked around his morning hard-on.

"You feel like one for the road?" she asked, running her fingers along the shaft.

Was he at the Waldorf? No, he always stayed at the Plaza when he was in New York. And he was with… what the hell was her name? Ann? Ali? One of those names, definitely started with an "A"?

With his free hand, he reached for the condom box from the nightstand beside him. When it fell to the floor, he broke the kiss and reached down to pick it up by the flap.

Empty.

"Hey, ah..." Ari? Alice? Shit, what was it? "Honey, it looks like we're out of luck." He held up the shredded box. "All gone."

"Well, we certainly were ambitious last night, weren't we?"

He glanced down at the three wrappers on the floor beside him. "Looks that way."

"Well, I'm on the pill. And I'm clean."

He let his eyes wander over her. He hated to assume the worst of every woman he brought to bed, but, unfortunately, it came with the territory. Never mind the STDs. He probably deserved a horribly painful disease that rotted his cock. But women saw dollar signs when it came to came to prospective Baby Daddies like him. Not that he cared about the money. It was more about sparing a child the torment of having him as a father. So he did what he always did when this plot-point arose. He smiled, lowered his voice to the soft gravelly one he used in his love scenes and said, "Honey, I'm not worried about me, I'm worried about you. I've been on location in pretty remote places these past few months. Drinking bad water, eating weird food. Who knows what's in me. I'd hate to pass it on to you."

He snuggled in close, caressing her cheek. He waited a beat, then another for drama's sake, than gave her one last kiss.

She looked up at him with swooning eyes, her fingers winding in his hair. "You know, I don't care what those tabloids or that crazy ex-wife of yours says. You're a real gentleman, Ty."

Yeah, right. If he was truly a gentleman, he would have at least remembered the poor girl's name.

"How about a bath?" she asked, with her tongue in his ear. "I can run you one."

Amy? Andrea? "Sounds good, honey. I'll be there in a minute."

He admired her honey-tan profile as she walked past him to the bathroom. Other than the boobs, it was obvious she had worked hard for her body. Toned, tight, petite. Perfect by any man's assessment. Except for Ty's. He'd had perfect, and Angie wasn't it.

Angie!

When she closed the door, he reached for the

remote on the bedside table and turned the TV on to the entertainment news network. His pathetic, but necessary, morning ritual. The pretty talking head usually had more of a clue about his exploits than he did, and like anybody else, he liked to keep up to date.

Sure enough, lead story. He pushed the "up" arrow on the volume control.

The creak of the bathroom door alerted him to Angie's return. Still naked, she sauntered past him, then curled up beside him like a kitten. "You ready, baby? You don't want the water to get cold."

He nodded as if he heard her. Her chin rested on his shoulder, her fingers traced the outline of his tattoo on his left bicep.

"Whatcha watching?"

"Entertainment news," he said. "I just wanted to hear what they're saying."

"Oh, I bet they're talking about *Undercover Heat* again. It's probably not big news in Italy, but everyone here has been talking about the DVD release."

He shook his head. "I can't understand why the world is still so into a TV show that's been off the air for five years."

"Are you kidding? That had to be the most addicting show of all time. You and that girl were so good together. What do they call that?"

"Chemistry," he said.

"Yeah, I remember. Jax Sinclair and Lexie Love. Two secret agents hopelessly in love with each other. Pretty hot for network TV." She giggled as her hands wandered south. "When does the DVD come out?"

"In a few weeks. It's the ten-year anniversary since the show premiered. They're making a big deal about it. That's why I'm in New York. There's a press tour, and then there's a big launch gala next month."

"And then there was all that controversy about your costar leaving suddenly at the end. What ever happened to that girl, anyway? Didn't she get sick or something?"

He bit his lip. The memory of the nightmare he just had still lingered, and he pressed his eyes shut in an effort to erase it. "I'm not sure," he stammered. "We just worked together. I don't know anything about her personal life."

"Well she fell off the face of the earth. Although I shouldn't talk. I haven't had a single callback in three weeks." Angie slid her legs around him, planting kisses on his neck. Her hand found his hardened shaft, rubbing the tip with a gentle finger.

He closed his eyes, and his mind flashed images of Grace. The long red hair, the deep blue eyes, her pink lips, glossed against the paleness of her skin.

"Take me please, Ty."

He felt her again, her skin grazed his, her velvet touch aroused his deepest desires. He moaned, letting the urges take over, and followed her wherever she wanted him to go.

"Please, Ty. I need you."

A loud bang on the door drove them to opposite sides of the bed. Ty jumped up and cursed. He scrubbed his stubbled face. "What's up, Manny?"

"Hey Ty, it's nine thirty."

He craned his head around, straining to see the red digital numbers on the bedside clock. "Yeah, so?"

"You have an interview at the *Entertainment Now* studio, remember?"

"That's today? How the hell…" He ran to the window, then threw open the curtains. The blinding sun stung his eyes. "Damn it!"

Angie laughed, retrieving her bra from the bedpost. "So you're late for an appointment. You're kidding me, right? You're Ty Hawthorne. I'm sure they'll wait for you."

"You better get moving, Ty." Manny called through the door. "We can cab it over to the studio."

Ty looked down at the city below. People lumbered shoulder to shoulder on the sidewalks, and cars idled on top of each other in the streets. Rush hour gridlock. If he was lucky, maybe he could get to the studio in an hour. That was if he skipped the shower.

Today, that wasn't an option.

"Listen, Angie, I'm sorry but I got to get going." Ty grabbed his jeans from the floor and slung them over his arm. "Big appointment."

"Yeah, with me, lover." She grabbed him by the arm when he attempted to breeze by her. "Come on, one more time. I know you want it."

"I can't."

"Please, Ty?" She planted her lips on his chest and slid her tongue down his stomach.

"Angie…"

Her mouth slipped over him. His body went stiff, his muscles flexed, the teasing temptation no match for his half-ass resolve. With each caress his mind narrowed, until there was nothing there at all. Only animal instinct to bury himself further. The better it felt, the less he existed. No thoughts. No feelings. Just numb.

He screwed up again.

She flipped her tongue across the tip and took him deep, as if she swallowed him whole. His building climax was a blissful punishment, and he sealed his eyes shut in submission. His fingers grasped the back of her head and weaved in her brittle hair. He was irresponsible, greedy, conceited, and angry. He groaned, pumping harder and faster into her. And when he came, he came hard. Letting whatever he held inside him spew like venom.

She wanted it, so she got it.

When it was over, he left her kneeling on the

floor and moved around her to the bathroom. He hoped she'd get the picture. Some girls were denser than others. When he finally heard the suite door close, he thanked God and cursed for thinking so badly about the poor girl in the first place. Who the hell was he to pass judgment on anyone? He turned the shower on full blast, and let the water scald him.

In minutes, he had a towel around his waist, and a toothbrush jammed in his mouth. He grabbed his jeans and leather jacket from floor and bolted out of his suite.

Manny waited, like any dutiful assistant should, sporting stylishly nerdy bifocals, frosted hair, and a vintage Sex Pistols T-shirt. He gave his boss a once over then gasped a few attempts at speech before he finally succeeded. "Are you freakin' kidding me? What are you doing? Put some clothes on!"

"I will on the way."

"You know, this is precisely why you get in the gossip magazines." Manny scolded from a few paces behind. "Running naked through a five star hotel is a bigger story then a Paris Hilton sex tape."

"I wouldn't have had to if you had gotten me up earlier."

"I thought I was doing a favor letting you sleep. Looks like you had pretty interesting company last night. I just saw her leave."

Ty chuckled and shook his head. "You can tell me about it later. Right now, I'm in a hurry." When he got to the elevators, Ty pressed the "down" arrow and waited in between for the nearest available car. The doors to his right opened first, and two older ladies stepped out and gasped.

Ty winked. What the hell?

"Can you at least put your pants on before we get to the lobby?" Manny pleaded. "You'll cause a riot."

"Sure." Ty shed the towel just as the elevator

doors behind him opened. Jaws dropped and women applauded. He smiled when the camera phones flipped open.

"That's what I mean," Manny said over the feminine squeals. "Behavior like that is what gets you in trouble."

"Manny, this is New York. People run around the city naked all the time."

"Well you aren't 'people.' You're Ty Hawthorne. Moments of tact would do wonders for your image."

Ty zipped up his jeans and stepped into an empty car. Manny held open his leather jacket.

"Didn't you bring a shirt?"

"Oops."

Ty knew where this scene was going. He could feel a classic Manny "I-am-not-your-nanny" speech coming on. An emotionless monologue that he knew by heart and hated, because it was the truth. Ty braced himself and leaned back against the elevator wall.

"This is self-destruction. Pure and simple." Manny pressed his thumb and middle finger against the bridge of his nose. "I mean, I know you're going through a divorce and all, but this behavior of yours." He shook his head. "This is why God invented therapists."

"Where I'm from, Jack Daniels and Jim Beam count as a therapists."

"Where the hell did you ever find the discipline to do a TV show? Eighteen-hour days, six days a week, almost year round." He sighed and stared at the panel of lights above the doors. "Thank God, you're a big movie star now. No one would put up with all your bullshit otherwise."

Ty let the words roll off. No point in disputing them. The assessment was correct.

"I called ahead to the studio. Grace Ann is there, and I guess, if you don't make it, she can do the interview herself."

"I'll get there." Ty pushed himself off the wall. "I don't want her to do it alone."

"What do you care? Less work for you, right?"

Ty took a sideward glance at his disgruntled assistant. Jesus, he could nag. But to his credit, he never ever judged, and that was a huge reason why he hired the kid in the first place. The wild and crazy lifestyle wasn't something they learned in the Business Management classes at Yale, and he could tell the kid secretly didn't mind the on-the-job training.

"Look, maybe I can clear your schedule next week," Manny grumbled. "You were invited to that thing in South Beach. It would be a shame to miss it."

"I'm not skipping out. I have an obligation."

Manny looked at him and flicked his earlobe as if adjusting a hearing aid. "I'm sorry, but did I just hear you use the word 'obligation' in a sentence?"

The car lurched to a stop. Ty squeezed through the elevator doors before they completely opened. He dashed through the lobby, out to the line of cabs in the front loop. The late November chill made him regret he didn't wear a shirt. Remembering his shoes would have been nice, too. His bare feet numbed in the slush.

"I'll head back to the suite and pack up your clothes and stuff," Manny said as they piled into a yellow cab. "You can't go all day half-dressed."

"*Entertainment Now* Studio, please," Ty told the cab driver. "And there's an extra grand in it for you if you put a rush on it. Ten minutes ago would have been great."

"Ty..."

"Just drive!"

****

Grace sat on the leather greenroom couch going

over her "To Do" list for the third time. Usually her daily lists filled almost a whole legal page, but leaving her sister, Lizzie, in charge of the bed and breakfast required one or two more at least. She gnawed on the end of her pencil, wondering if she should call. If she did, she'd just get a lecture. Lizzie's usual "stop being a Control Freak" mantra.

A check of her watch told her the interview was already an hour behind schedule. Not surprising, given the world of show business thrived on always being "fashionably late." One of the many reasons why she didn't miss her old career. It made her appreciate the freedom of making her own schedule. One she needed to get back to ASAP. Again, she looked at her watch. At this rate, she wouldn't be back upstate until after dark.

She stood up and paced, stopped mid-step when she glanced in the full-length mirror. A short, redheaded antithesis of Hollywood glamour stared back at her. She probably should have let the *Entertainment Now* stylists fix her hair down instead of pulled back like she had it. And maybe the short black tank dress wasn't the best wardrobe choice. But wearing it felt like a declaration that all the old demons were no longer present. Who cared that her calves looked thick and hopelessly unattractive. It wasn't normally an issue, given her daily attire of baggy overalls and knee-high boots. No need for micro-minis and three-inch heels when you chopped wood and shoveled snow.

Closing her eyes, she stepped away from the mirror, making a mental note to hide her calves from the glare of the camera.

"Grace, are you still in here?" The door flew open, revealing the panic stricken face of Earl Simmons, the Executive Producer and mastermind of *Undercover Heat*. At forty, he looked every bit his age, plus an added ten for stress, and another five for his chubby build and practically bald head. Grace was glad to see he had given up on the comb-over.

He slammed the door behind him like someone chased him, and beads of sweat formed on his shiny scalp. "Thank God, you haven't left," he panted. "At least I have one star for the interview."

Grace held her hand out to him. His clammy palm stuck to hers. "Earl, you have to calm down. This isn't good for your blood pressure."

"I'm so glad we aren't live. Can you imagine if it was live? I'd really be in trouble."

"Earl, no one is in trouble. It's just an interview." She led him to the couch and sat down beside him, trying not to cringe at the pit stains, the size of dinner plates, soaking his shirt.

"Has Ty called you?" he asked, with a whine that could rival a five-year-old's. "Tell me you know where he is! Tell me he has some incredible excuse why he's late."

"Earl, calm down. I'm sure he'll be here."

"How do you know? Really? Maybe he decided not to show."

"Maybe he got stuck in traffic. There was a fire truck down..."

"Maybe he got stuck under last night's fling." Earl put his head on Grace's lap and took a pill bottle from his shirt pocket. "This is why I have heart problems. This guy is going to kill me."

"Well, even if he doesn't show, I can do it myself."

"I hate working with movie stars," Earl said. "I'm glad you're a nobody again, Grace. You were always so good to me. You're like a really nice, sexy, babysitter."

She smiled. "Thanks, Earl."

"Really, when I first saw you dance in the Nutcracker, I knew you were a gem. God, you were still a teen when I hired you, but I had a hunch you could act. I have good hunches, don't I, Grace?"

"Yes, you do."

"Boy, was I upset when you were sick, even if it did end the show. Who knows, maybe now that you're better, this release will steamroll into other things."

"Maybe," she said through gritted teeth. Earl had hinted to her over the phone at the possibility of a reunion movie. A two-week press tour with Ty was one thing, but being in close quarters for months playing his romantic partner was something she'd had enough of years ago.

Earl rolled over and looked up with moon eyes. "Grace, what time is it, honey?"

She checked her watch. "Ten forty."

"Over an hour. God, he better be dead. If he's not, I'll kill him myself."

There was a soft knock at the door before it opened. *Entertainment Now* host Sally Hartman peeked in, extending her hand to Grace when she saw her. "Well, well, well, Grace Ann Langley. How wonderful it is to see you again."

Grace took her hand, amazed how Sally's forehead didn't move when she smiled. Her blonde hair plastered her head like a helmet, and Grace made out the faintest purple incision marks right on the edge of her temples. "Good to see you again, Sally."

"I'm glad you're here, but I wish I could say the same about your costar."

"He'll be here," Earl said and dragged a handkerchief across his brow. "He signed a contract. He has to be."

"Well even so, I'd like to have you on the set in five minutes. I'm doing a piece on celebrity dogs for tomorrow's show, and I'm due at the ASPCA in an hour."

"No problem." Earl held the greenroom door

open for the three of them. “We’re ready.”

“Great, and if Ty shows up, even better. Now that the divorce is final, I’d like the scoop on the whole ‘Layla-Ty’ breakup.” Sally winked at Grace. “That’s the biggest story in Hollywood.”

Grace followed Sally down the stairs, with Earl lumbering behind her. Taking her place on the soundstage couch, she glanced around the darkened studio. It had been a long time since she’d been in front of a camera. Acting on a TV show was one thing, but unscripted interviews were quite another. Pretending to be someone else offered a strange sort of protection. Any flaws or shortcomings could be assigned to the character. She took a deep breath, reminding herself to hide her fat calves close to the couch. Couldn’t blame Lexie Love for Grace Langley’s cellulite.

Sally smoothed her hair and stepped up onto the stage. She took her seat beside the couch and thumbed through her papers. “Okay, you remember how this goes, right? I’ll ask a few questions to prompt you, but otherwise just keep talking.”

Grace adjusted herself on the couch, watching the people move around her. Her face powdered, her hair sprayed, and someone set a glass of water on the table beside her. The director said something then stepped behind the camera. A green light suddenly snapped on, alerting Grace’s attention.

“Hi, everybody. Sally Hartman with an exclusive. We’re here with two-time Emmy winner Grace Ann Langley, star of the hit TV show *Undercover Heat*. The DVD release of the series hits stores next week, and we’re glad she’s here to tell us all about it.” Sally turned to her and smiled, touching her arm as if they were old friends. “So, *TV Weekly* has just named you and Ty Hawthorne “The Most Romantic TV Couple of All Time.” How does that feel?”

So that's why Lizzie hid it when it came in the mail. "I'm really flattered," Grace said. "We worked hard on the show, and it's great when the audience responds. I can't wait to get the cast and crew back together again."

"There were mumblings that you wouldn't participate in the DVD release, given your abrupt departure from the show."

"I wouldn't dream of missing it!" Grace laughed and nudged Sally's arm for good measure. "That was five years ago, and everyone's in a different place now." She congratulated herself for the response. Vague and polite and suitably bubbly that went along with her Lexie Love persona. Maybe she still had the acting chops after all.

"What about Ty Hawthorne?"

"What about him?"

"Are you looking forward to working with him again?"

From the corner of her eye, she noticed the studio door open. An entourage of people filed in. Security, some guy with headphones and notepads. Crew members whispered and dispersed, meeting the newcomers behind the camera. She turned back to Sally, forgetting she was speaking. "Of course I'm looking forward to it." Her voice cracked. "He's a wonderful actor."

"So is there any truth to the old rumors about you two?"

She took a breath. These were questions she had fielded a million times, but being out of practice they were hard to navigate. "No, not at all. We're just really close friends. Ty and I worked side by side every day for five years. We got to know each other very well."

"But no romantic connection?"

In that moment something came over her. A presence. Something heavy and thick that seized her insides. When she looked toward the camera, she knew why.

Ice blue eyes. Her heart stopped.

"No, no romantic connection at all."

She sensed his gaze on her, and suddenly a rush of memories flooded her mind. Things she had sworn she'd never think about again.

"Grace, what about your illness? There was a lot of speculation about your sudden departure from the show. What's the truth behind that?"

She thought she was prepared for this, but the tremble in her body told her different. Tucking her legs tighter against the couch, she again wished she'd passed on the tank dress. "I had a health crisis, but I'm fully recovered now."

"Some reports said it was cancer. Was it cancer?"

His eyes had claimed her. Intense. Commanding. What a fool she'd been.

"No, it wasn't cancer," she managed.

"Stop tape."

The sudden baritone echoed in her chest as Ty shoved his way around the camera. He reached down the front of her dress, snagging the small mike from the fabric. "Its okay, I'm here now," he whispered. "Just sit tight, and let me take care of this."

"Ty, what do you think you're doing?" Grace demanded.

"She doesn't have to answer these questions." His voice didn't invite disagreement. "She's here to talk about a TV show, not her personal life."

Earl came behind him and grabbed him by the shoulder. "Are you crazy, Hawthorne? She was doing a great job."

"Why the hell is she up here by herself anyway?"

"She was here on time. Dressed appropriately. Which is more than I can say for you."

Grace knew from experience that it was easier to let the two men have it out than to try to interject. But part of her was angry. Angry, hell—infuriated! How dare he be so arrogant to think she needed him to save her?

Ty stood with one hand on his hip, the other held in front of her, like a father making a case for a stricken child. His height and his build made him look menacing, but Grace knew better. The Ty she knew was more apt to stop trouble than cause it.

"This wasn't live," Ty told Earl. "They could have waited for me."

"Since when are you such a publicity hog?" Earl asked. "I'd think a gossip magnet like you would be happy for a break."

"Grace is in no condition to do this by herself."

"Wait a minute!" She pushed herself off the couch, strained her neck to meet Ty's gaze. "I am perfectly capable of conducting myself in an interview, and I was doing just fine until you showed up."

"But you don't have to now. I'm here."

"So what?"

"Grace, I don't like you getting upset. Everything is okay now."

He spoke softly, like he had when she was sick, as if the slightest spook would destroy her. She'd been fragile then, but that was years ago. She was over all that, and over him. "Fine then," she spat. "If you think I'm so damn incapable, do the interview yourself."

She pushed between the two men and bounded off the soundstage as fast as she could in her numbing stilettos. She threw open the studio door and bolted back up the stairs, ignoring the heavy footfalls echoing behind her.

"Grace, wait!"

Maybe agreeing to do this was a big mistake. No

amount of money was worth reliving the hell of five years ago. She was beginning to understand why parolees never made a habit of visiting old cellmates they'd left behind. It was easier just to forget they ever knew each other at all.

"Gracie?"

He stood behind her in the greenroom doorway. She closed her eyes and kept her back to him, afraid one look would stymie her resolve.

"Grace Ann, please look at me. I just thought you'd want company up there."

"I don't want anything from you."

She heard him shut the door, and the knowledge that they were alone scared the hell out of her. His large hand slipped over her shoulder, and when she opened her eyes he stared back at her. "Just hear me out."

"No."

Her brain screamed for her to move away. Somehow her feet wouldn't budge, trapped in the incredible presence that was Ty Hawthorne. The sun-kissed complexion, the short dirty blonde hair, a perpetual five o'clock shadow that framed his chiseled smile. No picture in a magazine did justice to the real thing, and his proximity crippled her best intentions. Finally she managed to step back, picking up her jacket and purse from the coffee table.

"Don't leave."

"Get out of my way."

"Gracie, please." He jumped into her path, his rippled bare chest peeking out at eye level from under his black leather jacket. "Please, not like this."

He touched her face. He traced the line of her jaw. Strong but gentle. Her skin tingled like it had a memory all its own. "I really have to get home," she stammered, hating the obvious tremble in her voice. "I have a million things to do."

"Look, I'm sorry for being late, and for how I look. Manny's finding me a shirt."

"Who's Manny?"

"He's my assistant."

"Oh."

"I know you were counting on me, and I should have been here. I let you down, and I'm sorry." He ran his fingers through her hair. Her breath hitched in response. His words were exactly what she wanted to hear.

Five years too late.

She drew away from his hand and exhaled when it dropped to his side with a thud.

"Hey, you two, what the hell is going on in there?" Earl pushed open the door. He had that expectant look, like he was waiting for a tea kettle to boil. "Time is money, folks," he said. "Can we film now and talk later, please?"

Grace pulled her jacket on and slung her purse over her shoulder. "Earl, I'm sorry. I thought I could do this, but I can't."

"Okay, so maybe you're a little out of practice."

"Grace needs to get home," Ty said.

"Can I speak for myself, please?"

"People!" Earl wiped his brow with a handkerchief then dabbed the back of his neck. "I don't mean to yell, but I would just like to remind you that neither one of you would be where you are today if it wasn't for the money and fame this TV show brought you. I deserve some gratitude. This DVD release means a lot to me. I put up with you people for five years. You can put up for two weeks."

Grace shrugged, and Ty chewed his lip. The usual response to Earl's scolding.

"Now, I can get over what happened here today, but you two have to promise me that you can pull it together by Tuesday morning, nine a.m. We are booked for *The Olivia Godfrey Show*, so I expect you both to show up happy, smiling and willing to talk by then. Got it?"

"Got it." Ty shoved his hands in his pockets.

"This is Thursday, so that gives you a five-day weekend. My suggestion is that you two get reacquainted. Go get some burgers or coffee or something."

Earl didn't wait for a response. Instead, he stormed out the door, pulling a pill bottle from his breast pocket as he went. Grace moved to follow, but Ty grabbed her arm. "Where do you think you're going?"

"To get him some water for his pill, and then I'm heading home."

"How about you leave him alone and worry about yourself for a minute?" His careful tone had returned. Soft. Warm. Irresistible. "Grab your things," he said. "How about if we head to the diner a few blocks down. Talk."

"Ty..."

"Come on, Gracie, please? For Earl?"

His breath hit her already heated cheek, and by God if she didn't feel herself swoon. "Fine," she heard herself say as she flipped her scarf over her head. "I'll go for Earl."

## Chapter Two

The noontime traffic was thick, as usual. Clouds of exhaust and the stench of diesel mingled with the damp promise of snow. A noxious concoction that was classic winter in New York City. They predicted a decent snowfall overnight, and by the swirl of the clouds converging above that the storm would move in earlier than Grace had planned. She cursed. It was a good two-hour ride back home, and she wanted to make it in the daylight. North Country white-outs were doubly nasty in the dark.

Her heels were unsteady on the slushy pavement, so she made sure to walk just out of Ty's reach. A painful tumble into oncoming traffic would be preferable to having his hands anywhere on her, breaking a fall. She maintained the distance until she hopped the curb in front of Hoggins Diner. He moved in front of her to hold open the door. Ever the southern gentleman, he had impeccable manners. Although she noticed earlier at the studio that he lost his accent.

When they stepped inside, Ty kicked the snow from his borrowed sneakers. Somehow the move attracted every eye in the place. The clanking of silverware and coffee cups ceased. Lunchtime chatter dulled to silence.

"What happened to indifferent New Yorkers?" Grace said through the side of her mouth. "I thought they were used to seeing celebrities out in public."

"Wouldn't that be nice," Ty said. "I thought I'd be pretty incognito looking like this."

She lifted her gaze and assessed his newly

donned baseball cap and a few-days-old beard. High profile celebrity or not, possibly he drew attention simply because he was that good-looking.

"There, behind that plant." He gestured toward a vacant booth on the back wall. Pulling the "Bama" cap farther down over his eyes, he nudged her through the sea of patrons. On her way past, Grace glanced at the clock over the counter. "I know the snow is coming," he said in her ear. "Don't worry. I'll make sure you're out of here in plenty of time."

Ty slid into the booth across from her. He took off his hat and raked his hand through his hair before jamming the thing back on. A nervous habit of his. Good. At least she wasn't the only uptight one. "Again, I'm sorry about the audience," he said. "I really thought we'd go unnoticed."

Fat chance. Two women giggled over French fries in the next booth. One whipped out a digital camera from her purse and took aim. "God, how can you live like this all the time? Don't you get sick of it?"

"I'm used to it by now." He cocked his head and scratched his chin with his thumb. "Forced myself to get used to it, I guess."

"Better you than me."

"Come on, don't tell me fans don't still stop you on the street."

"Not in Middle Valley. Up there I'm just the same Grace Ann who shovels her own driveway and drives an old pickup. Celebrity doesn't hold much credence."

He nodded. "Don't forget, I grew up in a small town, too. I know what it's like. And you don't have to sell me on Middle Valley. I liked it up there. And now you've put the place on the map with that bed and breakfast of yours." He reached across the table and brushed his fingers across hers. "I'm proud of you, Gracie. Really."

The tone was back. The one that reeked of pity. She tugged her sleeves down over her hands and sat back in her seat. When she looked up, she noticed him staring, a curious smile straightening his lips.

"You look beautiful, Grace. I noticed at the studio. Good and healthy."

The added weight of his deep blue eyes somehow made her all the more self-conscious. She cast a sideward glance around the diner. A thin-haired man with a mangy goatee lifted his coffee cup and smiled.

"Why don't you take your jacket off, Gracie? It's warm enough in here."

Her gaze shifted to the linoleum table. "I'm okay, still a little chilled from the outside."

"Grace..."

"I told you. I'm fine." She couldn't fool him. His scowl told her as much. Acting came naturally to her, hell, she had the awards to prove it. But she couldn't lie, and no part of Ty bought her lame attempt to do so.

"There he is. My favorite semi-regular!" A waitress with long dark hair and unnaturally tinted contacts popped her bubble gum as she approached their table. When she touched Ty on the shoulder, he started at the intrusion. "Ty Hawthorne! Boy, have I missed you." She bent down and kissed him on the cheek, then placed the menus on the table.

"Hey, Stacey." He winked and flashed a red carpet smile. "How have you been, honey?"

"Better now that you're here. How long has it been—two, three months?"

"That's about right. I've been on location. In Italy."

"At the gym, it looks like."

"Played a boxer. Had to put on some mass."

"No kidding." Stacey slid her fingers down his arm, and made a show of squeezing his biceps. "Is that why you're strutting around in the dead of winter with no shirt on under that biker jacket of yours? Showing off?"

"I was in a hurry this morning."

"Well, let me speak for my whole gender and tell you we don't mind." She pulled a pencil and pad from her apron pocket. "So, how long are you in town? Maybe we could catch up, you know what I mean?"

Grace did. It never ceased to amaze her how women blatantly threw themselves at him, any time any place, even in mixed company. She chuckled and buried her nose in the list of lunch specials.

"Wait a minute! Is that...? Are you...? It is! Grace Ann Langley!"

Grace peeked out from behind the menu. Stacey looked at her, red-faced with her hand covering her mouth like she'd seen the Ghost of Elvis. "Oh, my God," the girl gushed. "I love you so much. Really!"

"Thank you," Grace said in a polite whisper, a tone she hoped Stacey would emulate. No luck. Instead she squealed and did a strange little dance that looked almost like a seizure.

"God, and your show *Undercover Heat* is my number-one favorite ever. You two were so good together. It was like you really were madly in love."

Ty smiled at Grace. "We were that convincing, huh?"

"Oh, yeah. I love the episode when you guys are being chased by those drug dealers, and you end up hooking up in that refrigerator thingy."

"Um, I think it was a meat locker." Grace corrected, surprised she suddenly didn't mind the stroll down memory lane. "That was Ty's method acting stage, and he insisted we actually do the scene in a gigantic freezer."

"Yeah, and I was sick in bed for a week after that."

"I told you it was a bad idea."

Ty leaned across the table and smiled. "I didn't mind. I may have been in bed, but I did have pretty good company."

The waitress had slipped away, but Grace was sure any idiot could tell by her blush that they weren't talking about the weather. The spell was broken when a shutter clicked on a high speed camera. Ty scowled at the table beside them. "I'm a top story now," he grumbled. "They follow me like flies on shit."

"I know. The whole Layla thing is pretty big news. I'm sorry, by the way. That must be hard to go through something so personal so publicly."

"What can I say? I do my best to keep the world entertained at all costs." He tilted his head to meet her gaze. "Come on, Gracie. Don't tell me you're surprised. You were the one who warned me about her."

"Where did you meet up with her again, anyway?"

"Vegas. At one of those burlesque shows. After she left her assistant job at *Undercover Heat*, she worked at one of the hotels out there. Anyway, we met up one night. A few bottles of wine and a drive-thru chapel later, we were married. Eight months after that she left me for Marcy the dog walker."

"Wow. That must be hard to deal with."

"Yeah, I miss the dog like crazy."

He tweaked the bill of his cap and sat back in his seat. Flippant had never been Ty's style, especially about something like marriage. Although it was obvious the man in front of her was a variation of the original. His eyes looked tired, his shoulders hunched. His smile looked like he worked at it. What a sharp change from the charismatic man she remembered.

A burst of winter air followed a breathless man

through the door. He held a white T-shirt in his hand and scanned the room before jogging to their table. "I found you a shirt. I stole it from wardrobe at *Entertainment Now*."

"Hey Manny, this is Grace Ann Langley. Grace, this is my assistant, Manny Pipher."

"Amazing Grace is more like it. Incredible to meet you." He extended his hand and smiled.

Ty stood up and slipped off his leather jacket. A collective female gasp filled the diner when he revealed his incredible tanned physique. Grace averted her eyes. No need for her to look. Every inch of the man's body was etched in her brain. Even so, seeing him in person instead of her dreams was something she wasn't prepared for. Again, she went back to the lunch specials.

"I brought two of your usuals." Stacey slid a tray full of burgers and fries in front of them. Soda sloshed over the sides of the plastic cups when she caught a glimpse of Ty's sculpted pecs. "You need anything else, give me a holler."

"Thanks." Manny snagged Grace's plate and scooped the burger to his mouth.

"Hey, what the hell do you think you're doing?" Ty shoved him on the shoulder, knocking the bacon clear from the bun. "That was for Gracie."

"It's okay," Grace insisted, pushing the plate closer toward Manny. "Go ahead. I had a big breakfast."

"Gracie, I'm ordering something else for you." Ty signaled for Stacey across the diner. "It's a long ride back to Middle Valley, and I want something in your stomach."

"But..."

"How about a piece of pie. Apple's still your favorite, right?"

"Ty..."

"How about some ice tea. Lemon and sugar?"

"But it's not necessary."

"Damn it, Gracie. Yes, it is!" His fist landed on the table, knocking the silverware to the floor. Something flickered behind the whites of his bloodshot eyes. A strange variation of anger, maybe fear, even sadness, that had her glued to her vinyl seat. Manny too, it seemed, had appeared to have stopped chewing mid-bite.

The roomful of people probably still stared, but it didn't matter. The world always seemed to fade away when she was with him. She opened her eyes wide, daring him to blink. Who would back down? Not her, and stalemates were not their style.

"Hey Ty," Manny mumbled. "You have big plans this afternoon, and Grace seems to have stuff to do, too. Maybe we should wrap this up."

"Damn it, Manny, I'm having lunch with an old friend here."

"No, he's right." Grace refused to look away first. "I need to get going. And I don't want to wreck your schedule. I'm sure you have other things to do, business meetings, appearances. Right, Manny?"

Manny took her cue and whipped the Blackberry from his pocket. She watched his fingers flip over buttons until relief registered across his face. "You're already late for a lunch date about a film project across town. Then MTV has you later on this afternoon, after which you'll catch a quick dinner, and then back to Manhattan for the Late Show."

"And I know how you are about keeping commitments, and I don't want to mess you up." Seeing a quick out, Grace picked up her purse. "I'll see you next week, Ty. Good to meet you, Manny." She wound her scarf around her and slipped out from the booth.

"Grace, wait!"

She squeezed through the crowd, shoving harder and moving faster when curious eyes focused over her shoulder. When she pushed opened the door, horns blared and cars raced by, tossing sprays of slush into the swirling air.

"Hey, Grace!"

This was precisely the kind of scene she wanted to avoid. People would speculate and reopen old wounds. Why did she think it would be any different? The heavy footfalls echoed behind her, urging her strides to a jog. Her shoes skidded on the pavement.

"Grace Ann, slow down!"

The cement dipped at the crosswalk and her heel caught in the groove. She stumbled and braced herself for the fall, but fingers laced around her arm before she hit the ground.

"Don't take off on me like this."

Her eyes met his, and a jolt of anger zipped through her. She was taking off on him? Again her feet gave way, and again he caught her, this time slipping his hand around her waist.

"Stay with me tonight."

"What?"

"Call Lizzie. She still lives up in Middle Valley, right? Tell her to watch the place."

"Are you crazy?"

"Please?

Back then he could talk her into anything. He had. He would. But not anymore. She slipped away from his grip and eyed an idling cab across the street. Her pickup was parked only a block away, but the taxi offered a quicker getaway. She'd drive around the block if she had to. Anything to get off the sidewalk.

Mercifully, the traffic stalled, and she bolted from the curb to the crosswalk. She knew he still watched when she jumped into the taxi, leaving him in a cloud of exhaust.

She leaned against the window, the cool glass

stinging her blushed cheeks. Tears welled in her eyes, so she pressed them shut, right after she saw the slimy man from the diner snap her picture from the sidewalk.

****

Gigantic snowflakes zinged out of the darkness like darts bombarding the windshield of Ty's borrowed Hummer. His back was sore from leaning forward in his seat, and his eyes felt like they'd been dragged in sand from the strain. But he could crash and be torn into a million pieces, and he wouldn't care. That was the nice thing about self-loathing. Dying didn't seem that bad, when existence was the bleaker alternative.

That's what Grace had done to him.

A quick check of the dashboard clock told him it was close to eight p.m. In a few minutes, he was supposed to talk music videos with the deejays at Total Request Live. Manny nearly cried when Ty announced his change in plans. Blowing off a whole demographic for a joy ride upstate was what Manny called "a poor business decision" and in a snowstorm as bad as this, an even worse one. But in truth there was no decision to be made. Ty was a selfish bastard who couldn't help wanting to share the space with the one woman he had no business wanting. Hell, after what he'd done, he deserved to be bashed with a shovel and buried in a snow bank. If she was half as smart as he knew her to be, she would do just that, and at that moment, giving her the opportunity to do so seemed a lot more important than yukking it up with pre-teens at MTV.

Again the back tires fishtailed. He skimmed the roadside ditch before righting himself. His absent mind allowed a heavy foot, which was especially risky between Hanson's cornfields where black ice usually formed. Ty hadn't driven these roads in over five years, more than enough time to forget the lay of the land, but somehow it was etched in his memory. The windmill on the hilltop told him he was minutes from the town proper. "Welcome to Middle Valley," he muttered, surprising himself when he heard the Southern drawl mix with his words.

The last time he made this trip it was spring, a few weeks before the show was due for hiatus. Grace was too weak to leave her bed, and he had been working by himself. He remembered a balmy moonless night, and the two-hour ride from the Brooklyn set seemed longer that usual. It was three in the morning by the time he reached the farmhouse.

Ty had sensed something was wrong as soon as he pulled in the gate. Every light in the place was on, and the front door stood wide open, with just the screen keeping the bugs out. The TV displayed a snowy test screen, the volume turned down to a mute. He remembered calling her name, and the lump in his throat that impeded his words. An inhuman force propelled him though the house to the foot of the back stairs.

He smelled it first. The putrid metallic scent of an open wound that would tie the steadiest stomach in knots. She lay sprawled on the hardwood floor. Her skin as pale as the satin nightgown that covered her. Above her left eye gaped a deep gash, from hitting the railing, he figured. Blood matted her hair and pooled beneath her. He could tell by the way it stuck to his fingers that it had been there a while.

When he took her in his arms she felt cool and limp, and at first he thought she was dead. He kissed her purple lips until she opened her eyes, then cleaned her up and carried her to his Blazer. On a referral he'd secretly scored from a fashion model friend a few weeks earlier, he made the three-hour drive to the hospital in Connecticut in ninety minutes.

She lost the baby the next day.

He tapped the brakes when he read the sign that said 'Whisper Grove Farms.' The old one had been smaller, with black faded paint on rotting white wood. Now it was majestic, inlaid in stone, and illuminated by a spotlight placed on top.

Simple and classy. Very Grace.

He plowed up the driveway in a cloud of powder. If this was one of the most popular bed and breakfasts in upstate New York, it certainly looked the part. The whole damn place had been spruced up. A large addition to the old farmhouse, paint, new windows. Even in the deep snow, it was obvious she'd hired landscapers. He smiled, mentally correcting himself. Never in a million years would Gracie hire anybody to do her gardens. Whatever she could possibly do on her own, she did. Hell, he wouldn't be surprised if she had built the addition with her own little hands.

He parked beside the east barn, behind Grace's pickup, the same place he always parked. There was another truck next to the back door of the farmhouse. His heart stopped.

Maybe she didn't live alone.

For a moment he just sat there before stepping out of the car. Man, it was cold. The moon was hidden, and he smelled a storm in the air, mingling with lingering chimney smoke. The hum of snowmakers from the ski resort across the way competed with the whine of the wind. Very ominous. The snow he'd encountered on his ride up must have just been a preview for the main attraction.

Spying the light on the back porch, he broke into a clumsy jog. Snow jumped from under his heavy feet, stuck to his face and hung on his lashes. He stopped mid-stride at the foot of the steps, lifting a shielding hand to his forehead. Through the sheet of white, he made out a very pregnant woman standing on the porch steps with an arm full of bed linens tucked under her chin.

"Lizzie?"

Ty shuffled toward her and stood in the lamp light. "Lizzie, it's me."

"Ty?" Her brow wrinkled, and he wasn't sure if it was in surprise or disgust. At least it wasn't anger. Despite their small stature, the Langley girls had tempers. Even a guy the size of him feared to be on the wrong end of it.

She exhaled in a sigh, her breath clouding the night air. "God, I feel like I just saw a ghost."

"Tell me that's a good thing."

"Tell me why you're here."

Lizzie meant no harm. She was protective of her younger sister, and he suspected more so since their mother had died two years before. She had the same red hair as Grace, but shorter, and darker eyes that Ty always thought made sense. She was world-weary and practical. The opposite of the naive dreamer Grace was. In the past, Lizzie had been his biggest fan. She was the one who secretly corresponded with him when Grace was in the hospital, even after the fiasco with her father. He thought if anyone would be halfway happy to see him it would be her. So far he wasn't getting that impression.

"Listen, do you have some gloves or maybe an old winter jacket lying around? I'm not dressed for winter in upstate New York." He rubbed his hands together, then did a little cold-man dance for effect. Maybe playing pitiful and hypothermic would pull at her heartstrings.

"You should have called first."

Or not.

"You know, we're not open to guests for another week or so. Grace likes to close down the few weeks before Thanksgiving to prepare the place for the winter season. But you do look like you could use some coffee."

Ty shifted his feet and hugged his leather jacket around himself. "If you're offering."

"Well, I can't say there isn't a part of me that wouldn't mind seeing you freeze to death." Her chest heaved with a sigh. "Come on in. I just made some fresh."

Ty didn't give her a chance to change her mind. He jogged up the stairs, following her through the elegant stained glass door, a definite change from the rotted out screen he remembered. The mud room on the other side also looked updated with new drywall and paint. The only thing that looked the same was the crucifix that hung conspicuously over the entrance to the kitchen, and the scent of cinnamon and cedar that wafted in the space between.

"So this is a surprise visit, huh?"

"You could say that." Ty whipped his baseball cap from his head and stuffed it in his back pocket. "I hope I didn't interrupt anything."

"Not really. I was just waiting for Grace to finish up in the barn. Russ is in the city at some pediatric convention for the week, so we're having movie night." She held up a worn VHS copy of *This is Spinal Tap* and chucked it back on the counter. "I'm on a weepy love story kick, but she insisted on classic comedy."

"Hey, I know how you feel. Thanks to her, I still have *Blazing Saddles* committed to memory." He went to the cupboard next to the fridge and pulled out two mugs. After filling them with coffee, he handed one to Lizzie.

"You know, she's been worried about seeing you."

"Really?" Ty leaned against the counter and wrapped his hands around the warm ceramic cup. "She seemed pretty put together today."

"Did you forget her profession, Ty?"

He pursed his lips. The jab met its target. Square in the gut.

"So, I haven't heard anything from you in a long time," she said. "I guess I don't blame you. I know my family didn't make it easy on you."

His insides curdled at the thought of her father. Lizzie didn't know the half of it, and that's the way it would stay. "Yeah, well, I figure I had it coming. I knocked up the Deacon's baby daughter. I'm surprised I wasn't pelted with brimstone or set on fire at the stake."

"Well, then, you'll be relieved to know that Daddy isn't here. He travels a lot now, organizing retreats for the Archdioceses of New York. He's on retreat for the week."

"It's not just your Dad I pissed off. That husband of yours caught me pretty good with a right hook, you know."

Lizzie winced. "Yeah, I'm sorry about that."

"And I'm sorry about your mother's passing."

She set her mug back down on the counter and folded her arms against her. "Now how did you know that?"

"Just because I haven't kept in touch doesn't mean I haven't kept up." He brought the cup to his lips then took a long gulp, remembering how he felt two years ago when he happened upon the obituary in a New York paper. He almost called her. But after two hours of staring at his hotel phone, he decided that pickling himself in bourbon was the better alternative.

"Speaking of family, looks like you and Russ are expanding yours. Congratulations."

"Thanks." She rubbed her stomach through her wool sweater. "Another month and I'll be a mom. We can't wait. Neither can Grace."

"I bet. She loves babies."

"Yeah, she does."

Ty's smile faded along with Lizzie's, and he figured he could do one of two things. Launch into a ten-minute monologue about how sorry he was about everything, or stand there and suck down his French Roast like a coward and opt for a lame change in subject.

"God, you certainly have cleaned this place up," Ty blurted, shifting his attention to the refinished hardwood floor. "I remember chipped linoleum and rotting wood."

"Don't look at me, it's all Grace Ann. She rebuilt the whole thing piece by piece. The landscaping, the outbuildings, she even refurbished that old caretaker cottage for my Dad. The only thing left is that dilapidated barn out there." She nodded to the east side of the property. "She's got big plans for the place, I guess. Too bad her bank account isn't the same size."

Ty stepped into the huge living room, newly expanded from when he was last here. It resembled a log cabin, with exposed knotty pine beams and a stone fireplace that climbed up to the cathedral ceiling. A picture window looked out at the valley and the dull glow of night lights from the ski resort across the way.

"Looks like ski season will start early this year."

"That's what Grace is hoping. I think she misses her winter regulars in the summer off-season."

In the corner by the window sat a Steinway baby grand piano. He pressed middle C and smiled. It had been tuned since the last time he'd been there.

"Listen, I told Grace I would bring her a cup of coffee." Lizzie came up behind him and placed her hand on his shoulder. "Why don't you take this to her? She's in the barn."

When she handed him the thermos, he knew it

was a peace offering that he didn't want her to reconsider.

He leaned down and kissed her cheek before heading across the kitchen toward the door.

## Chapter Three

Grace stood in the middle of the barn, assessing the project in front of her. The place had been under restoration for three months, and the only thing that had been done was the stall removal. That's what she hated about hiring people to do things. They took their own sweet time, and it was never exactly as she wanted it. The place was now one big two-thousand-square-foot empty space with a questionable foundation. It would be perfect for the five-star restaurant she had planned if the roof didn't collapse on her first.

From her research, many of the world's best bed and breakfasts had separate restaurants on the grounds for both the guests and people not staying on the property. The project was actually a secret gift for Lizzie. Grace knew she missed the hustle and bustle of New York and her job as banquet manager at the Waldorf Astoria. Not that Lizzie wouldn't be busy with a newborn. But at this rate, the kid would be in college by the time the place was anywhere near finished anyway.

She lifted her head toward the ceiling and squinted at the sections of exposed sky. Snowflakes floated between the ill-fastened shingles, right next to the fluorescent lights, no less. She had a few do-it-yourself books on roofing, but electricity was something she left to the experts.

Doing a one-eighty, she studied the loft at the far end of the barn. In her mind she pictured the place as a private dining area, or at least a quieter one. The carpenter she'd consulted told her the wood was too rotted for anyone to go up there to check the integrity of the weight-bearing beams.

But she was curious.

The stairs to the loft were torn down, so she dragged a ladder over. Fully extended, the top rung was just high enough to reach. Tightening her boot laces for safety's sake, she carefully scaled the steps to the top.

Gently she stepped up, the dry bowed wood creaking under her leather soles. The area was larger than she pictured, but also in worse shape. The holes in the untreated planks indicated carpenter ants. If that were the case, the boards were probably hollow.

Maybe the professionals weren't always wrong.

The floor shifted underneath her. She held her breath when she heard a crack, and a small cloud of dirt lifted in the air. In an effort to disperse her weight, she dropped to her knees, then lay flat on her stomach. Sliding along the floor, she made her way to the ladder.

"Grace Ann, are you in here?"

The deep gravel voice was unmistakable. When she got to the ledge she peeked over. Her heart hammered in her chest, and her mouth was cotton dry, but she suspected that had less to do with her fear of falling to her death and more about the gorgeous man twice that distance away.

"Ty?"

When he saw her, he cursed then jogged to the foot of the ladder. "Grace Ann, what the hell are you doing up there?"

"Trying to get down."

He scowled, adjusting the cap on his head. "Well the quicker the better, that wood looks rotted out."

"It is." A carpenter ant crawled over her glove. She left it, afraid the sudden movement of flicking it off would send her plummeting to the floor.

"I'll hold the ladder."

"Forget the ladder, I'll jump."

When she said the words, she almost laughed. A drop from this distance would break more than a few bones, but it would be worth it to prove a point. She could do anything without anyone's help, although if her potential helper was anyone but Ty, this was one time she would have made an exception.

"Grace, there is no way in hell you can jump."

"If you remember correctly, Jax Sinclair, you aren't the only one who did his own stunts."

Ty put his hands on his hips and smirked. "Well, I can't think of an episode where a stunt coordinator would send you falling thirty feet onto concrete covered in ants."

"What about the time in that episode where we were hiding in a deer stand?"

Ty cocked his head as if trying to remember. "That was about half the distance on a sound stage, and I'm pretty sure you landed on an air mattress."

"Close enough."

"Shut up. I'm coming after you." He started up the ladder.

The last thing she needed was this jerk thinking he needed to save her. Taking a breath, she gritted her teeth, and with one fluid motion, she swung herself onto the ladder and quickly stepped down. "Happy now?" she asked, wiping her hands together with pride.

His dimples deepened in his day-old stubble. "Yeah, I'm happy."

She flinched when he pulled something out of her hair, probably an ant. Who knew where else they had settled. "Why did you come here, Ty?"

"To bring you this." He unscrewed the thermos and handed it to her. "Lizzie just made it."

"That's not what I meant." She smelled the contents of the thermos. She was explicit in telling

Lizzie she wanted it black, no sugar no milk. Coffee on its own was a diuretic, but everything else added calories. If she wanted to slim down, no extras. "What's in here?" she asked, trying to peak inside. "I wanted black."

"I don't know."

She felt his eyes sizing her up. He knew all her games, and she only looked stupid trying to hide them, but somehow it made her feel good to try.

"Grace, it's cold out here, and this will warm you up."

When she put the thermos to her mouth, she smelled the heavy cream. She pursed her lips damming the liquid, then pretended to swallow, making her throat feign the outward motion.

"What were you doing up there anyway?" Ty walked underneath the loft, studying a few of the beams. "This looks pretty unstable."

"Not that it's any of your business, but I want to turn this place into a restaurant. I was curious about the space."

"Ever think of hiring someone to do that for you?"

"Ever think I could do it myself?"

He banged on the walls and shook a few of the weight-bearing beams. After running his boots over the small piles of sawdust, he came back to her. "I'll tell you what. I'll go up there tomorrow and check things out. I also noticed a few loose shingles on the north side. You'd be wise to fix those before the snow flies."

His southern accent was back. The sweet, slow-as-molasses drawl that in hushed tones could stir her as much as his touch. And she thought he'd lost it. "The snow's already flying, Ty."

"Which is why I'll get started first thing in the morning." He winked at her then stared up at the gaping hole in the ceiling. "It's supposed to be sunny tomorrow. It should warm enough to melt the roof, even on the north side. I think I can do it in a day."

She folded her arms. If this was his way of manipulating himself back onto her good side, it wouldn't work. "I don't think that's such a good idea."

"Why not? You know I grew up on a farm. I did this kind of stuff all the time."

"It's not that." The thought of his staying overnight in the farmhouse was too much. How many nights had she ached for his touch and hated herself for thinking about it in the first place. How many times would she scale those farmhouse stairs and run her hand over her empty womb. She'd hear his name on TV or see his picture in magazines and have to look away. He was her savior and enemy all in one, and if one could negate the other, he'd be nothing. But Ty was anything but nothing.

When he touched her cheek, she closed her eyes, his fingers burning her raw skin. "You really can't stand to look at me, can you?"

"Ty..."

"I mean really look at me. Like you used to."

As if responding to a dare, she pushed her lids open. His azure eyes gazed down at her, and in that moment, she was brought back to the last time she allowed herself to linger there. When he carried her into the hospital in Connecticut and told her he loved her for the last time.

Her eyes clamped shut. She held her breath until he pulled away, and she heard his retreating footsteps echo in her ears. "Where are you going?"

He pulled the car keys from his jeans pocket. "Back to the City. I'm sorry I bothered you. I'll see you next week."

"Wait."

She came towards him in the doorway. Suddenly feeling hot, she pulled the wool hat from her head.

"Look, I'm sure the roads were bad coming up here, and I don't need Ty Hawthorne's fan club blaming me for your demise." She sighed, hoping she wouldn't regret her decision. "Go get your things and bring them upstairs."

"You sure?"

She blew out a clouded breath. "No, but you're staying anyway."

He smirked. The Million Dollar GQ expression that could melt the coldest heart. "Thanks, Gracie." He winked at her before disappearing into the white fog.

****

Ty thought it best to leave his things by the porch. There were twelve bedrooms upstairs, and he had no clue where Grace planned on putting him. Besides he heard the water running in the shower, and he didn't trust himself wandering around upstairs, knowing she was naked and wet. He'd take the time to search for something to eat instead.

He hadn't eaten since lunch, and he wasn't one who could sleep on an empty stomach. After wolfing down a few of Lizzie's cookies, he looked through the cabinets and fridge. In his recollection, the only food ever brought into the place was when he had shopped. Toward the end, he noticed that he was the only one who actually ate it. But the stocked kitchen reminded him how things had changed. He grabbed a can of soup from the pantry and dumped it in a pan on the stove. When he heard the shower turn off, he decided to add a second.

He found a stack of bologna in the fridge. He pulled it out and made a couple of sandwiches, on white for him and wheat for her. When she padded down the stairs, he spooned the soup into two bowls and took them to the kitchen table.

"Tyler, what do you think you're doing?"

She came into the kitchen, clad in a thick, white

terrycloth robe better suited for a man his size than a tiny woman like herself. The sleeves draped over her hands, and the tie wrapped around twice. She looked like a child wearing grownups' clothes, save for the small triangle of cleavage and the red strand of hair that stuck in the moisture in between.

Searching for his voice, he stalled by licking the mustard off his thumb. "I was starving, so I thought I'd make myself something to eat. There's a ton of food here, by the way. I thought this place was closed for a few weeks."

"It is. Lizzie's been cooking non-stop. Casseroles, stews. She's vacuum-packed most of it for the guests."

"Wow. What got into her?"

"I think she's nesting. It's a pregnant woman thing."

He closed the refrigerator door. "I've heard that."

She looked away, pulling the robe tighter around her. "I um, guess I'll just head back upstairs."

"How about a cookie?" He snagged a gingerbread man from the stove and took a healthy bite

"That's okay. I'm not hungry."

Her monotone voice told him she hadn't even considered the offer. "Suit yourself. I just thought after all that work in the barn..."

"Don't act for me, Ty."

He stopped chewing mid-bite. She'd caught him, and it surprised him that he was surprised. Grace was a smart woman. She knew him better than he knew himself, and she always saw past any game or any line. It was some consolation that hadn't changed.

"I know what you're doing. And you don't have to."

He groaned, flipping the cookie back on the

table. "Grace, I was just making small talk."

"I'm better, Ty. I have been for almost five years."

He took a moment to study her, but there really wasn't much to see with her swimming in the robe. She looked healthy enough, but he knew from experience that didn't mean much. When she worked on *Undercover Heat* she followed a strict training regimen and carried a fair amount of muscle. She never looked like the classic anorexic, but he had learned the hard way that didn't mean a damn thing. "I told you today that you look beautiful. I meant it."

"Thank you. I suppose that's a pretty big compliment."

"Why?"

"I've seen the women you hang around with. Tall, tanned blondes with huge silicone breasts. I'm surprised I'm even on your radar screen."

A slap in the face would have hurt less. He held his hands up in resignation. "Fine, you win. You're right. It's none of my business. "

He expected her to head back upstairs, but she surprised him by meeting him at the table. She pulled the chair out beside him, the legs scraping against the hardwood. When she ran her fingers through her wet hair, the sweet scent of lilacs tickled his nose.

"Ty, I'm not going to deny that I was sick back then, and I admit I depended on you probably too much. I'm sorry for my part in what happened, but its over and I've moved on. Just like you."

Her clear blue eyes dulled, in a way he recognized all too well. She took the piece of cookie from the table, but only ate the crumbs that stuck to her fingers.

He wasn't the only one with acting chops.

After a long moment, she stood up from the

table and headed for the stairs. "If you grab your bags, I'll show you to your room."

"I'm fine on the couch."

"You might be, but I'm getting up early, and from what I've heard you've turned nocturnal. I don't want to tiptoe around the house in the middle of the day worrying about waking you up."

The insult hit him just fine. At least she cared enough to bother. Ty lugged his bag up the front staircase and found the light burning at the far end of the hall. Following the oriental runner, he made his way to the last door on the right. It wasn't lost on him that the bedroom was the furthest point in the house from hers.

He lingered in the doorway and watched Grace replace the linens on the bed. Her robe had loosened around her, giving him a decent flash of her breasts. A silver cross on a thin chain slipped out, sticking in her damp strawberry locks.

"Gracie, I want you to go dry your hair. It isn't right to run around this drafty house with a wet head. You'll catch your death."

"Didn't I just finish telling you I don't need your two cents?"

He rolled his eyes. "Fine, catch pneumonia."

While Grace fussed with the bathroom towels, he walked around the room, checking out the accommodations. Grace was a stickler for detail, and he remembered when she'd conceived the place that she wanted each room to have a theme. This must be the music room. A music box, with a tiny ballerina on top, sat on the dresser, and the ceiling border had black and white dancing silhouettes in mid-pirouette. Even the desk had a glass inlay with yellowed sheet music displayed underneath. He smiled when he saw the title. Elton John's "Tiny Dancer." He used to play it for her all the time on the downstairs piano.

The sleigh bed, large and soft, was almost a replica of Grace's, with intricate designs carved on the oak headboard. He ran his hand over the velvet comforter. It was thick and rich, and the deep burgundy color seemed to suit Grace's personality. Warm. Inviting. Soft.

Perfect.

A framed black-and-white photo of a young ballerina in mid leap hung on the wall beside the window. He walked to it and smiled. "This was always one of my favorite pictures of you, Grace."

She stepped out of the bathroom and squinted across the room at the picture. "Thanks. That was from when I was in *The Nutcracker*. I think it has the New York City Ballet emblem at the bottom of the picture."

"I know. It used to be downstairs by the piano."

"I thought it worked better up here." She shrugged. "I put some of our publicity pictures downstairs instead. The guests really like them."

"Really? I didn't see them."

"I took a lot of them down to dust. Not a small project by the way; there's a lot of them."

"You don't have to remind me. I moaned and groaned through every single one."

"You know, I never understood why you didn't like them," she said, walking around the bed toward him. "I thought it was fun getting all dressed up and having our pictures taken. Easier than memorizing lines and blocking."

"Dressed up? Undressed is more like it. It took all my self-control not to break the freakin' camera." He looked down at her, remembering how they used to doll her up in negligees and paint her with makeup. He preferred her natural. Pure. Just like this. With a slow and careful step, he went to her. The light cast gold highlights in her hair, her eyes the lightest shade of blue. "You're beautiful, Grace, you know that?"

The question didn't warrant an answer, and he didn't wait for one. Instead he closed the distance between them, and slowly brought his mouth to hers.

Her cherry lips were as soft as he'd remembered. She tasted sweet, like the finest wine he ever sampled, and the rush it brought to him was just as intoxicating. He cupped her face, tracing the line of her jaw with his thumb. Desire teased him, taunted him, urged him to search her mouth with his tongue, but when he felt her push against his chest, he reluctantly broke the kiss and covered her hand with his. "I'm sorry," he croaked.

Her back was to him now, and her shoulders hunched over in a shrug. "It's okay."

"Grace..."

"Okay, I guess that's it," she said and moved around him toward the bathroom. "Towels are on the sink, and you know where everything else is."

"Gracie..."

"And if you need an extra blanket, closet at the end of the hall."

"Grace Ann." She had to still know that when he used her full name he meant business. Not in a menacing kind of way, but one that indicated he needed to be heard. Grace had a way of shutting others out, and in the past he'd mostly let her have her way. He reserved his battles for times when it really mattered, like insisting she eat when she hadn't in days, or times like this when he'd done something stupid and needed her to know he was sorry.

He sat down on the bed and shook his head. "That was inappropriate. I promise you it won't happen again. It's just been a long day and all. And seeing you..."

"I understand."

The words were obligatory. He could see confusion in her eyes, and maybe a little of the sadness that he felt himself.

He wished the smile back.

"What about tomorrow?"

She raised her brow. "What do you mean 'tomorrow'?"

"I figured besides that barn roof you could find something to keep me occupied. A walk in the woods or ice skating on the pond."

"Hmmm. I don't know about that," she said. "From what I've heard recently, this place might be a little low-key for you. No exotic dancers or blackjack tables for a good hundred miles."

She said it with the disgust of any good little Irish-Catholic girl, and he felt the dutiful shame. "I'll be on my best behavior."

Mercifully, she slid out the door. The scent of fresh lilacs lingered in her place, and the warmth of the space dispersed to a chill.

He sat on the bed and stared at the door, her taste still on his lips.

****

Harvey Tillman tossed his piece-of-shit camera into the empty passenger seat. You get what you fucking pay for. What he really needed on an assignment like this was one of those high-powered lens jobs that all the good paparazzi sported. But east L.A. pawn shops weren't known for their high-tech equipment, and he'd told Layla he had the scratch to invest in this gig.

So far he had gotten by just fine. He got his ass to New York, even took some choice shots of the duo in the diner. Not bad for a guy whose only experience in a job like this was advice he got in city lockup from a psycho who set his girlfriend's beauty salon on fire.

But Tillman was a bullshit artist, and,

thankfully, Layla was as stupid as she was crazy. The perfect combination, in his opinion, to make a hell of a lot of money and get crazy laid. But the money and the perks were only half of it. He had his own agenda, and if all went to plan…

He squinted through the darkness, at the glow in the upstairs window. They were in there. Probably doing it. He closed his eyes, picturing Ty on top of her, giving it to her good. Harvey loved small women, and Grace Ann was as sexy as they came. Petite, but built in all the right places. She was probably tight, too. He could tell. He imagined himself slipping into her. Jesus, did Hawthorne know how to pick his women.

He opened one eye and again looked up at the window. Not a damn thing to see. He wished he could figure a way to plant a camera in there. Like the ones they used on those news shows, like "How to Nail a Nanny" or some shit like that. Christ, a freaking sex tape of Ty and Grace. That would really blow Layla's mind, and he'd bet his piece-of-shit camera that she'd be more than happy to show her gratitude. Her and Marcy both.

The bedroom light turned off just as flurries dotted his windshield. Fucking figured. The place was winter hell, and he'd head back to the city if he wasn't driving a decade-old Dodge Shadow with bald tires and half a muffler. Nah, he was better off camping out right here in his car. There had to be a parking lot around where no one would hassle him. Maybe across the way at the ski resort. He could get a few hours shuteye and probably pick up some coffee there, too.

He checked his watch, then looked into the darkness in front of him. The wind whistled around his car, blowing clouds of snow across the pavement. The plow had just gone through minutes ago, and the cops would be on him if they figured him for a disabled car on the side of the road. But before he did anything, he'd have to check in. Staying on the boss's good side was the key to his success. He pulled his cell phone from his pocket and pushed Two on the speed dial.

## Chapter Four

Grace rolled away from the morning sun pouring through her bedroom window. Yesterday, when she was inspired to take down the venetian blinds to dust, she didn't think she'd have the sun to contend with. It was November in the North Country, after all. The job probably would have been a whole lot easier if she had just left the stupid things up in the first place. But that's how most of her life went. A search and discover mission all her own, that sometimes taught her lessons the hard way.

Ty Hawthorne, case in point.

Last night she tossed and turned, her bed feeling larger than usual. Lonely. More than once she had closed her eyes and imagined Ty lying beside her. Holding her, touching her. Dragging his lips down the nape of her neck, kissing her softly on the mouth...

The muffled sound of an ax striking wood snapped her out of her thoughts. Blinking back tears, she went to the window. Ty stood in the middle of the yard over a pile of wood, dressed in jeans, work boots, and a tan Carhartt jacket. God, he was handsome. Big and solid, but soft and gentle. At least that's what she remembered. Back then they were inseparable. Friends first, then much later lovers, secretly holding tight to each other while the wild ride of fame tossed them about. No one had a clue about their relationship. Not even Earl, and especially not her parents. They were already mad that she'd left the New York City Ballet to work on

*Undercover Heat.* And for people who considered eight o'clock network television pornographic, they would never have understood her relationship with a poor southern boy who in their eyes could never measure up to their perfect daughter.

Ty was thrilled when she told him she was pregnant, and she was too, until the fear overtook her. It would affect the show, expose their relationship, and no way would the Archbishop award a high-up position to a man with a notoriously illegitimate grandchild.

Somehow, her terror had manifested in a strange sort of contest of how little she could eat, and how much weight she could lose. A game she played casually as a dancer, but at five months pregnant mastered. She didn't recall the tumble down the stairs, but she imagined the physical pain was far less than the emotional agony that followed. Pulling through it was no small feat, but she came out okay. Even through her mother's death, she managed. Yes, Grace Ann Langley was a new person, and this one didn't need Ty Hawthorne in her life. In a few weeks, a month tops, she wouldn't ever have to lay eyes on him again.

"You want me to get a towel to mop up the drool?"

Grace clutched her chest and spun around. Lizzie stared back at her in the doorway. Her arms folded as if she was angry, but the smirk told her Lizzie was more amused than anything else. "Shut up, Lizzie."

"What? My sister is gawking at the Sexiest Man Alive two years running, and I can't make a joke?"

Lizzie wasn't naturally funny. Grace was actually the family comedian, not a hard fought title, considering the stoics her parents had been, but a quality she was proud of, nonetheless. This was Lizzie's attempt to let her know she was here for her, and Grace appreciated the gesture.

"So I'm sure you didn't miss me when I slipped out of here last night." Lizzie came up next to her and leaned on the windowsill. "That was pretty gutsy of him to drive all the way up here. Did he say anything to you? I mean, about why he's here?"

Grace ran her hands down her arms, feeling the chill from the window through her white cotton gown. "Not really," she shrugged. "Just small talk. Earl probably sent him. Make sure I don't jump ship on this whole publicity thing."

"Are you thinking of doing that?"

Grace looked across the way at the dilapidated roof on the east barn. When her mother got sick, most of Grace's savings from the show went for her care. Of course, she didn't regret spending it. She just wished she had a little left. "I can't. The money is too good to pass up."

"I guess you have to make the best of it then." Lizzie's lips bent into a smirk, and her eyes twinkled with laughter. "You didn't 'make the best of it' last night, did you?"

"Lizzie! Of course not!" Grace made a point of staring at her before waiting a beat and turning away. She learned that from Ty when they were running lines once. It was his "how-dare-you-question-my-conviction look." She had tweaked it and kept it for her own.

"I had to ask. It's not like you to sleep past eight."

Grace looked at her watch, but realized she hadn't put it on yet. "Past eight? Wow, I must have been tired."

"Well I hope you're rested now, because I'm leaving at noon. Russ is coming home, and I want to spend some quiet time with him while I still can."

Grace didn't reply, her gaze fixed on Ty. His agile body, the soft grunt he made when the ax struck the wood. She breathed deep to steady herself. The man could be jumping around like a monkey, and she bet he'd still be sexy doing it.

"Please don't tell me you require a chaperone."

"Of course not," Grace answered, too quickly for even her ears, then pulled the curtain closed. "Listen, I thought I'd run into town before the snow starts again. You need anything? Maybe some sparkling grape juice for your little tryst." She winked. "Russ is probably going to be very happy to see you."

"Don't you worry about me, baby sister. You keep your mind on your own dramas. That guy out there is red hot, and if he gets too close, he'll burn you like he did before." Lizzie squeezed her shoulder, her face softened to a motherly smile. "By the way. Daddy is due home in a few days. I don't know how long Ty's staying, but if he sees him..."

"I know," Grace said, the thought of last night's kiss passing through her brain. "Don't worry. It won't be an issue."

The loud crack startled them both as a large log tumbled to the ground. Ty picked up another and set it up, positioning his ax over his shoulder, and took a swing.

"Tell you what," Lizzie said, heading out the door. "I'll make a list of things we need in town, but before that, we should take him some water. He's been at that woodpile since I got here an hour and a half ago. He's probably parched."

"I'll do it," Grace called after her. She pulled on a flannel shirt and overalls and hastily threw her hair up in a ponytail. When she was downstairs ten minutes later, Lizzie had a thermos of ice water waiting.

"You should ask him about breakfast, too," Lizzie said. "I have a batch of peanut butter cookies in the oven if he wants some."

"I'll let him know." Not bothering with a jacket, Grace pulled on her gloves and jogged out the door with the thermos tucked under her arm.

****

Ty picked up another log and set it up on the stump. With his one swift swing, it split in half and tumbled into the snow in a cloud of powder.

Lizzie seemed impressed that when she pulled in at six thirty he was already shoveling the walk. Truth was he actually missed this kind of work. Funny, because when it meant his survival, it felt like torture. After his father died in the Kentucky coal mines, and before his mother passed, he supported her by working as a farm hand outside Birmingham, Alabama. He was at a mall hardware store buying pliers when a talent scout discovered him at age 23. A year later, he landed the role of Jax on *Undercover Heat*. A year after that he won his first Emmy.

He always thought having loads of money would make life cake, but so far it had done nothing but complicate it. Someone always wanted a piece of the pie. He missed the simple existence, where people were genuine and time passed slowly. Like the time he'd spent here at Whisper Grove. Some of his happiest memories were of just lying on the porch swing, watching the grass grow, with Gracie asleep in his arms.

"Ty?"

He stopped mid swing, her soft voice stealing his strength. When he set the ax down, she stepped closer, her delicate stature barely denting the fresh snow. "Grace Ann, how long have you been standing there without a jacket?" His thick Southern accent startled him. He'd noticed it last night, too. Where the hell did that come from all of a sudden?

"Not long, I just didn't want to interrupt you. You seemed to be on a roll." She pointed to the pile of freshly split wood. “You really got through that cord in a hurry.”

“Yeah, well, I could use the upper body workout.” Her hair looked even redder against the white landscape; the breeze blew strands across her pale face. He brushed one aside and tucked it behind her ear. He wished his hand wasn’t gloved, so he could feel her skin. “That for me?”

“Huh?”

He nodded toward the thermos tucked under her arm.

“Oh, yeah. It’s ice water. Lizzie thought you might like it.”

He unscrewed the cap and took a long gulp. When he was done, he smiled down at her. “Did you have a good night’s sleep?”

“Sure, I love a cool night.”

He remembered. Ten degrees outside, she’d crack a window. “It was still dark when I got up. I was careful not to make too much noise stumbling around.”

“Wow, when was the last time you saw a sunrise?”

“I see it all the time. Usually I haven’t been to bed yet, though.”

The porch door swung open, and Lizzie appeared. From fifty feet away, Ty saw the panic on her face. “Grace! We’re out of chocolate chips.”

Grace laughed. Ty loved it when she laughed. The way her cheeks reddened, how her lips curled at the sides. Something stirred inside him, and he brought the thermos back to his lips.

“So you’re telling me you’d like me to head into town sooner rather than later,” Grace called back.

“It’d be nice.”

“Can I tag along?”

Grace looked at him, with deep wrinkles creasing her forehead. He recognized the expression.

It was the one she gave when she sized him up or questioned his motives. And rightly so. After kissing her last night, all he could think of was how he wanted to do it again. “Get your jacket, and I’ll start the Hummer.”

“Fine, you can go, but we’re taking my truck. If people see me in that monstrosity of yours, I’ll be the talk of the town.” She felt around her overalls pockets before pulling out the keys. “I’ll be right back.”

Grace disappeared into the house, but Lizzie lingered. She leaned against the doorframe, her arms crossed over her swollen belly. Ty felt the daggers from her eyes clear across the lawn. Sensing she had something to say, he jogged up to the porch, but stopped on the second step when she lifted her hand in front of her. “Um…is there anything else you want us to get?”

“Cut the nice-guy crap.”

He looked past her on into the house. When he didn’t see Grace, he took a step closer. “What? What’s wrong?”

“Plenty, if you’re not careful with her. You know, you’re not the only one who can swing an ax around here, Hawthorne. Watch your step. “

This wasn’t the first time he had angered a woman enough to threaten his life. This was, however, the first time he absolutely believed it. With a growl that reminded Ty of an angry pit bull, Lizzie pulled a folded piece of stationery out of her apron and shoved it into his chest. “See you two in a bit.”

Grace stepped out the door and patted her sister’s shoulder on her way by. “If you think of anything else, call my cell,” she said. “And remember, no lifting.”

Ty followed Grace out to the truck. Grace sat at the wheel, rubbing her ungloved hands together to warm them. He knocked on the frosted glass and motioned for her to roll the window down. "How about you move over," he said. "The roads are bad, and I'd feel better if I was the one behind the wheel."

"Excuse me, but who's the native New Yorker here. I'm driving."

"But, Grace."

"Get in."

The power window hummed to a close, and just like that, the conversation ended. He took a step back, not so much in compliance, but at the shock of her words. Grace Ann had just given him an order. It had been a while since anyone had told him what to do, except a director, of course, but even then, Ty ultimately held their fate in his hands. It was refreshing and strangely arousing. Grace Ann was taking control, and God damn, he was happy to let her have it.

He jumped in the passenger side and pulled off his work gloves. Warmer ones would have been his choice, but as he rubbed them together, he was beginning to think they felt better frozen. His palms burned, heralding the bloom of blisters. He looked at them and scowled. A decade of easy living had dulled his calluses.

"Are your hands okay?"

"Yeah," he said and blew into his palms. "I guess I should have worn better gloves."

"You should have used ones like mine. I rarely get a blister."

He reached across the seat, bringing her palm to his cheek. "You're right. Smooth as ever."

"Which is more than I can say for your beard." She replaced her hand on the steering wheel. "So tell me, is this unshaven, unkempt look of yours all part of your dangerous playboy persona, or are you just lazy after long nights of carousing?"

"Jeez, you make it sound like I'm Grizzly

Adams."

"I'm just kidding with you."

He leaned against the door and looked at her. Her stiff shoulders, the slightest blush to her cheeks that he knew wasn't from the cold. Teasing was her favorite form of self-defense, and he could tell just by sharing the space she was on guard. He frowned. "You really have a hard time being around me, don't you?"

He heard her breath hitch before she answered. "I don't know, Ty. How do you expect me to answer that?"

"Are you happy?"

"What?"

"You heard me."

The lack of an immediate answer told him what he already knew. There was a glow about her before that was so intense, many times he'd likened it to a beacon. Everyone saw it. Earl, her fans, and especially him. It still was there, but it had dulled, like whatever fueled it was no longer at a premium. He wondered if he was to blame. "Look, Gracie, I know you've been through a lot, I mean with what happened with us, and losing your mom and restoring the farm. But you came through it, and I'm glad to see that."

"Don't do that."

"Don't do what?"

"Pity me."

He shrugged. "I wasn't. I was just saying..."

"I know what you're saying." Her knuckles blanched as her grip tightened on the steering wheel. "I just worked so hard to get past everything. I can't think about it anymore."

Ty stared out the windshield and fixed his gaze on the horizon. The memory of her limp in his arms at the bottom of the staircase flashed through his mind. Her pale face, her eyelashes black against her white cheeks. "I don't blame you, baby."

"And please don't do that."

"Do what?"

"The pet names," she said. "It may impress all those silicone-filled Barbie dolls you sleep with, but I don't want to hear it."

She was right. Who did he think he was? She may have put him up for the night, and let him ride shotgun while she ran some errands, but that didn't mean she had to like it. She should give him a hard time. He deserved nothing less.

The snow came down in giant clumps now, blurring the landscape into a grayish haze. The pickup fishtailed, but she righted it. "What about you, Ty. Are you happy?"

He turned back toward her. "Huh?"

"You heard me."

Ty pushed himself up in his seat and chewed the inside of his cheek. No response was necessary. Just by asking the question, he could tell she already knew the answer.

She tapped the brakes and turned a corner into the parking lot of Wellman's Grocery. It looked just like it did five years ago, with a sagging roof, chipped paint job, and a neon "open" sign with the "p" burnt out. The lot consisted of five parking spots out front and an area for snowmobiles around the back. Mavis Wellman, owner and proprietor of the store, had won the pink Cadillac, parked in front, for selling cosmetics. It told Ty she was working that morning.

"Mavis is totally going to know who you are," Grace grumbled under her breath. "Do me a favor and stay in the car. I really don't need the fanfare right now if someone recognizes you."

"Grace, I don't even recognize myself. I've got a hat on, I haven't shaved in days, and I'm dressed like a freakin' Eskimo. I think it's fine."

She rolled her eyes. “Fine, just let me go in first.”

He pulled the list from his jeans pocket and handed it to her. When she was safely inside, he counted to one hundred before following her path up the wooden stairs.

A bell announced his entrance when the door slammed behind him. His eyes watered immediately, partially from the sudden heat, but mostly from the overpowering smell of cedar competing with stale coffee. A mangy sheep dog, named Duke, he thought, looked up from his slumber on the splintered wood floor. Unimpressed by Ty’s presence, he laid his head back down with a groan.

Taking a quick glance around, Ty headed to the magazine rack beside the front counter. The small town staples were all sold out. *Field and Stream, Outdoor Life.* The entertainment ones, however, were in good supply. They were all a week behind, and most had his picture somewhere on the cover. One with some blonde girl in Italy, another with a brunette in New York. He picked up the one with a half-naked Layla superimposed next to him on a beach. The headline read “Reunited?” He laughed. Were they ever united in the first place?

“You’re following the Tyla breakup too, huh.”

A girl peeked out from behind the register, cracking her gum. She flipped her dark hair over her shoulder, revealing her SUNY Stonybrook sweatshirt. He smiled in relief. It wasn’t Mavis.

He waited a moment to answer, taking a quick scan of the store. Empty. Even Grace had disappeared. Perhaps he was incognito after all. “Tyla?” he asked.

“Oh, yeah!” the girl said. “You know—Bradgelina. TomCat. All the big couples have nicknames like that.”

“Hmm, I don’t know much about that. I just

thought that Ty Hawthorne guy was a pretty decent actor." Feeling brave, he picked up another magazine and held it out in front of him. "His ex-wife seems a little screwed up, though."

"Yeah, well can you blame her? If my boyfriend cheated on me like he cheated on her..." She held her hand up in a fist. "That's why I'm glad I came here with his family for the holidays instead of mine. I can keep an eye on him."

Not everyone was a fan, he figured. But it couldn't hurt to defend himself. He walked up to the counter and leaned against the candy display, crossing his arms against his chest. "Do you really think he's all that bad? I mean Ty Hawthorne, not your boyfriend. I thought Layla was the one who ran out on him, with the dog walker?"

She giggled. "Maybe he drove her to it. You know what I mean?"

Again, he scanned the front aisles. No Grace. And that was fine. No sense being slandered in front of her. He smiled at the girl as if he agreed, then turned his attention back to the magazine rack.

"Wait a minute. I know you!" The girl snapped her gum when she leveled a pointed finger at him. "You're Amy Miller's older brother! I'm Kelly. I know Amy from school. Your picture is hanging in her dorm room."

Ty shifted his weight, and the rotted floor whined underneath him. Whoever this guy was, she seemed happy to see him, and he never liked to disappoint a pretty girl. His decision made, he cleared his throat. Improv. Just like when he hosted *Saturday Night Live*. "Hi. Yes, that's right." He extended his hand to her. "It's good to be home. I missed this place."

"Todd, right? I've totally heard so much about you."

Grace came up to the counter, spilling her

handful of items in front of Kelly. She looked past Ty like she didn't know him, and he picked up on her cue. Either she had overheard his conversation with the girl and was keeping out of it, or she had an agenda all her own.

"Well, tell Amy I said Hi," Kelly chirped. "I forgot she lived up here, too. You can totally come out with us if you want. I'm not sure there's a whole lot to do up here, but I'm sure we could find something."

The smile widened on Grace's face. He moved over when she reached in front of him, pulling a magazine from the rack. "You know, I just overheard you two talking about that Ty Hawthorne." Grace held up the *Celeb!* magazine and read the headline out loud. "Layla Plays It Straight. I Want My Husband Back."

"God, do you blame her?" Kelly said, punching the buttons on the register. "The guy might play around, but he is, by far, the hottest man ever."

"He's not bad." Grace shrugged. "He just seems like sort of a jerk."

"I've seen all his movies. And he was on that TV show. What was it?" Kelly looked up to the ceiling, waving Grace's twenty in the air. "Undercover... something."

"*Undercover Heat*." Grace supplied, pulling the zipper closed on her wallet and stuffing it back in her pocket.

"Oh, yeah," Ty said, leaning against the counter facing Grace. "And his costar. Was it Grace Ann Langley?" He folded his arms, seeing a challenge in her little game. "Wow, she was a beautiful woman."

Grace smirked. "Really, you thought so?"

"Hell, yeah, and talented. I think she won an Emmy."

"Hmm, just one?" She took the change from Kelly. "I thought it was two."

Ty brushed his beard with his hand. A dramatic pause, but also a moment to contain the laughter. "You know I remember reading somewhere that they had a thing."

Grace raised a brow. "Really, you mean like a romantic thing?"

"No way," Kelly said from somewhere behind the register.

"For real." He leaned over, with his elbows on the counter. "Yeah, and I also heard that he was so heartbroken over their breakup that he never got over her."

Kelly put her hand over her heart. "Oh, that is so romantic."

"And I don't blame him," Ty added. "Grace Ann Langley... Wow." He extended his hand to Grace, and she took it. "I'm Todd Miller by the way, and forgive me for saying so, but you remind me a lot of her."

"Really?"

"Does she?" Kelly giggled, piling the food into a paper bag. "I don't really remember her."

"She had incredible eyes and a smile that'd melt ice." He looked up at Grace. "I always had a thing for her. Still do."

"That's sweet," Kelly said.

"And a little scary," Grace added, taking the bag off the counter. "That show has been off the air for almost five years. Move on, Todd."

She breezed past him, her elbow bumping his shoulder. When he heard the bell on the way out the door, he paid for a pack of gum and followed. By the time he made it down the stairs, she had already pulled the truck around back. He went to the driver's side, and she jumped across, collapsing in a fit of laughter, when he opened the door.

"I see you're at least letting me drive. That's nice of you."

"No one's made me laugh like that in a while," she said, wiping a tear from her eye. "You earned the right."

"Great. You can abuse me all you want. As long as you don't lose that smile."

"You really do know the right thing to say at the right time. I can see why you're so successful with the ladies."

"Successful?" He chuckled, as he turned out on to the road. "You're a strange source of positive reinforcement."

"I'm not reinforcing your behavior, nor do I think it's positive. I'm just stating a fact."

The comments struck him funny. He realized that he didn't like talking about other women with Grace. It felt dirty and pathetic. Stealing a glance beside him, he watched her pull the grocery bag onto her lap. She buried her head inside and rifled around in the contents.

"Grace, you know all of them aren't true, right?"

"All of what?"

He drummed his fingers on the wheel. "The news stories. About me. The things you've heard."

She looked up at him, her hooded eyes conveying disappointment. Grace Ann took sex very seriously, partially from her upbringing, but mostly because control over her body was hard for her to relinquish. This was her calling him morally disgusting, and he hated that she was absolutely right.

"Grace, I know this probably doesn't mean anything now, but while we were together, I was faithful. I mean that."

Her gaze drifted out her window. "What about Layla?" she asked after a moment. "Did you cheat on her?"

The fact she was asking the question at all told him how far he'd fallen in her eyes. He had been faithful to Layla, painfully so, until a few months ago when she decided on a "discreetly open marriage," whatever the hell that was. But that didn't justify his behavior. "My marriage to Layla was a sham for the whole eight months we were together. It was a drunken night in Las Vegas that I regretted from the start."

She shook her head. "How could you marry someone you didn't love?"

"Trust me; it's much easier than leaving someone you do."

"Damn it! Prenatal vitamins!"

Ty blinked, his train of thought totally shifting. "What are you talking about?"

"Lizzie's vitamins. I knew I forgot something." She picked up the list from the seat and looked it over. "I wrote it down, too."

"Don't worry about it. I'll turn around."

"I remembered everything else. Chocolate chips, shortening. Canned frosting. Yuck, how can she eat this stuff?"

"She's pregnant, Grace. She has cravings."

"I never did."

Ty smiled; he couldn't resist.

"Well…maybe not for food."

She slowly lifted her head out of the bag, her smirk telling Ty she caught his drift. "What are you suggesting?"

"Nothing. It's just that I remember suffering from dehydration for a good week after you told me you were pregnant. I had no bodily fluids left. I'd touch you, and you'd throw me into bed."

"Tyler James!" She slapped him on the arm and laughed. Jesus, did he love that sound. A childlike giggle with the deeper timbre of a woman. Used in the right setting, he was convinced it could be a weapon.

When the moment passed, her face clouded again, and Ty knew her thoughts had shifted. "What is it?" he asked, playfully, patting her knee.

"I'm sorry I didn't crave food."

"I know," he said softly. "I know."

He pulled into the parking lot, not bothering to kill the engine. "You wait here," he said. "I'll be right back." Ty headed back inside and made his way to the medicine aisle. He picked up the familiar bottle and headed up to the register, wondering what the hell Kelly would think of his purchase.

But it wasn't Kelly at the register. It was Mavis. Her grey bobbed hair just like he remembered, her glasses balanced on the bridge of her nose. Her back still turned to him, enabling a getaway if need be. He considered it, given what he held in his hand.

He dropped the bottle on the counter, and she scanned it without looking up. He figured he was home free, until he reached in his back pocket. His money clip was back at the house. All he had was a credit card.

Thankfully, he could slide the card himself, and when it asked for his signature he scribbled it fast before snagging his purchase and heading out the door. He hopped back into the car and was about to congratulate himself on his slick getaway when he realized his fatal flaw. He'd left the receipt behind.

It was probably paranoia, or years of getting used to looking over his shoulder, but in Los Angeles or New York making a purchase like that would be tabloid fodder. He could see the headline now: "Ty Hawthorne and his Secret Love Child."

But Middle Valley wasn't Hollywood. People weren't out to get each other. Besides, Mavis was a nice person, she wasn't an opportunist. A gossip, yes, but not vindictive. It would never occur to her to call a tabloid or news reporter.

"Ty? Everything okay?"

He looked at Grace and threw the car into gear. "Of course. Let's get the hell out of here."

## Chapter Five

Grace set the phone down beside the stove and sighed. Phew, at least that's over with. She'd been stressing all day about the dinnertime check-in with her father. Usually they just chit-chatted about the weather, a funny story about a local parishioner, or tidbits of news from the Archbishop. Not a daily interrogation, but if the subject of Ty and the press event came up…

If he didn't ask specifically about Ty, she sure as heck wouldn't mention him. So if she was guilty of lying by omission then so be it. It wouldn't be the first time.

The angry wind rattled the frame on the kitchen window, so she pulled on the crank to tighten the seal. Installing new windows was next on her to-do list, but the barn took priority. Ty had been out there banging away since they came home from the store. Not that his diligence surprised her. What would, however, was if he didn't come running when he smelled his favorite meal.

She pulled the pot roast from the oven and basted it, taking a deep whiff. Even though eating sometimes was a struggle, cooking was not. She considered it an art. When Lizzie told her Russ was coming home, Grace insisted on cooking them dinner. She slid it back in the oven. It should be done in an hour. Then she'd pack it up and drive it down the road to them, hopefully before the snow started again.

Grace retrieved the strainer from the cabinet and went back to the sink to peel vegetables for the relish dish. She was stuffing the cucumber skins down the garbage disposal when the door creaked open behind her.

"Something smells good in here," Ty said from the mudroom, his voice carried on a rush of cold air. "If I didn't know better I'd say it's pot roast."

Her heart skipped when she heard the thuds of his boots falling to the floor. "I hope you're hungry."

She heard him rub his hands together before opening the oven door behind her. "That's one hell of a slab of meat, darlin'. What army are you feeding tonight?"

"Lizzie."

"Damn, and I was hoping for leftovers."

She smiled, her attention still fixed on the veggies. "I made two, actually. The small one is for you. I thought I'd feed you first before I took the rest over to Lizzie and Russ."

"Feed me first? What am I, a poodle?" He came up behind her and reached around for a carrot in the strainer. She smelled the snow on his sweatshirt, mingling with his musky aftershave. Her stomach stirred at the familiar scent, her eyes fluttered to a close, and she forced them back open.

He moved about the kitchen, setting the table, stirring the gravy. Things he used to do before. Years ago she loved moments like these. No rehearsed lines, no characters to play. Just the two of them co-existing, operating as a real-life, everyday couple.

Except now, things were different. Her lines were rehearsed, even if just in her head, and the space they shared was now clouded with regret. But maybe forcing herself to keep her distance was pointless. So what that he had abandoned her? Who cared that she cried herself to sleep for months after he left? Big deal. She sliced the carrot hard, taking a hunk of her skin along with the vegetable's.

"Damn it!" She dropped the knife into the sink. Ty pushed around her and took her hand in his. "What'd you do?"

"What does it look like?"

He turned on the water, adjusting the hot and cold knobs. When the temperature satisfied his own hand, he held hers under the stream. "I think you might live, Lexis Love. It just looks like a flesh wound."

She rolled her eyes at her character's name. "Thanks, Jax, you're my hero."

"Let me put a bandage on it, so it doesn't get infected." He winked at her and opened the cabinet next to him. She stared at her small fingers held tightly by his large ones. Gentle and kind at times, but also strong and agile. She gulped, remembering the pleasure they conjured.

"You know, I snuck in here earlier for a glass of water, and you were in the other room on the phone." He smoothed the bandage gently over the wound. "Sounded important."

"It's nothing," she mumbled.

"You didn't tell him I was here, did you."

He said it like a statement rather than a question, and somehow the presumption irked her. "You're not always the first topic of discussion, Ty."

"When's he coming home?"

"Tomorrow or the day after. He's not sure."

He nodded like he understood and turned his attention back to her bandaged hand. "Well, I think you won't have to amputate, but the carrots are a casualty. You bled all over them."

She looked into the sink at the tainted vegetables. "Sorry."

"No problem with me. You know I'm a meat and potatoes man." He picked up the strainer and dumped them into the sink. "How about you sit at the table and look pretty, and I'll finish up here."

"Ty…"

"Hush, girl," he said, pulling the dinner plates from the hutch. "You've been putting me up in your house. The least I can do is serve you dinner."

Grace sat at the table with a cup of tea, watching Ty move around the kitchen. In minutes, he carved the roast and arranged the fixings on the table. He helped himself to some merlot from the wine closet in the pantry and handed her a glass.

"Looks good." Ty rubbed his hands together before sitting down across from her. His smile made it impossible to protest when he spooned a healthy helping of mashed potatoes and a thick slice of meat onto her plate. If she didn't have to worry about the camera's scrutiny over the next few weeks, she'd eat at least some of it. But the power in defying her hunger was far too liberating. If she couldn't control the hold Ty still had over her, at least she could take heart in resisting a piece of beef.

"Grace Ann, I'm not trying to boss you around, but I really want you to eat a little of that."

The yellow pond of butter in the potatoes and the perfectly pink meat looked incredibly appetizing. It made her feel even better when she pushed the plate away. "I can't."

He stared at her, balancing his fork in his fingers.

"And I know what you are thinking, but it's not like that. I just want to lose a few pounds before I go in front of the camera, that's all."

"No." He took a sip of wine and shook his head. "Absolutely not. I like you the way you are."

"I don't care what you like. I care what I like, and I want to look my best."

"Grace Ann, are you kidding me? You could crawl out of a mud puddle and still be gorgeous. Now have a little something to eat."

He stabbed a bite of meat, and shoved it in his

mouth. His calm was a practiced tactic she remembered well. When her emotions got to her, he always steadied his. Crisis never rattled him. He was always lucid and methodical. At times the strategy frustrated her, and at this moment she almost resented it.

Her gaze fell on the *Celeb!* magazine lying at the far end of the long table. Somehow they had ended up with it after their visit to the grocery store. The corner picture showed a dark-haired model in a string bikini hanging on Ty at some European beach. She bit her lip and regarded Ty sitting across from her. "You know, Ty, you're used to sharing the screen with beautiful women. I would think you'd want me to look my best."

He dragged his napkin across his mouth, and his forehead wrinkled in the center. When he spotted the magazine, he dropped his fork to his plate. "Okay, that's it. I think we need to clear the air here."

"Oh, yeah, about what?"

He leaned back in his chair and cleared his throat. His pursed lips told her he chose his words carefully. "Okay, I know it may be your intention to lose a few pounds, but I don't trust you can leave it at that."

"That's not fair."

"Oh no? Look at your track record."

"And don't you think I've learned my lesson?"

"I don't know, Grace Ann. You tell me."

She wasn't sure if she was offended by his boorishness or grateful for his patience. She looked down at her plate. The sight of the gravy turned her stomach, so she closed her eyes and took a breath.

When she felt his hand caress the side of her head, she flinched. "Can I ask you something?"

"What?" she croaked.

"Remember we had our little ritual? Can we do

that?” The palm of his hand slipped across her cheek, his thumb brushing her chin. “Please.”

At first the idea of doing something so intimate scared her, and then it angered her that he had the audacity to ask. Confusion swam inside of her. What would a stronger woman do?

If it meant proving she was okay, there was no reason to balk. Her decision made, she lifted her fork, and with painstaking effort took seven bites of each food. Minutes felt like hours as the food stung her mouth, pushing down her throat in a tasteless lump. She felt defeated and weak. Her palms moistened, and her breath thinned. Again, she closed her eyes, this time to steady herself, and when the last bit of food passed her lips she took the glass of wine Ty offered.

When she pushed the plate away, her heartbeat slowed to a gentler pace. She followed Ty’s shadow across the floor, and when he stood next to her, he offered his hand. “Come on,” he whispered, his voice as soft as his touch. She rose and forced one foot in front of the other until she found herself in the great room, with Ty standing beside her in the darkness.

The outbuilding lights across the yard hit Ty at his back. It reminded her of standing on a soundstage, the stillness of the room, the silence collecting around them. In front of them, the gigantic stone fireplace. It was the only one in the house still not equipped with a gas insert, and the sweet scent of smoldering oak swam around them like a spell. The embers were little more than a glow, and he released her hand to add another log to the fire.

When the flames danced to life, he brushed the dirt from his hands and straightened the long mirror above the mantle. He turned back to Grace, his fingers lingering at the top button of her shirt. “You ready for this?”

His breath hit her in the face, and her lips parted in response.

"Open your eyes," he whispered. "You know the rules."

He smiled down at her, the firelight twinkling in his azure eyes. She heard each button release with a snap, the sound deafening in her ears. Sliding his hands to her shoulders, he pushed the fabric to the floor. The sudden rush of air brought a hiss to her lips. He chuckled and ran his hands over her goose-pimpled skin.

"You're shaking."

"I'm cold."

"You're scared." He touched her face, his thumb running down her throat. "Don't be scared, baby. It's just me."

That was precisely the problem.

Holding her by the hips, he slowly turned her toward the mirror. It took a moment for her eyes to adjust, but just as they did, they clouded with tears. She turned her head against his chest, grabbing his shirt in her fists. Gently he released her, his long fingers running circles on the nape of her neck. "You're okay," he soothed. "Just look at yourself. Tell me what you see."

She gawked at her own image in the mirror. The white lace bra and panties looked virginal, and considering who was next to her, it seemed silly and embarrassing. Her hair was loosely bound, and tendrils curled around her face. People liked to describe her as a nymph, and while she couldn't say that she thought it was inaccurate, nothing else really came to mind. She had the hips and breasts of a woman, but on a childlike frame. In Hollywood, she wasn't voluptuous enough, and as a ballerina she was too big. Never just right. And that's how she wanted things.

"Work in progress," she mumbled.

"Really? I was thinking 'perfection.'" His mirrored reflection dropped his head to hers, and he gently kissed her temple. "Come here."

He led her to the couch and lay down with her in spoon fashion. Her head rested on the inside of his thick arm, her cheek tingled as his breath teased her skin. The heat of the fire hit her face, but despite the warmth she shivered.

"Relax." He brushed his fingers though her hair. "I'm right here."

They were the exact words she had dreamed of hearing for years after he'd left, but tonight they offered more confusion than comfort. There had been so many things she'd wanted to say if ever she was given the chance, but at this moment there was only one thing she could think of. "Everything is different now," she whispered. "So different."

"Hush, darling.'" He pulled her closer, his southern drawl thick against her ear. "It's all over. The past is the past."

"If I could change things I would. You have to believe me when I say I would never do that to myself twice. I'm stronger now."

"You were always strong, Grace." His fingers splayed against her belly, teasing the edge of her panties.

"Ty really, I mean it." She rolled over on her back so she could look him in the eyes. "Running this place has been like a weird therapy. I make my own decisions, and live how I want. Plus, I get to take care of people instead of everyone taking care of me. It gives me a sense of control."

"I'm glad, Gracie."

She took a deep breath, suddenly realizing she'd let her mouth run off. "Sorry, sometimes I go all 'pop psychology'."

"I remember." He chuckled and laid his head on her chest. "Keep talking, darlin'. Lord knows I could use some."

She touched his face, her fingers running over the dark stubble. In her whole life the only person she had ever been completely honest with was Ty. Even at times when she lied to herself, Ty knew the truth. It wasn't until that moment she realized how much she had missed that, and how much she needed for that to still be the case. "My weight is something I can control, Ty. Even if other things around me I can't. This whole thing with the show, and seeing you, and worrying about my dad and the press..." She took a deep breath. "I don't have much control over any of it, and I just want you to know that I know that."

"You don't have anything to prove, Grace Ann. Leave that to me."

She felt his hand run the length of her body, down her side, over her hip. It felt good. Almost right. She let her body ease into it. "Do you remember when we used to lie here and run our lines?"

A puff of air tickled her breast. "Sure." Ty chuckled. "Earl was always impressed with how well we knew our stuff. At least the love scenes, anyway." His voice deepened; his breath grazed her eager skin. "We were good together, Gracie. So good."

Her body tensed when she felt his mouth on her neck. Kissing her gently, scattering her thoughts and assaulting her better judgment. Instinctively, her hands wandered south and reached for the fly of his jeans.

"Gracie, no."

She jumped when she felt a vibration against her hip. Ty cursed, then moved around behind her, retrieving his cell phone from his pocket. "It's Earl. Should I take it?"

She looked at him over her shoulder. "If you don't, you know he's just going to keep calling. I have to take dinner to Lizzie anyway."

"You're the boss." He put his finger to his lip and pressed the "answer" key. "Earl? What's up?"

Grace lifted her head, straining to hear Earl on the other end. Ty still held her against him, his hand rubbing her arm while he spoke.

"Yeah, I talked to Grace after we left the studio Friday. I haven't seen her since, but she seemed okay." He smiled down at her. "I think we smoothed things over at least a little."

The statement offended her for some reason. She pushed herself up from the couch and threw on her clothes before heading back into the kitchen to wrap up the food.

"No." Ty laughed. "I think she looked great."

She ripped the tinfoil off the roll like it gave her a reason. How long would she have to put up with people talking about her like a science project? Like she was a time bomb or an invalid. Who was he to decide what she was ready for?

And how many times would she let Ty Hawthorne reject her?

He hung up and came into the kitchen. He scooped up some dishes from the table and deposited them in the sink beside her. "Well, Earl's glad to hear we made nice. By the way the story is I'm still in New York, and you're here safe and sound.

"You could have told him the truth. We don't need to lie to him anymore."

"You're probably right." He came up behind her and squeezed her shoulder. "Habit, I guess."

"And he could have called me himself and asked how I was."

"Put yourself in his shoes, Gracie. Before you signed on to do this press stint, the last time he heard from you, you were in a Connecticut hospital with an 'undisclosed ailment.'" He quoted with his hands. "He's just concerned."

"Concerned I'm going to jump ship." She dropped the basket back on the stove with a thud. Turning toward him, she squared her shoulders, trying to look as imposing as possible with more than a foot disadvantage. "Just because you were my mouthpiece in the past doesn't mean that you are now."

"What did I say so wrong?"

"And I don't need a babysitter. I was fine without you before, and I'm fine without you now." She stomped around him to the mud room, jammed her feet in her boots and threw on her jacket.

"Grace, if anyone in this room needs a babysitter it would be me. I know how capable you are."

"Good, then I don't need to explain myself any further." She picked up the food and stomped out the door, unsure if she had a point in the first place.

****

"Marcy, come quick! I think I'm blind!"

Layla Hawthorne ripped the cucumber slices from her eyes and chucked them over the lanai. A pool boy in a leopard print Speedo ducked. He still sported a knob on his forehead from where an avocado had hit him earlier. "And didn't I ask for a pitcher of margaritas an hour ago? I'm parched, people! How come no one around here can follow directions?"

An army of assistants scattered like ants, doing their best to get out of her way. Figures, Layla thought. Good help was hard to find in Los Angeles, even if you paid top dollar. And Layla Hawthorne never paid a penny less. It wasn't her fault. Her ex-husband had spoiled her, and now he'd pay for her affliction.

Dearly.

"And can someone bring me my fucking phone? I need to make a call."

She looked up at the sky to spot the sun and

adjusted her chaise lounge accordingly. Late afternoon rays were still strong enough to get some color. She tucked her short blond hair behind her ears and undid the top of her Versace bikini. "Three o'clock here, six in New York," she mumbled, drumming her freshly manicured fingers beside her.

She should have heard from Harvey by now. When he called earlier, he promised some big news on the way. Something about a backroom tryst with a lady in a convenience store. She smirked at the thought. It almost seemed like a lame attempt to make her jealous. Hell, she'd be anything he wanted her to be, as long as the pervert got the job done. Honing her acting skills wouldn't hurt in the least.

"Did I hear you were looking for me?" Marcy stepped out the sliding glass doors with a tray of margaritas and Layla's rhinestone cell phone. She set them down on the table and pulled up a chair of her own.

"I don't suppose it's possible that the phone rang, and I missed it?"

Marcy brushed her short, dark hair aside and shrugged. "Not that I heard. But I was out walking the Spellings's Pomeranians."

Layla leaned back on her chair and sighed. "Ty's been with that redheaded whore for two days. What is it about that woman that sucks people in?"

"I don't know."

"She's a manipulator, Marcy. She screwed me out of the role of Lexie Love, and she's been screwing me ever since. If it wasn't for her, I'd still be married, and you and I wouldn't have to live like paupers." She wiped a smudge from her Waterford crystal glass. "At the very least, Ty would have been on board with an open marriage."

Marcy chuckled then slid her sunglasses over her eyes. "Fine, but if this little revenge scam of yours is going to work, you better light a fire under

Harvey. He has some good leads, right?"

"Who knows," Layla said. "Last night when he called he was in the middle of a snowstorm, bragging about his stalking skills, and today I got the Quickie-In-The-Back-Room story. He says he has a few tricks up his sleeve."

"Considering his past history, I don't doubt it," Marcy said. "That's why I don't think you should trust him."

"I'm not. My deal with Harvey is cash on delivery. I don't pay unless he produces. And believe me, I'm hard to please." Layla took a gulp of the drink and licked the salt from her lips. She wasn't stupid. Ty was the last man who'd ever take advantage of her. Hell, she had made drastic lifestyle choices to ensure that.

More than once Marcy tried to cool her down about the whole thing. She was more interested in living a quiet life and moving on. But Layla didn't see this arrangement as permanent. The only person she now considered she had a lifetime commitment to was herself.

Marcy sat up and turned to look at her with sad brown eyes that reminded Layla of her furry clients. "Look, I don't know if this is more about revenge for the pain Grace has caused you or just plain old extortion from your ex-husband. But if your plan is to make Grace's life a living hell in an effort to force Ty's hand, you better up the ante. The divorce is already final, and the only way you're ever going to see another red cent from that man is if you scare it out of him."

'That's what I've been telling you all along," Layla said. "The key to Ty's wallet, and my vindication, is all centered on one objective. Ruin Grace Ann Langley. Believe me, if Ty ever thought that woman was in danger, he'd pay top dollar to prevent it."

"Well then," Marcy chirped, raising her glass in toast, "I think you have your plan of attack."

"Always have, honey. Hand me my cell phone. It's time to give Harvey a little pep talk."

## Chapter Six

Ty surveyed the scene around him from his perch on the top rung of the ladder. Ghostly clouds swam across a silver moon, casting shadows over the tin barn roof. It was dumb and incredibly unsafe to do a job like this without the advantage of daylight. One false move and he could maim himself with a nail gun or plummet thirty feet to his death. The snow pack was too thin to offer much buffer if he slipped.

It was frigid, hardly above ten degrees, but tonight he found the cold more refreshing than torturous. The moments on the couch with Grace awoke an acute need to expend some energy. Now. Not that banging a hammer was the activity he had in mind, but it would have to suffice. The alternative was unquestionably and painfully out.

Holding himself back wasn't something he was used to. He didn't have to, and most times he didn't want to. It had been a while since he even cared about a woman's perspective or making love versus getting laid. He shook his head and laughed at himself. "Making love" was a phrase he only used when he was paid to. It seemed like a legend or an old wives' tale. In his whole life, sex had been purely a physical act, a stress reliever, a mind clearer, a cure for whatever ailed him.

That is, except with Grace.

"Making love" was the only way he could describe what passed between them when they were together. It was always sensual and intense. Like a piece of them fused into something greater than each alone. He was ready for that. Missed that. Needed that. But Grace—he wasn't so sure. Grace had a tendency to follow her emotions, to be whimsical and impulsive. At times she could be her own worst enemy. And for a woman as incredible as she was to give herself to a jerk like him, it required at least a little more than a few naked moments of consideration.

He positioned his feet on the top step of the ladder and anchored himself against the roof. The impact of the hammer hitting steel echoed in the darkness. When he reached in his jacket for another nail, he heard a squeak and the moan of snow grinding under the ladder's legs.

It was too late to right himself. On the way down, his arm seized with pain, like something sharp had sliced it. He landed on the snow with a thud, sending the powder into the air like a cloud. For a moment he stayed on his back, trying like hell to find a breath. When he did, he cursed and rolled over, his eyes staring straight at the leather toe of someone's work boots.

"Well, if it isn't the world renowned film star Ty Hawthorne," The man taunted. "Good thing you can act. Looks like you're pretty much a screw-up at everything else."

Ty tried to push himself up from the snow, but his arm gave way. It hurt like hell, a fact he was sure would please Russell Haines. Ty painted on his most sincere smile as he forced himself to his feet. "I didn't hear you pull up." And I thought Grace went there to take you dinner, he said to himself.

"I walked," Russ said. "Real people like us don't need eighty-thousand-dollar automobiles to get around in a few inches of snow."

The moonlight bounced off Russ's bald head, and his beady dark eyes simmered in medium-boiled anger. Ty didn't think a reunion with Lizzie's husband would be pleasant. The last time they'd seen each other was at the hospital, when Russ dropped him with a right hook.

"So Lizzie told me you came up to visit. What the hell for? Don't you think you've done enough?"

"This is none of your business, Russ."

"Yeah, just like it was none of my business five years ago, right? I had to watch my wife clean up your mess. She had to give up her job and her place in the city to look after Grace Ann."

"I did Grace a favor by leaving, and you know it," Ty said. "If I'd stayed, the press would have been on to us. Grace didn't want it in the papers, and you know for damn sure her parents didn't."

"She had to go through labor."

"I know."

"She had to go into an operating room all by herself and push a dead baby out."

"I know!"

Russ cocked his head in mock confusion. "And you think fixing a broken roof is going to make up for that?"

Ty had no right and no way to defend himself. In fact, he couldn't agree more with Russell's assessment. He was a coward. A selfish, weak, bastard who had deserted the one person who ever gave a crap about him. How do you put a positive spin on that?

"Grace was inconsolable for weeks," Russ said. "Lizzie couldn't even get through to her. Nor her parents. Nobody. What the hell were you thinking?"

Again Ty didn't have an answer. Of course, he could have told him how he snuck back in to check on Grace, and the kindhearted nurse who slipped him the piece of paper. Hell, he could even tell him about the business with her father. But defending himself wasn't a priority. Not then, and not now. He did what he did because he believed it was in Grace's best interest. If Russ didn't see that, the hell with him.

"If the Deacon was here, he'd run you out of here so fast."

"Well, he's not, and Grace is a grown woman. If she wanted to toss me out she would have, believe me."

Russ stared at him through the cloud of his breath, then stalked toward him until they were nose to nose. "Don't think you can come around here and charm her like you did before. She's not one of those tramps you run around with."

"Damn right she's not."

"You think you're entitled or something just because you're rich and famous. Well, around here that doesn't mean shit! People like you don't impress people like us."

Ty's blood bubbled under the surface. His skin crawled, his heart hammered. His gloved hands fisted at his sides.

"You know, Hawthorne, you're nothing but a poor piece of trash that got lucky. You found a weak woman to use and abuse, and when things got too tough you skipped town. You never deserved Grace, and you damn sure didn't deserve being a father."

The words socked him square in his gut. A sucker punch he wholly deserved, but he couldn't squelch the reflex to respond. As if something other than himself propelled it, his right fist zipped around, blasting Russ in the jaw. He fell back in the snow, and Ty rushed him, pulling him back up by the collar, and throwing him against the barn wall.

"You think this is like one of your movies, don't you?" Russ sputtered. His eyes bulged from their sockets. "You're the hero, and I'm the villain, and you beating the crap out of me will make everything better."

"It would make me feel better."

"That's what it's all about with you, huh? Instant gratification. Just as long as she's a good lay you'll stick around!"

Again Ty lashed out, this time a blow square to Russ' stomach. The man tumbled to the snow, landing on his back.

"You're a waste, Hawthorne," Russ panted as he struggled to his feet. "You're nothing but trouble."

Ty's knuckles burned from bone hitting bone, and in a weird, twisted way, he liked it. Russ brushed the snow from his jacket and rubbed his already purple face. At the moment Ty had no regrets, except maybe that he didn't nail the other eye, as well.

"I won't tell Lizzie or Grace about this," Russ said. "Oh, and you might want to get a doctor to look at your arm." He nodded to Ty's left side. "It looks pretty bad."

Ty watched Russ disappear into the woods, unable to believe the last ten minutes of his life. He felt like he'd just played a scene in one of his movies, and any second the director would yell "cut." His arm throbbed with stinging pain, and he smelled blood. The bitter stench that usually meant a serious wound. Good. The worse it was, the better. Maybe if he was lucky he'd bleed to death.

When he went back inside, he peeled off his blood-soaked jacket. The cut on his arm was deep, needed stitches probably. It hurt like hell, too. He glanced around the empty kitchen until his gaze settled on the liquor cabinet in the great room. He fished out a brand new bottle of scotch. Not bothering with a glass, he took a long gulp, then a few more until the pain dulled to that nondescript constant ache that somehow always plagued him.

Trouble found him again. Not that he tried hard to hide from it. Hell, Russ only pointed out the obvious. He sat down in front of the fire, remembering the last time he saw Grace in the hospital. It was after the scene with Russ. He'd snuck back in the hospital and peered through the door. Grace was asleep, tired from the induced labor but alive, and for that he was thankful. But the baby...

He couldn't resist seeing her just once. A sympathetic nurse brought him to the baby's room. She was wrapped in a blanket and still warm to the touch.

He pretended she was sleeping.

It was all his fault, regardless of what happened with her father. He had failed Gracie, something he promised he'd never do. He figured staying around would only make it worse, so he took off. But before he left, that nurse had slipped him a piece of paper, and he slipped her his money clip. After a trip to the tattoo parlor and a good few weeks in a drunken stupor, he attempted to put his life back together.

The crack of the fire snapped him out of his thoughts, and he lifted the bottle to the light. It was half gone, and still he could think clearer than he wanted to. He took another swig and dragged himself up the stairs.

He pushed the bedroom door open, and reached for the light switch, but stumbled. The lamp beside him fell to the floor and shattered into tiny pieces. He laughed, then hated that he did. A shock of anger zipped through him, and he hurled the bottle of Scotch across the room. It smashed against the antique wall paper, dripping down the wall in muddy trails before settling on the newly refinished hardwood.

Destruction. What he did best.

He should leave. Had to leave. Whatever reason he came here for, no good would come of it. Grace said it herself. She'd moved on. She didn't need him anymore.

With clumsy coordination, he pulled his duffle bag from the closet and jammed in the clothes Grace had neatly unpacked. He threw it over his shoulder and pulled the car keys from the outside pocket. If he left now, he'd be back to the city for last call.

"Ty?"

Her voice. Her sweet buttery voice that stirred every part of him. He turned, and through his blurred vision, he saw her standing in the doorway.

"Tyler? Are you okay? The barn ladder was in the middle of the lawn when I pulled up, and I saw blood next to your tools. I thought something happened."

Ty moved away from her, when she stepped into the room. He could tell by her face she smelled the liquor, and he could see the disappointment in her eyes when she spotted the broken lamp on the floor. "What's going on in here?" She stared at the glass at her feet. "How did the lamp break?"

He didn't answer. Couldn't answer. He tried to push around her to the door, but she jumped into his path.

"What's wrong with you?"

"Get out of my way, Grace. I'm leaving."

"Why now?"

"Because, you don't need me here."

"That may be true, but you don't need to drive out of here like a drunken maniac, either." She snagged the car keys from his hand and stuffed them in her pocket. Again he tried to shove around her, but she wedged her hand against the doorframe. "You're not going anywhere but to bed, Ty. I'm not letting you leave like this."

God she was sexy. A fucking angel. Those little pink lips, and those deep blue eyes. He remembered what it was like to slide himself inside her. How wet and tight she was. How she'd moan and scream and call his name. How he'd come so hard the room spun.

Just like it was now.

He dropped his bag and grabbed her, pushing her against the wall. He lifted her body so she was closer to eye level, his lips almost even with hers.

"Put me down."

"Then quit acting for me. Like you care what happens to me."

"I do care about you," she said. "Now, put me down."

"You sure you want me to do that, Grace Ann?" He raised his knee, pressing it in between her legs.

"You need to call it a night."

"I was thinking the same thing." He touched her cheek, running his fingers down her flannel shirt, across her breast. "I know what you really want. Just like what all the girls want. You want me to fuck you, don'tcha?"

"What?"

He waited for her to get angry but she didn't. Her self control excited him. Almost as much as the thought of making it unravel. "You liked it when I fucked you, didn't you? Remember how wet you got? I could make you drip."

"Stop it..."

"And you were so tight. You remember how much you liked my cock inside you, baby?" He lowered his lips to her ear, and his insides bubbled with heat. "You want it now, don't you?"

"Let go of me, Tyler."

"Come on, baby. You wanted it earlier."

In that instant, he caught a knee in the groin, followed by a fist that landed square on his mouth. He catapulted clear across the room and landed face up on the bed. His eyelids fluttered before falling shut.

"You sure have a way with words, Hawthorne."

When he opened his eyes, minutes, maybe hours later, Grace sat beside him on the bed, her hand pressed against the bandaged wound. The flannel shirt and overalls she'd had on earlier were replaced with a white lace nightgown, and her strawberry hair fell loose and long around her. At first he just stared at her, unsure if this was a dream or reality. But when their eyes met, heat raced through him. And suddenly, he was aware of just how real she was.

"You okay?" Her gaze focused on his arm. "This thing doesn't want to stop bleeding."

"Huh?"

"This is the second time I've dressed it." She cast him a disapproving scowl. "I don't think the alcohol in your system is helping your cause."

He couldn't agree more. His stomach lurched, and the stench of antiseptic burned his nose. When his eyes finally focused, he noticed the low burn of the fire.

"And in case you don't remember, the fat lip is my doing. I would offer my apology, but you deserved it."

He ran his tongue over the fresh scab. He'd forgotten about her years of martial arts training during the run of *Undercover Heat*. Her dancing skills made her a natural, and despite her size she packed quite a punch. Or kick, for that matter. "Sensei Bill would be proud," he said. "You still have a mean right hook."

"I keep up on the skills. It's good for self-defense. There's a lot of crazy people out there."

The wrinkle in her brow indicated she was referring more to the nut in front of her than anyone else. "Gracie, I'm sorry. You know I'd never hurt you, right?"

"I think you scared yourself more than me," she said. "You know, the first time I came in here to check your arm, you were tossing and turning. It was almost like you were having a nightmare or something." She glanced at him through the corner of her eye. "You want to talk about it?"

"Nothing to talk about."

"You're sure?"

When he saw Grace reach for the light, he pulled her back to the bed. "Don't do that. Leave it dark."

"Okay…"

He tossed off the sheets and climbed out of bed. Naked, save for his boxers. Wonderful, the poor woman had to undress him, too. How much more of a jerk could he possibly be? He jabbed the button on the side of the fireplace. The flames came to life, casting orange shadows in the dark room.

"It just seems strange," Grace scratched the side of her head. "I've never known you to have nightmares. You always sleep like a rock."

He leaned on the mantle, staring at the knotty hardwood at his feet. "I don't know. It happens now and them."

"Tell me about it."

He felt exposed. Like the most intimate parts of him were now on display. Baring his soul wasn't something Ty did. Hell, who knew he even had one. But Grace was the last person who'd tell anybody, and if she trusted him enough to sit in front of him, the least he owed her was a morsel of the truth.

"I heard you call my name. You thought I was holding a baby."

His eye traveled over her, and he was stunned how she was the exact incarnation of the image that haunted him. The porcelain skin, the bedroom eyes. He pressed his fingers on the bridge of his nose and turned back toward the fire. "It takes place here in the farmhouse, but not really. There's smoke but no fire, and I'm trying to find you. I can't, but you keep calling for help, and the baby is crying..." He exhaled. Guilt, shame, something cramped him. "No.

I don't want to talk about this."

"Please, Ty. I want to hear it."

His legs weakened under him, so he went back to the bed. He eased himself onto the mattress, flinching when Grace slipped her hand over his shoulder. "When I get to you, you're at the top of the stairs, holding the baby, and just when I think I get there in time, you fall. And my hands..." He held them out in front of them. "They're covered in blood."

That was it, as far as he could go. He scrubbed his face with his sticky palms and swallowed the lump that had lodged in his throat.

"Listen, Ty, I'm no dream analyst, but if you're carrying around guilt because I fell down those stairs, there's no reason to it. It was my fault. I admit I was angry when I woke up and you weren't there." She brushed a tear from her eye and shrugged. "I didn't know if you knew about the baby, and if you didn't I wanted to be the one to tell you. But then my father said it didn't matter because you had taken off."

"I thought I was doing you a favor, Gracie."

"Well, forgive me, but I didn't see it that way."

Ty wasn't sure what her father had told her. Probably something awful like he didn't want the baby in the first place, or that he was angry at her for being sick. Either way, he was sure it was the farthest thing from the truth. "I never should have left you that morning in the first place," he said.

"And I should have accepted your help a lot sooner. Just like you should accept mine now."

"What are you talking about?"

She climbed out of bed and knelt down in front of him. "I can't stand to see you like this," she said, reaching for his hand. "Something's eating away at you, and if you have something you need to get off your chest, now is the time to do it."

"Are you kidding me? After everything I've put

you through, you're worried about me?"

"There was a time when I knew you better than I knew myself. There used to be a passion in your eyes, and somehow it's faded. Dulled. I don't know."

He didn't, either. But it didn't seem to matter when he looked at her. "I can't stand seeing you self-destruct this way," Grace whispered. "The drinking, the wild behavior. It doesn't help anything."

"I know, baby. I know." Somehow she was in his arms, and like a drowning man hanging on to a life line he held her. If he could just stay right here with this woman in his arms, he'd be okay. He could feel it. The energy that passed between them. Just her closeness could heal him.

"You're bleeding, again." Grace pulled away and ran her hand over the gash on his arm. "This is really bad. Like, 'stitches' bad."

"It's fine. Don't worry about it."

"But I don't want it to get infected." Gently, she unwound the bloody gauze. "How did you do this, anyway?"

"The ladder slipped. I think I hit the metal girder on the way down."

She stood up to her full height and frowned. "Let me dress it again. The first aid kit is in the bathroom."

She came back with the box, towels, and a small bowl of water. Again, she knelt down beside him. "So last night, when I came home, you certainly were in a mood. Why were you going to leave all of a sudden?"

If there was a right answer, Lord knows he didn't have it. She turned back to her task. Grace's touch could calm any storm. He took a deep breath, letting the scent of lilacs pass over him.

"When did you get this tattoo?"

His body tensed. Never in his wildest

imagination did he ever think she'd see it. "A few years back."

"Who's J.H.?"

"A character in a movie I was in," he answered quickly.

"Well you're in luck. I think you just missed ruining it. Although I still think a doctor should look at this. When was the last time you had a tetanus shot?"

"Before I left for Italy."

"What if I call Russ?"

"Don't do that." That was the last thing he needed. Russ running over to play doctor, when they both knew he'd rather euthanize him. "It's not necessary. You fussing over me is more than enough. You done yet, by the way?"

"In a minute." She wrapped a bandage once and then twice around. He smiled at the way her little pink tongue stuck out the side as she concentrated on her task. "Okay, I think that will hold. Why don't you lie down? I'll get you some pain pills."

"Grace, wait." He grabbed the hem of her nightgown, bringing her back to the side of the bed. "About last night. When you left to go to Lizzie's, you were mad. And what I said to you when you got back..." He nodded to the doorway. "I was way out of line."

"Yeah, you were."

"Promise me that if I ever act that way toward you again, you treat me to another right hook."

She winked and slid her hand down the side of his cheek. "Deal."

His settled back against the pillow and his body drifted. He imagined her climbing in bed beside him, just like she used to. The way she curled into him and rested her head against his chest. God, he loved to hold her, and when she was pregnant he'd rubbed her swollen belly and whispered how much he loved her. "You would have been a good mother, darlin'," he heard himself say. "I mean that."

Their child. He would have had a daughter. A sweet little baby girl. He thought of the nurse handing him the envelope and finding what it held inside.

He took a deep breath and drifted further. "Jamie Hawthorne," he mumbled. "Daddy's little angel."

## Chapter Seven

"Darn truck."

Grace pulled the key from the ignition and blew out a breath through her chattering teeth. She should have stayed in bed. Had it not been for her perfect attendance record at Sunday Mass she would have considered it. Heck, if she'd known the truck wouldn't start, it wouldn't have been an issue in the first place. She drummed her fingers against the steering wheel, and uttered a curse she'd have to say a Hail Mary for.

Situations beyond her control drove her craziest.

She jumped down to the snow, slammed the door, and glared at the heap like her anger might change its mind. If it was summer, or at least a few degrees warmer, she'd walk. Two miles wasn't that far, but in a foot and half of snow, wearing a skirt, it might as well be a marathon. She yanked on her sleeve and glanced at her watch. Too late to call Lizzie and Russ for a ride. They'd already be there.

She scanned the overcast landscape before her gaze settled on the big yellow Hummer next to the barn. It was an eyesore for sure, but as ugly as it was, she bet it would start. She glanced up at Ty's bedroom window. She still had the keys next to her bed, from when she took them from him the night before. He wouldn't mind if she drove it. The rest of the town on the other hand might. A new car in Middle Valley was headline news, and if word leaked out about whom it really belonged to, she'd hear about it clear into spring.

She kicked an ice chunk with her suede boot.

Still this really was an extenuating circumstance, and maybe if she was willing to go to such lengths to get to Mass, the least God could do was bless her with anonymity. Her decision made, she ran upstairs and quietly retrieved the keys from her bedside table.

Minutes later, she slid into the pew beside Lizzie, for the most part unnoticed by the rest of the congregation. Father Lepchen had just finished his morning blessing, and the children were being dismissed for Sunday school classes. Frazzled mothers wiped faces and straightened collars before letting them loose on the million-year-old Miss Betsy, who waited in the atrium on the side of the altar. Grace made a quick sign of the cross, thanking God it wasn't her day to teach. The last thing she needed was a rectory full of wide-eyed six-year-olds asking about Miss Grace's big yellow truck.

"You okay?" Lizzie whispered, slipping the scarf from around Grace's neck. "Not like you to be late for anything."

"I'm sorry. The truck wouldn't start."

"You should have called. We would have picked you up." Lizzie motioned to Russ beside her.

"Good morning, Russell." Grace reached over and touched his leg. When he turned toward her, Grace gasped. His eye was swollen shut in a gory combination of purple, orange and yellow. "Oh, my God, what happened to you?"

"Shhh." He motioned with his finger in front of his lips. "It's no big deal."

"He went out for a walk last night and fell on the ice," Lizzie explained. "I would have insisted he see a doctor, if he wasn't one himself."

"Discuss it later, girls," Russ mumbled, nodding to the priest, who cast a damning look in their direction. Grace bowed her head with the rest of the congregation, and a hush settled over the church.

Father Lepchen opened his Bible and cleared his throat. Grace was midprayer when the heavy wooden doors behind her creaked open and slammed with an echoing thud.

The intrusion drew eyes to the source, and Grace looked, too, at the heathen latecomer. She blinked twice before her eyes widened in shock. "Hey, does anyone in here know where the driver of that Hummer out there is?"

The guy wore torn jeans, a leather jacket with chains attached, and neon-pink frosted hair. He scanned the crowd before he jogged down the isle in Grace's direction. "Sorry," he announced to the church while making a weird sort of sign of the cross-salute combination. "I don't mean to interrupt, Reverend...Priest...Your Honor, but I'm looking for..."

"Manny!" Grace jumped up from her seat and grabbed him by the shoulder. "What the hell are you doing here?"

The old ladies in the front row gasped, offended by her language, no doubt. She bit her tongue and apologized, then adjusted her volume to a stage whisper. "If you're looking for Ty, he's back at the farmhouse."

"Great. You about finished here? Because the sooner the better."

She glanced around the church. Every eye was fixed on her, except those of the old ladies, whose eyes were pressed closed in fierce prayer. For her benefit, no doubt, and she was oddly glad for the consideration. Lizzie and Russ sat silent beside her. Explanations would have to wait, although knowing her sister probably not very long. In fact, if Grace didn't want to be the hot topic in the church bulletin next week, she'd have to get out of there. Now.

"Let's go," Grace said, tugging on Manny's sleeve. He followed and even offered a genuflectturned-bow on his way out the door.

"God, why do churches always smell like rotten eggs?" Manny stood at the top of the steps and fanned his hand in front of his nose. "How can you sit in there for an hour?"

"It's incense."

"You mean nonsense."

"No, I mean the smell. It's incense." Grace shook her head. "What are you talking about?"

"I don't know. What are you talking about?"

Grace grabbed his shoulder and dragged him down the steps. She led him to the courtyard on the side and stopped in front of the snow-covered statue of the Virgin Mary.

"Look, I didn't mean to crash your party," Manny said.

"I don't suppose you did, but up here, Manny, we don't interrupt church services because you can't get through to someone on a cell phone."

"I'm sorry, but I saw the Hummer, and I figured I could snag him and bring him back to the city. He's been MIA for three days, and when that happens I get nervous." He jammed his hand in his pockets and kicked the snow from his Doc Martes. His pout reminded Grace of a child who'd been scolded, and in spite of herself she smiled.

"You look like you could use some breakfast," she said, then rubbed her hand on his sleeve. "Go get your car. You can follow me to the farmhouse."

"Car?" He raised his brow. "I didn't drive up here."

Grace took a deep breath before daring herself to glance in the direction of his nod. Across the street, sat a stretch limo, idling next to the faded "Bingo Tonight" sign.

She cringed and brushed the hair from her eyes. "Go get your stuff," she said. "And tell the driver there's a diner a few miles down. You can call him later from my place."

Grace watched him jog across the street and return with a huge official-looking briefcase. It seemed out of place in the hand of a guy sporting black nail polish.

The Hummer was still warm when they piled inside. Grace hunted for the wipers and waited for the defrost to disperse the fog, while Manny furiously rubbed his hands together. "Man, how do you live up here?" He sniffled. "I spent four years in Boston for college, but the winters were never like this."

"You learn to love it." She turned out on the road. "It's quiet. The living is easy. The weather isn't always great, but it's home."

He sat back in his seat and looked out the window. "I'm sorry, Grace Ann, I should have known better than to make a scene like that. People in show biz aren't the religious types. I just thought that after the stripper incident in Cleveland a few years back, he would have learned a lesson or two about letting his women drive his cars."

Ty's women? She considered being offended by the label, but let it go instead. "Well, he doesn't actually know I have it," she confessed. "But maybe, just this once, he'll make an exception."

"It doesn't look like there's much trouble to find up here, anyway. Maybe that's the key to managing Ty. Keep him isolated so he can't cause problems. My hat's off to you, Grace, for babysitting him. I needed the R and R."

"The job is that tough, huh?"

He shrugged. "Don't get me wrong. I love Ty like a brother, but sometimes it gets pretty hard to watch someone self destruct."

Her hands fisted around the wheel. As a person who'd experienced the dirty world of Hollywood gossip, she knew sometimes stories were embellished and fabricated. Over the years, she had turned a blind eye to the wild tales. But after last night, she was beginning to believe there was more truth to the gossip than she thought. “Manny, the stories in the tabloids. Are they really all true?”

He dragged his fingers through his fuchsia hair. “Grace, there are so many I really can’t keep them straight anymore.”

“Maybe he’s upset about Layla.”

“No way. He was like this long before she even showed up. She just happened to be conniving enough to get him to a Vegas chapel to say ‘I do.’”

She wasn’t sure why, but Manny’s assessment of Ty and Layla’s marriage offered her a strange sort of relief. She decided to file it away and think about it later. “You know he wasn’t always like this,” she said. “I mean his behavior. Back when we were working together, he was a different person.”

“Well, I don’t think he has a clue who he is now. He’s got some serious issues. Sometimes I think he just likes being lost. You know what I mean?”

She had a pretty good clue. Last night she saw a side of Ty she’d never seen. But she got the impression that the Ty she knew was a stranger to the man beside her.

“He’s different with you, Grace.”

She started, like he had heard her thoughts. “Excuse me?”

“He’s different,” he said. “Like at the studio when you were doing that interview, and then when we were in the diner. He just seems...” He tilted his head, as if searching for the words. “Mellow, centered. Like he’s all there.”

Grace laughed at the assessment. She liked Manny. He was brash and green, but she could tell he truly cared about his boss, a quality sometimes lacking in Hollywood assistants. Ty was lucky to have found him. “Well, maybe all the press stuff has gotten to him."

"Could be. That's actually the reason for my coming up here. More fires to put out." He pulled the leather satchel onto his lap. "You might be interested in it, too."

When she pulled into the driveway, Ty was under the hood of the truck. He tossed whatever tool he held in his hand back into the box beside him and met her at the car door. "So the Hummer isn't so bad after all, huh, Langley?"

"Extenuating circumstance."

"Yeah, I can see that." Ty nodded to the open hood of her pickup. "Truck needs a starter, by the way. So did Father Lepchen like your new ride?"

"I didn't stay long enough to ask." Grace tossed him the keys and slid down from the seat into the snow. "I left halfway through."

"I hope not on my account."

"Nope, not yours." She nodded toward the passenger side. "His. You've got company."

The far door slammed, and a tuft of pink hair made its way around the hood. Ty laughed out loud when he saw its owner. "Christ, Manny, what the hell did you do to your hair?"

"Party in Soho last night. You like it?"

"Soho, huh?" Ty braced himself on Grace's shoulder and laughed some more. "Looks more like *Sesame Street* to me."

Manny rolled his eyes. "Look, I'm freezing. Can we please go inside and talk?"

"Of course." Grace cast a disapproving glance at Ty. "Let me get you some coffee and something to eat."

Ty still snickered, while they headed into the house. Pleased to see the coffee already brewing, Grace went straight to the pantry to retrieve the banana bread she had baked the night before. When she came back to the kitchen, Manny sat at the table, his jacket still on and his head buried in his open briefcase.

"This better be good, Pipher," Ty warned, delivering Manny his coffee and heading back to the counter to retrieve the other two. "I had my eye on that bread for breakfast. And I'm not into sharing."

"Neither is Layla."

Ty lowered the mug from his lips and leaned against the sink. "What the hell is that supposed to mean?"

"Look, I don't mean to be a smart ass, but I really think you need to give this your full attention."

The smile faded from Ty's face. "What are you talking about, man?"

Manny went back to his briefcase and riffled through it until he found what he was looking for. He pulled out a stack of newspapers and slid the one on top across the table. "This appeared yesterday morning in the *Times*. It's been the talk of the town ever since."

Ty pushed himself from the counter and picked up the paper. Grace watched his eyes scan the page before he passed it to her beside him.

Movie news. Society gossip. Standard entertainment fare, but it was the picture that caught her attention. It was of the two of them in the diner a few days ago. They were smiling at each other, and his hand was touching hers across the table. The headline read, "Not-So-Undercover Heat?"

She sat down at the table and skimmed through the article below it. Old news. Rumors and speculation. That was the whole point, after all. Even her father would understand that. "And so it begins," Grace said and slid the paper back at Manny. "I figured we'd make a tabloid here and there."

"I'm sorry," Ty said.

"It's fine. Like I said, I was prepared."

Grace waited for relief to register on Manny's face, but it didn't. Instead he went back to his pile and whipped out another paper. This time *The Daily News*. "This appeared just this morning."

Ty reached for it, but Grace snagged it first. Phrases like "real life lovers" and "secret affair" caught her eye, as did the photo of Layla that graced the top of the page. Her face scowled in anger, with a fist superimposed as if sounding a battle cry. The headline read "He Drove Me To It! My Husband's Secret Love Affair with Costar Grace Ann Langley."

Her face burned. This was way more than a picture in a restaurant. This was the truth.

"Can I see it, Grace?"

Ty slipped it from her fingers and sat down at the table beside her. His expression gave away nothing, and when he finished, he flipped it back on the table. "Manny you drove all the way up here for nothing. This is old news. There were headlines about us being romantically involved all the time, back then. You had me going. I was expecting major dirt."

"I'm glad you said that, because I think that's what's coming."

Manny shifted in his seat, and Grace could tell by the way he looked at her, his concern was for her benefit, too. She squared her shoulders and took a deep breath. "Okay, so lay it on us."

"Something about a secret rendezvous in upstate New York and a purchase of prenatal vitamins from a convenience store. When I caught wind of this, I figured Layla was blowing smoke as usual. So I made some calls. Got a hold of a guy at *It* magazine. Turns out they are about to run a story about Ty Hawthorne's weekend rendezvous upstate where he purchased prenatal vitamins for his pregnant ex-costar." Manny looked at Grace then back at Ty.

"You two have something you want to tell me?"

Ty slammed his fist on the table. "Damn it! I knew I was in for trouble when I bought those stupid vitamins. I forgot my money clip back here at the house, so I used a credit card." Again, he cursed and ran his hand through his hair. "Jesus, I'm not new at this. What the hell was I thinking?"

"Oh, man!" Manny dropped his head to the table. "So it's really true. You're pregnant, Grace?"

"What? Me? No!" she stammered. "Manny, maybe if you calm down—"

"God, Ty, you've been in Italy! I know you're good with the ladies, but even you can't knock a girl up a continent away."

"They were for my sister," Grace said. "Not me."

"*It* magazine, huh." Ty leaned back in his chair and shook his head. "See if I ever give them an interview again."

Manny held a hand over his heart and expelled a breath like he'd been holding it since he left New York City. "Thank God. So all this talk about secret romances and babies is just Layla stirring the pot?"

"Like you had to ask," Ty said. "Come on, of course it's her. She's unhappy about the divorce settlement, and she's trying to piss me off."

Ty had been nominated for three Academy Awards, but even his acting abilities couldn't hide the terror on his face. His voice had lowered the slightest decibel, and he tapped his foot against the hardwood. Instinct compelled her to reach for his hand, but before she could, he slipped his hand over her shoulder instead. "Where did she get her information, anyway?" he asked.

"I don't know. I contacted them, and of course they won't reveal their source. They did say, however, that they had a copy of the credit card receipt for those vitamins with your name on it." Manny cocked his head. "My theory is that the bitch finally cracked and hired someone to tail you."

"Come on." Ty rubbed his face and chuckled.

"She's crazy enough to do it."

Grace gulped and looked at Ty. Over the years, it had amazed her how nothing had been leaked to the press about what happened. She figured her father made sure it wouldn't, given his contacts in the church and his desire to protect his reputation. She also thought Ty had something to do with it. In some ways it made her feel better to think that, even though the man had left her, he at least kept her from public humiliation.

"We can always sue her for slander," Manny said. "But that's still going to cost you money."

The men's voices fell away, and her own heartbeat echoed in her ears. What if Layla was on to them? Her father was one of the most highly respected men in the New York Diocese. His career would be ruined. And what about her? The press would hound her, and she'd be forced to relive the nightmare all over again. There were a ton of reasons why a public debacle would have been torture, and even though five years had passed, it would be just as tragic now. Grace Ann Langley was not cut out for life in a fishbowl. She'd spent a year in a recovery hospital as proof of that.

"Grace Ann?" Ty put his hand on her back. "You okay?"

Maybe she could trust Manny. He seemed to have Ty's best interest at heart, and maybe if he knew the truth he could somehow prevent it from getting out. "Manny, you can't sue someone for libel if the story they're telling is true."

Manny's forehead creased. "What...what do you mean?"

Grace stood up and pushed her chair back into the table. "How about you two head out for something to eat. I think Ty would like to have a chat with you."

"I would?"

She sent a silent message with her eyes, and when Ty set his coffee cup down, Grace knew that he had gotten it. "You sure, Gracie?"

"Manny, get ready to earn your salary. I have a feeling you have your work cut out for you." She leaned down and kissed Ty's cheek before heading up the back stairs.

****

Harvey took a sip of coffee and studied the generous ass of the brunette waitress serving an English muffin to the man in the booth beside him. Not bad. One thing he noticed on this excursion up in this Arctic Circle, women here wore entirely too many clothes. It was hard to ogle when three layers of wool and heavy down jackets stood in the way.

But this breakfast had little to do with pleasure and everything to do with business, which was why he was glad when the waitress waddled out of sight. The success of this mission depended on him staying focused. Something he had done quite well so far. He contributed it to his sixth sense, and to his ability to act on a hunch. A hunch made him drive up to this snowy hell in the first place, and another made him follow Ty into that convenience store. Both had paid off, and the scene with the woman in the back room wasn't a bad perk, either.

Talk about customer service.

The brunette waitress topped off his coffee and headed to Ty's table behind him. It was ballsy to follow Hawthorne and his pink-headed assistant here and even more so to snag the adjacent table. But when he saw Grace leave church with that guy, he knew something was up. No way would Pinky make a trip all the way up here just to see how Ty was. Trouble was brewing. This morning's news must have hit right where Harvey aimed. Square in the nuts, and if he guessed right, this little meeting was their attempt at damage control.

Sure enough, the earful was simply too good to be true. A love affair, an eating disorder. His jealous lesbian wife. Even the part about hiding the truth from Grace Ann's family was interesting. He only had one question.

What was the truth Ty was talking about?

He'd find out. In the meantime, he'd dig a little deeper. Maybe use that cover as a reporter for *It* magazine. Somebody had to know something about the tale Ty told. Maybe someone willing to talk. He'd have to think about that one.

Moments later, Harvey heard the leather upholstery shift behind him. Ty and Pinky were leaving. He watched them head out the door, then cross the parking lot to the yellow Hummer. They drove away, going in the direction of the farmhouse.

He finished the last of his coffee and tossed a few bills on the table. Layla had told him not to bother returning to Los Angeles without something more she could use as ammunition. He smiled. Who needed ammo when you had a smoking gun, and he was on it. He could smell it like a shark smelled blood. And he was moving in for the kill.

# Chapter Eight

Grace awoke to pitch black and the sound of metal striking metal echoing in the distance. For a moment, she was disoriented, tangled in the sheets of a bed that wasn't hers. It wasn't until the scent of cologne drifted across her nose that she realized where she was.

Ty's room.

She rolled to her side and looked out the frosted moonlit window. After Ty and Manny left, she had tried to busy herself with mundane tasks like dusting and folding laundry. It didn't work, and somehow she'd ended up here. Her intention was to shut her eyes for a few minutes and try to wrap her head around the impending crisis, but evidently exhaustion took priority. Maybe a rested mind would yield a clearer perspective. She figured she needed all the help she could get.

Again she heard the rhythmic clanking. Probably Ty doing the same thing she was earlier. Busying himself. Taking everything in. Five years ago, she had lain in a bed a few doors down mulling "what ifs" and "worst case scenarios." Back then, she relied on Ty to sort it all out. What she didn't realize at the time was the worst case scenario was losing the baby, and she did that all on her own. Ty couldn't have prevented it, and in a way she actually worked against him sapping his strength while he fought a war on both ends. Her with her issues, and the ramifications they created for everyone else.

But things were different now. The new and improved incarnation of Grace had no intention of depending on others to clean up her mess. This Grace was capable. Competent. She had found what the therapists called "mastery," and if Layla, or anyone else, thought she was an easy target, they were wrong. This time she was ready for them. This time she wouldn't go down without a fight, and she would fight it with Ty by her side, not hiding behind his back.

Suddenly, filled with purpose, she tossed off the covers and headed outside.

Ty worked under the hood of her pickup with the sleeves of a gray Crimson Tide hoodie pushed up to his elbows. The light, attached above him, gleamed off whatever tool he held in his hand, and his eyes squinted in a snarl like he'd been at the task a while, and not necessarily enjoying it. "Hey, there, darlin'," he greeted without looking up. "You were dead asleep when..."

"I have something to say."

"Well go right ahead, I'm all ears." He nodded at the toolbox beside him. "But first, find me some clean rags in there. You got an oil leak worse that the Exxon Valdez."

She pushed around him and dug for the rags. When she found them, she shoved them in his face.

"Jesus, Gracie. This thing is shot. The belts are cracked, and the undercarriage is rotted. You're lucky the engine hasn't fallen clear out to the ground." He shook his head. "Does that guy with the lazy eye still service your cars? Because I'm not sure he's done such a great job."

"I service my own car."

"What do you mean?"

"I mean, I take care of my own vehicle. I change the oil, I rotate the tires. I even replaced those cracked belts in the first place. You'd be surprised at what I can do."

He looked at her with a wrinkled brow. "Why

would I be surprised?"

"The car may not run like a top, but the point is I tried. It needed fixing, so I decided to fix it. If there was a problem, I tried to solve it."

"Okay but…"

"I know the car is old, and maybe I'm not the best mechanic, but I can say I rose to the challenge. I'm not some helpless wimp, you know."

She saw she'd gotten his attention. He took a step back from the open hood and wiped his hands on a rag. "Well, hell, baby, we're not talking about the car, are we?"

She bit her lip and stared at the ground. "No, I guess I'm not," she said, drawing a circle in the snow with her toe. "You and Manny sure were gone for a long time. You two must have had a nice chat."

"Nice enough. Took him down to the Moo Cow for a cup of coffee. And before you ask, no, no one recognized me. Grizzly Adams might not be such a bad look after all."

"What did you tell him?"

Again, he leaned over the engine and inserted the wrench back into the slimy mess. "I told him about us. Our history." He glanced at her and shrugged. "I kinda had to. I'm sorry, Grace."

"I figured." She shoved her hands in her pockets. "So which was it? The thirty-second sound bite version, or all the gory details?"

"In between, I guess. I told him we had a thing, and about your hospital stay in Connecticut. We decided that maybe I should prepare you, in case it all comes out."

A wave of heat washed over her. They decided? Prepare her? What was she, an infant? "Don't do that, Tyler."

"Do what?"

"Treat me like I can't handle the situation."

"That's not what I was doing," he said casually.

"And besides there's nothing for you to handle. It's my problem to worry about. So let's not talk about it anymore." He stepped back out from under the hood and wiped his hands on a rag. "How about we head down to Hoagie Heaven? Meatball subs on me."

"And don't do that."

"Do what?"

She exhaled loudly, letting the cloud fester in front of her face. She knew his indifference was an effort to calm her, but now she wasn't interested in the consideration. "All I'm saying is, I don't want you to run interference for me. Am I scared to death that this whole thing will come out? Sure. Have I thought about the consequences, and the embarrassment it might cause me and my family? Absolutely. But what's different, and has taken me five years and a whole lot of treatment to realize, is that while I can't control the actual situation I can control how I react to it."

"If you think I meant to insult you..."

"I'd be insulted if you started lying to me." She tossed her hair over her shoulder and locked her gaze on his. "Tell me the truth, Ty. What's going on?"

He shut the hood and leaned against it. "Okay, fine, the truth is I don't know what's going on."

"Manny seemed pretty worried."

"Manny's always pretty worried." He studied his blackened hands then slipped them into his pockets. "Look, I don't know where these rumors are coming from. If it's Layla trying to stir the pot, I'll sure try my best to stop her. But if it's just some crafty paparazzi, that might be a little harder to police."

"How much does Layla know?"

"I didn't think she knew anything. She worked on the show, so maybe she suspected something. But we were always pretty discreet."

"And you never said anything to her?"

He looked at her like the question offended him. "That was our business, Grace Ann, no one else's."

A very small part of her relaxed. "Well, then, maybe we're worried for nothing."

"I don't know, darlin'. There's always someone somewhere who knows something about everything. That's the one thing I've learned in this crazy business." He fixed his eyes beyond her and sighed. "I know how much you love your quiet life, and I also know how this would affect that. There's a lot of pressure on you now, and I feel like it's my fault."

"And you can stop with that, too."

He cocked his head and took a step toward her. "Jeez, Gracie, now what did I say?"

With her hands on her hips, she squared her shoulders and shot him the angriest face she could muster. "You know, I realize that you're a big movie star and all, but even so the world doesn't revolve around you. I created this mess right along with you. I am half of the *Undercover Heat* duo, and when I signed my contract a decade ago, I knew I'd have to deal with the press. I agreed to the same thing when I signed on to do this press tour."

"Okay but..."

"And really, what's the big deal if all this gets out? I mean, sure, I'll be mortified, as will my family. My Dad will probably lose his job. We'll both have to relive everything all over again under the scrutiny of the media. But will the world end? No. But my point is, I'd rather it not happen that way, and as your co-worker and ex whatever-I-am, I'd like a shot at saving my own ass."

Ty ran his hand over his face, and Grace could tell it was an effort to hide a smile. That was fine. His reaction was unimportant. What mattered was she had put him on notice.

"Damn, darlin'," Ty finally said, "if I didn't know any better I'd say you were channeling a little Lexie

Love just now."

"Well maybe that's how we should approach this whole thing. Like Lexie and Jax would. Confront the problem methodically and rationally as a totally united front."

It sounded great to her own ears. Incredibly plausible and incredibly easy. She felt inspired and strong, but Ty's laughter indicated he didn't share the sentiment. "Grace Ann, this isn't a network crime drama. This is real life."

"I know, but all I'm saying is, the way I've confronted these situations hasn't worked for me in the past. I'm just trying to help my own cause."

"Yeah but I don't like you making yourself a guinea pig, either." He came to her and brushed his hand down her arm. "I want you to leave it to me," he told her. "And I also think we should reconsider you participating in the press events."

A snowball in the face would have been less offensive. "Thanks for the vote of confidence," she said, then spun on her heels toward the house.

"Grace Ann, wait a minute!"

Clouds of fine flakes jumped from her footfalls as she stomped across the crunchy snow. She heard him closing in behind her, so she quickened her pace to a jog.

"Listen, darlin', this is a little scary for me, too, ya know. You're important to me, and I don't want you to get hurt. Would you feel better if I didn't care how you felt?"

"I'd feel better if you'd let me express my own fears rather than assign them to me yourself."

"Is this the pop psychology again?"

"I don't know, is it making sense?"

"A little."

"Then I guess I've won the argument!" She stormed up the porch steps and slammed the door behind her. If he thought he could walk back into her life after all these years and push her around, he had another think coming. She kicked off her boots, dropping them in the corner of the mud room along with her hat and jacket.

Ty watched her from the kitchen doorway while she filled the teakettle and dropped it to the stove with a thud. "So you're just going to be mad at me the rest of the night?"

"I was thinking about it."

He groaned and rested his head against the door frame. "Okay, so, just so I have things straight, you're mad at me for trying to protect you. Is that where you're coming from, or am I totally misreading you?"

She pulled a mug from the shelf and slammed the cabinet door shut. Was what he said right? Was she really faulting him for his concern? There was a fine line between being assertive and irrational, and she hated to think she'd crossed it. "Okay, fine, I don't mean to be mad at you, but I'm just trying to make a point."

"Which is?"

"I acknowledge that I have a few issues in my past that might give a person a certain impression of me. I suppose given your colorful history, you can appreciate what I am talking about."

"Duly noted."

"So perhaps I have something to prove. Maybe to others, but mostly to myself, and if you truly wanted to," she quoted with her fingers, "protect me, then I suggest you give me the benefit of the doubt when I tell you that I can handle this situation."

She expected an adamant rebuttal. In the past he would have, but it occurred to her that he probably didn't know what to say. This was the first time she'd ever challenged him. She had asserted herself, and it felt pretty good.

"So, you think you want to come back outside

and help me fix the car?"

When he extended his hand to her, she knew he had gotten her point. This was his peace offering, and she was compelled to take it, but on her terms. "No, I was thinking you could stay inside and help me make some tea."

"Deal." He looked at her and chuckled. "So I guess Lexie and Jax reunite after all. Sounds good to me."

"Me too."

His slipped his hands around her waist and pulled her into his arms. She snuggled in close, resting her head on his heart. "Okay, baby," he whispered. "This is just like how it all began. You and me against the world. We get through this, we get through it together. You understand?"

She understood she had a lot to lose, but right now she felt so empowered, it didn't seem important. Heat radiated from him in a slow burn, and her fingers tightened around his sweatshirt in response. He smelled like spice and night and cold. A strange but enticing combination that tied her stomach in knots.

"We should go to bed, darlin."

Grace felt her face flush. "You think so, huh?"

"No, I mean to sleep. I didn't mean it that way."

"Well why not? I'm not tired. In fact, I'm wide awake." She traced her finger down his collar. "How about you, are you tired?"

"I could go all night." His voice had lowered to a grainy whisper, and a breath hitched in her throat. It amazed her how this man still affected her. Just a word spoke volumes, and a touch was a grand gesture. An intimate shorthand all their own, that transcended anything overtly sexual.

Her gaze followed her hands as they slid up his chest. He felt solid and strong, and real. She lifted her head, and his eyes locked on her. Blue beams of intensity that drove straight through her. She wanted him. Badly. Even as her brain screamed they shouldn't, her body hummed in disagreement. He licked his lips, and when his gaze fell to her mouth, his eyelids lowered to a close. She rose to her tiptoes and lifted her chin, silently urging his mouth to hers.

His kisses were as delicious as she remembered. Deep and soft, gentle and sweet. When she offered her tongue he accepted, tasting her, teasing her, softly nipping at her lips the way she liked it. Kissing Ty was something she could do for hours. She had even been lucky enough to be paid to do it. But here, tonight, it was nowhere near enough.

"We should stop," Ty breathed, his lips still grazing hers. "Really."

"No." She gulped. "Upstairs. Let's go upstairs."

Even his world class acting skills couldn't hide the shock on his face. Scooping her in his arms, he scaled the stairs in record time. When he turned the corner to her bedroom, she stopped him, prying her mouth from his. "The guest bed is bigger," she said.

"Yours is warmer."

"I bet with extra body heat, yours would be just fine."

He raised a brow. "You're kind of bossy tonight, aren't you?"

His hot breath swirled around her like a spell. She felt strong and sensual and so incredibly aroused. This is what she wanted. And she could tell by the way Ty looked at her he wanted it, too. "You were always good at taking direction," she teased, splaying her finger over his swollen lips. "Take me to your bed."

His grip tightened around her as he dragged her lips to his. His kisses were deeper, hungrier, and so incredibly clear with intention. He wanted her as badly as she wanted him, and she was up to the task of pleasing him.

Air rushed around her when he released her onto the bed. Her cheeks burned from the friction of his beard, and strands of her hair stuck to her moistened lips. Silently, she invited him to remove her clothes, and his hands moved over her with remarkable dexterity. Buttons released, clasps unfastened, and suddenly she was completely exposed.

It felt oddly empowering to know he watched her. Studied her. She arched her back, lifted her breasts in a tease, and she giggled when he growled in response. Stepping forward, he brought his hand to her leg, then dragged it down the swell of her calf. "You certainly got the Devil in you tonight, don't ya, darlin?"

"Not yet," she said in the sexiest voice she knew, pretending the line wasn't cheesy in the least. The trash-talking temptress was pure Lexie Love and not something that came to her naturally. Ty obviously remembered, given the smirk he attempted to hide. She rolled onto her side, propping her chin in her palm. "Do I amuse you, Hawthorne?"

"Among other things." His voice was ripe with sex. "How about you put your money where that dirty little mouth of yours is?"

Ty pulled off his sweatshirt and jeans and chucked them into the darkness behind him. He stood over her a moment in all his naked glory, the light from the hall hitting him like a spotlight. His muscle-bound body looked like cut rock, and his eyes and mussed hair made him seem dangerous. She gulped hard. This was exactly why he was the Sexiest Man Alive.

His chest heaved with jagged breaths as his gaze raked hungrily over her. In the instant their eyes locked, her insides churned. She was ready for him. Now. And even if this was the stupidest decision she ever made for the rest of her life, she simply didn't care.

"Gracie."

"Don't talk anymore," she whispered. "Don't say anything."

She reached for his hand and brought him to her. He was warm and hard and so incredibly masculine. She molded against him like a perfect part of a whole, his large angular body encasing her tiny soft one.

She exhaled slowly, as his hands traveled over her. Down her arm, over the rise of her backside, along the length of her thigh. He was gentle as always, slow and deliberate, relaxing and arousing all at once.

"You have the softest skin, Grace Ann. It's like milk."

She giggled. "Like milk? Now that's a line, if I ever heard one."

"I'm serious. Pale and pure." She felt his fingers behind her knees, then up inside her thighs. "Everything about you is perfect."

Her heartbeat echoed in her ears, as he dragged his finger along her breast. His hardness pressed against her belly, and she instinctively pressed back. She marveled at his self control. Judging by the headlines and TV news, it was something he'd lately lacked. She wondered if it was reserved just for her.

"Ty?"

"Hmm?"

"I'm glad you're here."

His lips hovered over hers, widening into a smile. The creases in his cheeks deepened, and his eyes gleamed in the dim light. "Me too, although I don't know how wise it is to reopen old wounds. But I suppose if they didn't heal right the first time around..." He kissed her softly and brushed the hair from her eyes.

"How did you get so smart?"

"Darlin', believe me it's easy to be smart about other people and be completely clueless about yourself."

There was a resignation in his voice that moved her, like he admitted something in a moment of vulnerability. Instinct made her touch his face, weave her fingers through his hair. Longing made her bring her mouth to his.

"Wait a minute." He pulled up slightly, to look at her. "Tell me you're sure you want this. I mean, I don't want you to give yourself to me because you think I expect it, because I don't. Not from a woman like you."

"A woman like me? Is that a compliment or an insult?"

"I want you to trust me, Grace."

She slid her hand down his cheek, then over the ripple of his solid chest. She felt his heartbeat inside him, drumming against her palm. "Tyler, you know I don't give myself easily, and I'm not here for any other reason except that I want to be."

"I just want you to be sure about it."

She stared at him before reaching across to the bedside table. Pulling open the drawer, she produced a condom and placed it on the pillow beside them. "I'm sure."

She lay down on his chest, her cheek replacing where her hand had been. When his arms closed around her, it seemed like déjà vu, his musky scent, the contour of his body, the same needful quiver her body made when against him. Time stopped and the darkness dulled. Each breath, each heartbeat in time with his.

"Relax," he whispered, nudging her body off his, his eyes raking her nakedness. "It's me. Just me."

He dragged her up to his mouth, taking her with a kiss. Long and lingering, his tongue probed and sought. In a bold move that surprised her, she trailed her pointer finger down his stomach, until she reached the tuft of coarse hair near his groin. When he sucked in his breath, she smiled with pride. He wasn't the only one with the carnal memory.

"You're a tease," he said through clenched teeth.

"You want me to apologize?"

"Hell, no, I want you to keep going."

His arousal heightened hers. With the eager clumsiness of amateur hands, or at least ones out of practice, she teased the thick hard shaft that pressed against her. She gripped it, stroked it, then found the swollen tip. Soft and moist under her caress.

"Like this?"

He groaned then settled beside her. His skin was slick with heat, and she bet it tasted as good as it felt. With devious intentions, she brought her mouth to his chest, and slid her tongue to the sensitive spot just above his belly button. When she heard his sudden gasp for breath, and his cock twitched in her hand, she knew she'd hit the bull's eye she aimed for.

"You like playing dirty, don't you?" he hissed.

"Oh, I'm sorry. I thought that's what you wanted."

"I do. I just hope you can handle the payback."

Easing on top of her, he nipped at her ear before tracing the curve of her throat with his tongue. Heat simmered inside her, bubbling white hot under her skin. He went lower, slower, until his mouth found her nipple.

In the past, she was convinced he had to have the most perfect mouth in the world. His smile, his kiss, and the things he did to her body made her weak. He lapped at her in hungry strokes, taunting with little nips of his teeth. She panted now, her limbs limp and numb. His breath floated over the curve of her belly, then lower to the inside of her thigh.

"Ty," she breathed, consumed by the incredible sensation. He stroked her hip in response, slowing his advancing pace.

"You don't like that?" His voice ragged and raw.

"I do, but it's too much." To anyone else she'd make no sense, but his eyes told her he understood. "I haven't, since you."

"Take it easy. We've got all night. We'll take it nice and slow. And if you want me to stop..."

"Don't stop. Please."

She could have been embarrassed by the admission. That he was the only man that had ever touched her, seen her, been inside her. For a moment she felt inadequate, afraid to disappoint. Tears welled in her eyes, and her throat narrowed. "Kiss me, please," she pleaded. "Just kiss me."

He did as she asked, slow but intense. She could tell he wanted her, needed her, and was happy to cater to any need. This time when his fingers wandered, she trusted the feeling. They parted her, searched her with gentle purpose, and when they found her, she surrendered. Her inhibitions slipped away as his finger eased into her weeping center.

She lifted her body to him. Pressing, grinding, bringing her core closer to his touch. With slow rhythm, he pulled in then slid out, one finger then two. She closed her eyes, concentrating on the sensation, knowing and liking that he watched her.

"That's right, just relax."

His sandy, soft hair tickled her chin, and his breath snaked over her cleavage. When he took a nipple in his mouth, she slid her hands around his head. She moaned and writhed, eager to rid her body of this strange purgatory between pleasure and pain. The edge of control. "Tyler, please," she pleaded.

Her eyes sealed shut when he settled on top of her, his arms braced around her head. He brought his lips to her ear, and took her right hand in his left. "I'm all yours, Gracie," he breathed, wrapping her fingers around his cock. "I'm all yours."

She was reminded of how big he was, but her desire chased away the fear. Her eager fingers placed his soft tip at her threshold, and slowly he eased himself inside her.

He groaned as he impaled her, at first in steps of progression. She felt her insides stretch to accommodate him, like her body had a memory all its own. When he was fully sheathed, he started a slow rhythm, his muscles straining with each movement.

Her body met his in a perfect syncopation, and her inhibitions fell away like clutter in her mind. Suddenly, she was keenly focused. Each touch, motion, kiss brought her higher and higher to a vortex where she teetered, hanging. He sped up at her urging. Her hands gripped the flesh of his back. She heard herself whimper, beg, plead—for what, she wasn't sure. But she was reeling, lost, her body no longer her own.

"That's it, let it come, baby."

She couldn't stop it, if she tried. Her orgasm came the same time his did, with a force that knocked the breath from her. All at once she drifted, spiraling and floating on a blissful cloud. He moaned her name, pushing himself into her deepest recesses. It went on and on, until neither could move. Breathless and spent, their bodies still connected, he lay on top of her.

"Are you okay?"

She sighed when he kissed her neck. "Yeah, I'm fine."

He slid out from the sheets and got rid of the condom before climbing back in and snuggling against her. "Can I ask you a question, Grace Ann?"

"Sure."

"You ever think about trying again?"

The question blindsided her, but in a weird way it seemed obligatory. She propped her head in her hand and gazed down at him. "You mean 'us' or having a baby?"

"Either one. There isn't a right answer, Grace. I just want to know."

"Have you?"

He brushed a hair from her face. "I asked you first. But I have to tell you—say 'no' and you break my heart."

She lay back down on the pillow, and stared at the shadows the moon cast across the ceiling. Thinking of Ty was something she'd trained herself not to do. Like breaking a bad habit. She supposed the clinical word would be denial. She had always wanted Ty. Even when every shred of logic told her she shouldn't. "Ty, do you remember when we found out I was pregnant?"

He looked at her, as if suddenly engaged. She saw his throat tighten, he swallowed. "Yeah," he croaked. "We were filming a scene in that rollercoaster episode we did. The one where the carnival guy was a mass murderer."

"And I had that scene where I was stuck on that Ferris wheel, and you had to come save me. I was so nauseous, and I couldn't understand why, because I never got motion sick. And then I thought back to that night in your trailer when we weren't so careful."

Ty chuckled. "I remember."

"I snuck off the set and got a pregnancy test at the store, but I already knew."

"God, I remember how beautiful you looked when you told me, downstairs in the kitchen after work. It took you three tries to get it out. Then I made love to you the rest of the night."

Her face burned at the memory. How he took her slow and easy, spooning her, kissing the back of her neck, and whispering sexy things in her ear. When her orgasm came it went on forever, stealing her breath and stunning her body. They'd slept in front of the fire that night, wrapped in a wool blanket and each other's arms. They both showed up late for work the next day. Earl wouldn't talk to them for a week.

He pulled her into his chest, weaving his hands in her hair. She hated how right his arms felt around her. Even when it had been scripted, his touch stirred her in ways no man had ever come close to. "I really wanted that baby, Tyler."

"I know, Gracie. Me too."

She had never been a believer in true psychology, and she still wasn't, clinically speaking. What she truly believed healed her was simply talking. Communication. Ty was always the open person. Receptive. The man beside her was the Ty she knew. In repose, unguarded. This was the man she had fallen in love with.

And it was happening all over again.

## Chapter Nine

Ty slept less than two hours, but it was the best sleep he'd had in five years. Dreamless and deep, and so rejuvenating that he actually twitched with unspent energy.

He had a good idea how he'd like to burn some off.

Grace's head rested in the crook of his arm, with the morning sun warming her pale cheek. God damn, did that feel right. To wake up with a woman and actually feel like he belonged there. If he could do this every day for the rest of his life, he'd die a happy man. But if the truth ever came out...

He couldn't imagine Layla knowing what really happened. Even Lizzie and Russ were in the dark. Deacon Langley had covered his bases, Ty was stupid enough to let him, and if Grace ever found out he'd lose her for good. Of course, that's exactly what he deserved. He was greedy, weak, and totally drunk on his desire. If he were a decent man, he'd level with her, and he definitely wouldn't have taken her to bed.

"What time is it?"

The soft, groggy voice jolted him from his thoughts. He pushed through the sea of red hair until he found her sleepy eyes. "Very early," he whispered. "Go back to sleep."

"Too late. I'm awake." She yawned and slid her arm around him. "I should get up and get to work. We open Thanksgiving weekend, and I have a ton of things to do."

"Grace Ann, that's two weeks away. If you had

to open tomorrow, you'd be more than prepared. Go back to sleep."

She looked up at him and smiled, her fair complexion ghostly against his darker chest. "You look tired. Didn't you sleep well?"

"What I got of it. Hard to think about sleep when you've got a beautiful naked woman beside you."

She raised a brow. "You say it like it's a rare occasion."

He tossed a pillow at her, and she tossed it back. It wasn't every woman you could have a pillow fight with at the ass-crack of dawn. But right now he wasn't interested in horsing around. Grabbing her wrist, he pulled her back under him.

"Let me up." She giggled.

"Say please, and I'll think about it."

"Tyler, really. I have so many things to do. I need to get an early start."

"Well how about if we hire more help," he said in between nibbles of her earlobe. "Like a college kid on break, or a friend from church or something."

"We?"

Is that what he'd said? He wouldn't be surprised. He was right where he wanted to be, with the woman he wanted to be with. "We" seemed as natural as breathing.

"Ty, 'we' would rather not spend the money."

"Well, I don't mind. Seems worth it to me, if it frees up some of our time."

"Our?"

He did it again. Possessive pronouns. Which seemed perfect to him because that was exactly what he felt. Possessive.

She slid out from under him and sat up. The sheets fell away, exposing her perfect breasts. He reached for them, but she batted him away. "Ty, I'm flattered that you're interested in helping me, but I really don't feel comfortable using your money."

He lifted his gaze, her eyes being the second favorite place to stare. "My checkbook is in my bag. What if just this one time—"

"Tyler, stop!"

He clamped his mouth shut when he saw the look. The pink puckered lips, the narrowed eyes. Her "giving notes" face. A term used between actors when critiquing a performance, and if his memory served him that was exactly what she was about to do. He lay back down on his pillow and prepared himself for the lecture.

"First of all, I'm not one of your 'women.' Second, I'm not interested in your money. And third, the words 'us' and 'we' don't flatter me."

He frowned. "I'm not sure I'm following you."

"Yesterday, Manny called me one of your 'women' and now you offer me money." She flipped her hair over her shoulder and shrugged. "I'm not a groupie."

He folded his arms behind his head, trying like hell not to smile. God damn, he had missed her. His little firecracker.

"I just don't want you to think that spending the night with you means more than it does. We were comforting each other, and I'd like to just leave it at that." She shrugged. "You know, like a one-night stand."

That caught his attention. "I'm sorry, what?"

She took a breath and tucked the sheet under her arms. "I'd like to approach this as two co-workers who just happen to enjoy each other's company, naked. No strings attached."

He felt like he'd been socked in the gut. This was the opposite conversation than he was used to having. Usually the woman irked him by using words like "we" and "us" or making cases why he and they were perfect for each other. He'd never been on the other side.

He didn't like it.

"Darlin', I just thought that after last night..."

"Last night was last night, Ty. You can't just assume things are different." She moved to get up, but he pulled her back.

"Last night had to mean something to you, Gracie."

"It doesn't have to. We were emotional, that's all."

Again she moved away, and again he pulled her back. "What's going on?" he asked. "Really, why are you acting like this?"

"I'm not acting."

"You're giving me the bum's rush, Grace Ann, and I want to know why!"

The sudden flush of her cheeks told him she was upset, and the glaze of her eyes warned tears. This time when he reached for her, she didn't resist. "I'm sorry," she whispered against his neck. "I guess after last night I'm a little scared."

The admission told him more about her feelings for him than anything else. He pulled her closer, brushing his lips against her temple. "No, it's my fault. When I offered you money, I didn't mean to insult you."

"I know you didn't."

"Let me make it up to you."

"And just how do you plan to do that?"

He kissed her forehead before meeting her gaze. "Well, we have to be in the city early tomorrow for *The Olivia Show*. What if we went in today and bummed around. Just you and me."

"Yeah right," she said, with a laugh. "You don't see the million and one things that are wrong with that idea?"

He shrugged. "Like what?"

"Didn't I just finish telling you about all the

things I have to do around here? And what about the paparazzi? We're already front page news."

"So? We're two costars catching up on old times. Besides it's good to be seen. That way no one thinks there's anything to hide."

"I don't know, Ty."

"Well, how about you let me talk you into it?" Gently, he brought her under him, pressing against her with obvious purpose. He kissed her and then dragged his lips down the slope of her throat. She tasted sweet, with a hint of spice that was so incredibly sexual he was sure it could make him come all on its own. "How am I doing?" he asked, his breath teasing a needy nipple. "You coming with me, or what?"

"You're making a pretty good case."

The strain in her voice excited him. What was it about this woman that he craved? The hell with foreplay. He couldn't wait. He needed her. Fast, hard and right now. "Where's that condom stash of yours," he stammered.

"I think there's only one left."

Her voice was as soft and as seducing as her body beneath him. His mouth went further down her belly. "Well then let's put it to good use, baby."

He pushed himself up and dove into the bedside drawer. "Aren't you Little Miss Resourceful. You got your own little condom stash."

"Mine?" She laughed through a sigh. "What would I be doing with condoms? Those were yours. When I unpacked them I put them in the drawer."

"My condoms?" He pulled it out and looked at it twice.

These weren't his.

He knew for sure he was out when he left New York, and Manny packed his bag when he left. Suddenly it dawned on him. That girl, Angie, had left them in the bathroom.

"Ty, is something wrong?"

"There will be if he doesn't get off you!"

The sound of Lizzie's voice drove them to opposite sides of the bed. Ty cleared his throat and pushed his hand through his hair, wishing he'd thought to close the bedroom door the night before.

"Lizzie!" Grace yelled, pulling the sheet up around her. "What do you think you're doing?"

"I was just about to ask you the same thing."

"Oh, my God, you're still here!" Manny leaned on the doorframe, and panted like he'd just run a marathon. He held his hand over his heart, and flakes of snow frosted his pink hair. "Why are you still in bed? You have a brunch meeting in the city at ten thirty with those indie film producers."

Ty looked at his watch. "Manny, where the hell did you come from, anyway?"

"The weather was too iffy to drive back last night," he said, while he scanned the room. When he spotted the suitcase by Grace's side of the bed, he jumped to retrieve it. "I stayed a couple miles down the road. I would have spent the night here, but I didn't think you wanted me around."

"You could have stayed here," Grace said, reaching out to his neon head. "I wish you would have asked."

"Jeez, darlin'," Ty said. "The guy just burst into the bedroom unannounced. Why are you even talking to him?"

"You're right. She should be talking to me." Lizzie stood with one hand over her eyes and the other in the air for emphasis. "You do know, Grace Ann, that this is asking for trouble."

"Oh, please. I know what I'm doing."

"Save it for Dad. I'm sure he'd love to hear it."

Ty watched the color drain from Grace's cheeks. "He's not home, is he?"

Lizzie sighed and dropped her hand from her

face. “He called this morning. He said he’d be home in a few hours, and tomorrow night he’s taking us all to the city to have dinner.” She scowled at Ty. “I didn’t tell him about your visit.”

“I think you caused enough trouble,” Manny told Ty, already stuffing clothes into the leather duffle. “Lets get moving. We need to get on the road if you want to make your appointment.”

“And Grace,” Lizzie added. “You have to show me how to work that new reservation database.”

Grace brushed the hair from her face and tightened the sheet around her. Her cheeks blushed, but he could tell by the twitch of her lip it was from amusement and not embarrassment. She drummed her fingers against the mattress. In the past, the trick was a weird sort of subconscious habit she did when she was highly focused. Preparing for a scene or getting into character. He wondered if that still applied.

“Wait a minute!” Grace suddenly blurted, flinging her hand in the air in protest. “What are you guys talking about? Don’t you remember about the change in plans?”

The drumming stopped, and Ty smiled as the room came to a halt. He had read her right. Lexie Love was up to something.

Everyone looked at one another. Confused, annoyed. Ty smiled and eased himself back against the headboard. This was her scene. He was happy to play the supporting role and fade into the background.

“I thought everyone was clear on our plans today,” Grace said. “Ty and I have some appointments this afternoon.” She turned to Ty, her eyes twinkling. “Isn’t that right?”

“Huge.”

“And Manny, remember, you agreed to stay here in my place, helping Lizzie?”

Manny stood up, sending an armful of clothes tumbling to the floor. "Pardon me, Grace, but what the hell are you talking about?"

"You agreed to help Lizzie while Ty and I went to New York. That's why you stayed overnight, isn't it?"

More headshaking and raised brows. Ty wasn't worried. Grace was unflappable in tense scenes. Breaking character was something he did, never her.

"That was really nice of you to offer to straighten out our new database," Grace said to Manny. "I'm sure you'll make quick work of it." She turned back to her sister. "Manny has a management degree from Harvard."

"Yale," Ty prompted.

"Yale. And he said he was really looking forward to organizing our reservation files and making the menu calendar. Right, Manny?"

Manny looked at Lizzie, then at Ty. "Well..."

"So it's settled." Grace clapped her hands together and smiled. "Ty, we should get moving if we want to make our appointments. Lizzie, thanks for the heads up on Dad. Manny, thank you so much for filling in for me. My sister will show you everything. And remember, if you have any questions you can just refer to the list I faxed you."

Manny scratched his temple. "I'm sorry, Grace. What list?"

"The list I faxed to you at your hotel last night."

"I didn't get a list."

Grace shook her head. "Well that's what happens when you stay in second rate places. I guess I'll just make up another one."

Ty smiled with pride. This was precisely why she was a two-time Emmy winner. The woman had talent. No doubt about it.

"Great," Grace chirped. "Now that everything is straightened out, we'd like to get dressed."

“Fine, Lizzie mumbled. “Although the first order of business is to clean up in here and change the sheets. Manny, I’ll meet you in the computer room in fifteen minutes.”

Her sister followed Manny out, slamming the door behind her. When Ty looked at Grace, she smiled, and his heart swelled with pride. He raised his hands and clapped, once then twice, coaxing her smile to a laugh.

“And scene,” she breathed, bowing her head dramatically. “Now let’s get the hell out of here.”

****

Harvey squinted through the frost-covered windshield when Grace and Ty piled into the yellow Hummer. He had been staked out in the ski resort parking lot for hours, waiting for nothing in particular. He had a hunch he’d be rewarded for his patience. And what a reward it was! His instincts were dead on. Ty and Grace were on the move.

He rubbed his frozen hands together and turned the key in the ignition. The engine sputtered then roared, discharging a huge cloud of exhaust. His bald tires skidded when he turned out to the main road, but he gunned the gas anyway. Moments later, he was a few car-lengths behind them, following like he’d seen it done in movies. Hell, like he’d seen Hawthorne do himself.

He turned on the defroster and it hissed to life, slowly pushing the fog from his view. Looked like they were headed toward the city. Was this a business trip? As far as he knew, the duo didn’t have an appearance planned until tomorrow. No. This was for pleasure. Every instinct in his body told him so. His hands tightened around the wheel. There was a story about to unfold. He could feel it.

They reached the city about noon. Heavy traffic, pissed off drivers, usual lunchtime bullshit. The sun shone, and Harvey realized he hadn’t seen it in days.

He counted it as a good sign as he followed them to the Waldorf.

He hit the lobby just in time to see Ty check in, while Grace hung back in the gift shop. A few minutes and a few hundred dollars later, Harvey secured a room just below their penthouse suite. With any luck, they wouldn't spend much time there. He bought a paper and parked himself in the lobby, directly across from the elevators.

A few minutes later, they emerged, both in a change of clothes. They wore jeans, but Ty had a thick, black winter jacket and an "I Love New York" baseball cap over his eyes, and Grace sported a yellow parka and matching ski hat. They breezed out the door with more than a few arm-lengths between them. A casual observer wouldn't even think they were together. But Harvey knew. They were together, all right. In more ways than one.

Harvey dropped the paper and followed them out the door, hanging a few yards back. The day was a blur of window shopping and aimless walking. Even the stroll through Central Park didn't produce anything juicy. They behaved like old friends, throwing snowballs and laughing. The highlight came when Ty eased an arm around Grace to help her over a snowbank. So what? Certainly nothing worth a front page photo op.

After a hot chocolate, they ended up on Fifth Avenue, hitting the overpriced boutiques. In one shop Harvey had a good view as Grace eyed a long black gown that cost more than a small house. She held it up against her, and Ty smiled with approval. When Grace's back was turned, he motioned to the manager, and slipped her something from his pants pocket. A wad of cash, probably. They came out of the store moments later, but they left the dress behind.

Big Deal.

As night fell, Harvey, discouraged, cold and angry, figured he'd wasted the day. But he reminded himself why he was a journalist. He was a warrior on a mission and, just like any good soldier on a special operation, waiting was a big part of the game. His diligence would be rewarded. It had to be.

A hundred yards ahead, the duo entered another store. Harvey followed, half interested, daydreaming about a decent bacon burger and the pot of hot coffee he'd order from room service. But that was forgotten when he read the name of the storefront. Leslie's Layette. His eyes narrowed, and through the cloud of his breath, he saw the merchandise in the window.

Baby clothes.

Hot damn!

He pulled his collar up around his neck like he'd seen undercover agents do on TV. It was ballsy to actually follow them into the store, but he couldn't help it. The possible rewards were simply too great. Taking a deep breath, he walked through the door, the bell on the knob alerting his entrance. The smell of talcum powder and some sort of flowery baby scent invaded his nose. He held back a sneeze and smiled at the proprietor, who was folding blankets in the back.

"Can I help you, sir?"

"No thanks," he said. "Just browsing."

Harvey looked around, peeking through clothes racks and between crib railings. The place was empty except for his pair. Mumbles came from somewhere in the back. He followed the sound until he spotted them huddled near the newborn clothes. Harvey stood behind a tall teak wardrobe, his ears poised in their direction.

"Aren't these the cutest little dresses you've ever seen?" Grace cooed, holding one up for Ty to see. "I can't believe how small they are. And I can't decide if

I like pink or purple. Which do you like?"

"Either one." He chuckled. "But don't you think we're jumping the gun a little? We don't know if it's a boy or a girl."

"You're right, I guess." She put the dress back on the rack and snagged a tiny pair of shoes from the counter. "But look at these little boy sneakers. God, I could get a dozen pairs."

"Wait a minute, darlin'. I think we should think more gender neutral."

Grace frowned. "Fine, but that's not nearly as fun."

*Darlin'*? Harvey thought. When the hell did Ty develop a Southern accent?

The two moved to a display of ridiculously priced blankets. Grace ran her hand over the fuzzy pink one draped on the wall. "Wow these are beautiful," she said. "And so soft. They're big enough to put on my bed."

Ty looked down at her and smiled. "I have a feeling that if you had your way, the baby would spend more time there, anyway, than in its crib."

"That's not true!" Playfully, she jabbed him in the ribs. "A baby can't sleep in an adult bed. They might suffocate. Don't you know that?"

He leaned over, meeting her nose to nose. "Well how about this—you get that blanket for yourself, and you won't have to worry about me suffocating. How does that sound?"

Harvey's ears perked up, as their voices lowered. In an instant he had his camera poised, just in time to snap them as Grace batted away Ty's kiss.

"Are you crazy, Ty? People could see us."

"Baby, there isn't a soul around, and even if there was, they wouldn't know who we were."

"Excuse me. May I help you find something?" The dark-haired woman pushed her glasses up her nose and smiled pleasantly at the couple.

"No, thank you," Grace said, taking a step away from Ty. "We were just browsing."

They left the store, and Harvey followed soon after. Undetected, like a shadow or a spook. God, was he good.

Not a smoking gun, but maybe a prelude to bigger things. They were definitely more than old friends, and this scene, combined with Ty's prenatal vitamin purchase, convinced him. Grace Ann Langley was pregnant with Ty Hawthorne's baby. Everything pointed to that fact. But he had to be sure. No need to get sloppy now and risk a lawsuit because of lack of patience.

He followed them back to the hotel and through the lobby to the elevators. Just as he did before, he sat on the bench with a copy of the *Times* in his hand, just in case they appeared for dinner. Odds were, they wouldn't bother. The lovebirds probably wanted some private time. He felt for his camera phone in his pants pocket and started on the evening edition.

****

Grace awoke in the bathtub with a mouthful of bubbles and a crick in her neck. Judging by the icy chill of the water, she'd been in there a while, but despite being cold she was in no hurry to get out. She couldn't remember the last time she felt so at ease. Peaceful. Like everything in the world was just as it was supposed to be.

And it had a lot to do with Ty.

The thought drove her eyes wide open. What the heck was she thinking? This was just a fling. She'd never had one, and it seemed very empowering. There was also the added advantage of knowing there was a definite beginning and an end when the press commitment was over. Just like a role in a movie.

If she kept telling herself that, she might start

to believe it.

Seeing him again was hard, but being with him was surprisingly easy. She could understand Ty's willingness to forget the past and pick up where they left off. It was tempting, but she wondered if he'd feel the same way if he knew the truth about her father.

A knock at the bathroom door startled her, sending the now ice cold water over the sides. She wiped the soapy drops from her eyes, and when her vision righted itself, Ty stood over her in a tuxedo.

"What are you doing in here, woman? I was beginning to think you drowned."

"I'm sorry, I guess I fell asleep."

"No need to apologize," he smiled and came toward her. "I'm glad you're enjoying yourself. Besides, it's good you took a catnap now. I can't guarantee you'll get much sleep tonight."

His eyes raked over her, so she leaned against the side of the tub to distort the view. "Where did you get the monkey suit?"

"Called Barney's. They hooked me up." He ran his hands down the lapels. "Told them I had some big plans."

"You do, huh?"

"I promised I'd show you a good time, right?"

In that tux? She could think of plenty of ways he could have a good time without ever leaving the hotel suite. "What do you have in mind?"

He looked at his watch. "Well, we have reservations in forty-five minutes. So that gives you just enough time to get out of there and get dressed."

"Forty-five minutes?" She jumped up, grabbing a towel from the brass rack beside her. She wrapped it around her and tucked it under her arm. "Tyler, look at me. How am I supposed to be ready so fast?"

"Hey, I have no objections to you staying like that the rest of the night."

"Pig." Taking another towel, she flipped her hair over to dry it. "And what do you suggest I wear? I didn't bring a dress."

When he didn't answer right away, she looked up. Ty stared, smiling. His blue eyes twinkled as he bit his bottom lip. "Take that towel off."

"Excuse me?"

He took a step toward her and reached for the knot under her left arm. With one agile flip of his fingers, the towel fell in a puddle at her feet.

The dripping faucet echoed in her ears, and his European cologne teased her senses like the gentle fingers he traced over her breast. "Cold in that tub, was it?"

"Maybe."

"Well, then, come over here, and let me warm you up." He slid his hand around the nape of her neck, bringing her into his chest.

"Ty, I'm going to get you all wet."

"Shhh." He lifted her chin with his thumb and brought his mouth down to hers.

There was something very erotic about being naked in the arms of a sexy well-dressed man, and fantasies didn't come better than Ty Hawthorne. He raked his hands down her back, cupping her backside and lifting her against him. Her nipples dragged against the rough fabric, urging her stomach into needful knots.

"Feel better?"

She moaned in response. The cold chill left her, replaced with damp heat. His hands pushed through her knotted hair, exposing her throat to his mouth. In a heartbeat, his mouth was on her, forcing the air from her lungs.

"If you want me ready in forty-five minutes, this is not the way to motivate me."

"Well, would you put a rush on it if I told you I got you a present?"

“A present? What kind of present?”

“Go look in the bedroom. It’s on the bed.”

She scooped up the robe from the bathroom counter and pulled it on as she headed into the bedroom. A dress bag lay on the bed, with the name of one of the boutiques they had visited written in calligraphy on the side. “What’s this?” She held it up in front of her.

“Why don’t you open it and find out?”

She slipped the plastic over the hanger, revealing the long black dress she had seen earlier that day. The beading sparkled like diamonds, like tiny kaleidoscopes in the low light.

“I could tell you really liked it when you saw it.”

“I love it,” she said, running her hand over the silky fabric. “But it’s so expensive.”

“Darlin’, don’t you worry about that stuff. Now go put it on. You’ve made me wait long enough.”

She slipped back into the bathroom and looked at herself in the mirror. In five years she had never indulged this side of her, the girlie-girl that liked to dress up in designer clothes and fix her hair and make-up. Magazines used to call her “sexy,” but the word used most to describe her was “fiery.” Back then she was naïve enough to think it was in reference to her hair, but she had come to understand it was actually an impression she gave. She remembered one article that Earl read out loud on the set. “Grace Langley is the rare type of vixen that makes a man feel like a man.” She had no clue what that meant, but Ty had told her that it was a compliment.

As she slipped the fabric over her, she truly felt like a woman. Her curves pushed the dress to its limits, her breasts spilled over the top as if in offering. But she wasn’t inclined to cover herself. She looked good, felt good. Confident. Real. She swept her hair up in a loose bun, allowing tendrils to fall around her face. Her makeup was sparse by Hollywood standards. Just a light foundation, some mascara and lip gloss.

When she came out from the bathroom, Ty lay on the bed with the remote in his hand. He tossed it to the side when he saw her, whistled and motioned with his finger to turn around.

"Do you like it?" she asked, indulging him with a second pirouette.

"You're gorgeous." He rose to his feet, half laughing. "But as long as you wear that smile you could sport a garbage bag, and I'd still think you were the sexiest woman alive."

"Sweet-talker." She stood on her tiptoes and reached up for a kiss. "So you said forty-five minutes and I made it in..." she checked her watch, "thirty-two. Are you impressed, or what?"

"As a matter of fact, I am. And to reward you for your efforts, you get a bonus prize." From behind his back, he produced a long leather box. He placed it in her hands and smiled. "Open it."

Her fingers trembled, as she pulled the box open. Lying on the white silk lay the largest sapphire she'd ever seen, surrounded by a cluster of flawless diamonds. She stared at them a moment before Ty eased it out of the clasp. "Tyler James," she stammered. "Goodness, this is beautiful."

"The lady said it was vintage. That's a good thing, I think."

"Good and expensive," she said. "I can't accept this."

"What good is money if you can't spend it? And besides, a woman like you should have the best."

He spun her around and lifted the necklace in front of her. When the cool gems fell against her skin, she swallowed her protests in a gulp.

"Now let's get going," he whispered in her ear. "The limousine is waiting."

# Chapter Ten

Ty lifted the champagne to his lips and took a long sip. He couldn't remember when he'd last had such a great meal, and with someone he could actually relax and enjoy it with. The restaurant, quiet, dimly lit, had a violinist floating from table to table. He stared at the redheaded beauty across from him and smiled. Couldn't beat the view, either.

"You're staring, again."

"Was I?" He set his fork down and picked up his napkin. "I was just thinking what I wanted for dessert."

"I'm surprised you chose a French restaurant. Since when did your tastes get so fancy?"

"I don't know. When I was filming in Italy, we had a small hiatus, so I bummed around the south of France for a few weeks. Developed a taste for it, I guess."

"Well, I'm glad I let you order. I don't know what I just ate, but it was excellent."

"I wish you'd eat a little more of it."

Her eyes darted around the room. When they landed back on her plate, she slid her wrap up over her arms. Ty knew both the look and the gesture. She had a thing about her arms. Those and her legs. He swirled what was left of the champagne in his glass and fixed an easy smile on his face. "Grace, if people are looking, it's because they can't help themselves. You're beautiful."

"Thank you," she said, bringing a small bite of asparagus to her mouth. "I'm just a little nervous. It's been a while since I've been out in public with you. I mean in a position where we're so obvious."

"Obvious?" He chuckled. "This is what Manny calls 'hiding in plain sight.' Renting out a private dining room would have been obvious. This is two old friends catching up."

Again, he scanned the dining room. Earlier today, he could swear he saw one of those vulture paparazzi hanging around at some of the places they visited. He hadn't mentioned it to Grace, and he wasn't going to now.

"Tyler?"

"What, baby?"

"I asked you about Manny. Was he mad that we ditched him with Lizzie?"

When Ty called him earlier, he expected at least a little attitude, but he was surprised that Manny actually enjoyed himself. "No. He said Lizzie was a quick study. They were done long before your father came home, and then he rented some skis and took off to the hill."

"That's good. I was wondering how we were going to explain him to my dad."

"Are you going to tell him about us?"

She looked at him over her water glass. "Listen, Ty..."

"I'm sorry." He held up his hand in apology. "I know, I'm pushing you. I'll stop."

"You're not pushing anything. I wouldn't have come to New York with you if I didn't want to spend time with you."

She shifted in her seat, and from over her shoulder, Ty saw him. He sat at the bar, and now the hostess showed him to his table on the far end of the dining room. Far away, but with a perfect view of their table. Typical.

"Excuse me, are you Grace Ann Langley?"

Grace set down her wine glass and looked up at the man. "Can I help you?"

"More than you know. My name is Max Freeberg. I'm casting a show that I think would be perfect for you. I know you were with the New York City Ballet, and your expertise would be an honor for us. I don't suppose..." He took a breath and gave her a once-over. "Good Lord, you're even more stunning in person."

Ty stared at the tall, well-groomed man with the wide solicitous smile of a man on the make. He slipped a card from the breast pocket of his well-tailored suit and handed it to Grace.

"Hey, pal," Ty interrupted. "Have your people call hers. She's having dinner."

Max smiled at Ty, as if just realizing he was there, and extended his hand to shake. "Mr. Hawthorne, it's an honor to meet you, of course."

"Of course. Now get the hell out of here."

Grace kicked Ty under the table before addressing the man. "I'm flattered you thought of me, Mr. Freeberg, but I'm afraid I'm not interested. I haven't danced in years."

"I can see. You do look well fed." He chuckled. "If it's the preparation you're worried about, we'd be happy to accommodate you."

"Hey! Are you deaf?" Ty tossed his napkin on the table and jumped up from his seat. "She's not interested. Now can you find the door yourself, or do I have to help you?"

"Excuse me, Mr. Hawthorne, is everything okay?" The manager pushed between the two men. Ty shoved him back, still looking square in Max's face.

"We were having a quiet dinner before this jerk showed up."

"I'm sorry," the manager said.

"Yeah, me too." Ty tossed a wad of cash on the table, and took Grace by the hand. He hurried her across the dining room toward the front doors, right past the man sitting alone in the corner.

"Ty, stop it!" Grace hissed. "You're making a scene!"

People gawked and whispered as they passed, but he didn't care. He wanted to get her out of there before the jerk's words sunk in too far. Blowing off the coatroom, he headed straight to the limo. He ushered her inside and ordered the driver back to the Waldorf.

"What the hell was that all about?" Grace demanded, her head snapping back as the car pulled away from the curb.

"We'll talk about it back at the hotel."

"Are you crazy, causing a scene like that? That's going to be on every paper tomorrow."

"I heard what that guy said to you. I didn't want you to get upset."

She rolled her eyes. "I'm not going to shatter into a million pieces every time some guy gives me a backhanded compliment."

"And how do I know that, Gracie? This is hard for me, ya know? I'm used to taking care of you. Protecting you."

"Are you saying that you prefer me sick?"

"Of course not." His attention drifted to the bottle of bourbon on the bar in front of him. He poured himself a shot, and brought it to his lips before Grace eased it from his hand.

"Tyler, I'm flattered that you want to look after me. But there's a difference between treating me like a lady and treating me like a child."

"Believe me, I don't think of you as a child." He tossed his head back and covered his eyes. Grace wasn't helpless. In fact, she was one of the most capable women he'd ever known. Smart, talented, kindhearted, but she was also naïve and sensitive. The world was a scary place. Grace was vulnerable, and he'd do everything in his power to spare her from pain. It was a promise he'd made to himself long ago, and he had no intention of breaking it twice. "Look, I don't mean to insult your intelligence or anything else. But I guess I'm just used to looking after you, that's all. Old habit."

"I'm not your responsibility."

"Well, maybe I like to think that you are." He looked out the window and took a breath. "I just don't want to make the same mistakes I made before."

He felt her slide up against him, felt her fingers slip under his chin, turning his head to meet her gaze with his. Man, those eyes. He could lose himself there. The deep azure pools that turned his insides to jelly were now at odds with his composure. They bored into him like lasers, holding him to his seat.

"Tyler, you have always mattered to me, and I care about you enough to tell you this. I have forgiven you for any part you had in what happened. But now you need to forgive yourself, because I can tell this is tearing you apart."

Five years had done nothing to dull her perception. He felt exposed, like she stared straight into his soul. God, if she only knew. He didn't deserve forgiveness, not hers or his own. He was a useless liar, and if the girl required protection, it was from the person staring back at her.

But if he could only make it up to her...

He slipped her hand from his face and held it in his. "All I know is, when I saw you again, something snapped inside of me. I can't describe it, but for five years I have been walking in a blur, and then there you were, and suddenly everything came back into focus. Like it all just came together."

"That's what they used to say about *Undercover Heat*, remember? That there was something about it that was bigger than any single one of us. Maybe that's what this is. This thing you and I have. This weird sort of cosmic energy that just sweeps us off our feet, and there's no room for reason."

Something tickled his cheek, and when he dragged his finger across it, it was moist. Jesus, was he crying? Nice. Ty Hawthorne, Hollywood bad boy, had been reduced to tears by a five-foot pixy. He shook his head and smiled. "Grace Ann, I just want a chance. I know I don't deserve one. But you can't deny that there's still something between us."

He held his breath. It was like his whole existence depended on this very moment. The glutton in him wanted nothing more than to take her in his arms, but the shred of decency still residing within him held him stuck to his seat.

"I don't know how much of myself I can afford to give you," she said softly.

"Well then take from me what I'm offering instead. You can't break a heart that's already broken." It was a huge admission, but he didn't care. Their telepathy would betray him. Again, he reached for the bourbon, but she caught his hand in hers.

"I want the Ty that I used to know," she whispered. "The real one."

"He's yours, if you can find him."

"Oh, I found him. He's right in front of me."

His body quaked when she kissed him. Hard and long. Crippling. All his defenses failed. He felt it. The impenetrable wall he had haphazardly constructed crumbled like matchsticks. He had no resistance when it came to Grace. Somehow, just being with her, she exposed his soul, the places in his heart no one had ever seen. He suddenly realized there really was a difference between the real Ty Hawthorne and the movie star playboy the world expected. A kind of strange schizophrenia that became his method of self-preservation. Sometimes he wondered if he even still existed. But like a beacon, Grace had summoned his true self to the surface.

"You know, I was thinking maybe we should make the most of this week." She slid onto his lap and rested her head on his shoulder. "Do some catching up."

"You were, huh?"

"Yeah and a small town girl like me needs an escort around the big city. I was hoping you could show me a good time." The pitch of her voice rose to a chirp as she undid the knot of his tie. "I made a mental list of all the things I'd like to do. Want to hear it?"

"I'm all ears.'"

"Well, first I'd like to see a show or two. And I'd like to head to the ballet."

"I figured as much," he said. "What else?"

"I'd like to skate at Rockefeller Center, go to a Knicks game and..." She put a finger to her chin, as if she trying to remember. "Oh, yeah, and I want to make love to the Sexiest Man Alive in the back of a stretch limo while driving through Central Park."

"That's quite a list," he teased, nuzzling the slope of her neck. "And I hope you have me in mind when you do that sex-through-Central-Park thing.

She released another button and smiled. "There's never been anyone else."

After alerting the driver of their change in route, he pushed his fingers through her copper hair, letting the strands tangle between. Outside the tinted windows the city lights passed in blurs, shadowing her face in a gray-blue haze. Her translucent skin glowed. And her signature scent of spring flowers and pure woman honed his every sense to razor sharp. This was need. An acute and constant craving for this one woman. He couldn't control it and didn't want to.

He found the zipper on the back of her dress and slid the bodice down past her breasts. Now these were God's version of perfect. Round and soft, with eager nipples. He cupped them both before taking one in his mouth.

Her staccato heartbeat drummed in his ears, and he felt the cool heat on her dampened skin. He teased her with his tongue and nibbled with his teeth. Good God, what the woman did to him. "I love how real you are, Gracie," he whispered, more to himself than to her. "Everything about you is honest. I miss that."

To anyone else the words would be senseless, but they had always spoken a language all their own. Words were secondary to intuition and instinct. And the proof was in her kiss.

She tasted like wine and was just as intoxicating. Soft yet obvious with desire. He deepened the kiss, searched her mouth with his tongue, and ran his palms over her bare back. With the dexterity of a driven man, he gathered the fabric of her dress and hoisted it over her head. He tossed it onto the seat beside them, and her black lace panties soon followed.

New York City passed before them in oblivion and faded when they reached the park. Minutes passed in seconds, and soon his clothes were cast on top of hers, his smoldering desire now a full-on blaze. He laid her down on the seat and collapsed on top of her.

She wrapped around him like a ribbon of warmth, drawing him close and holding him tight. He kissed her belly, easing lower, wanting to taste her, drink her. His lips trailed down the inside of her thigh, and she tensed with anticipation.

He brought his mouth to her. She gasped at the sudden contact. Her fingers tangled in his hair, urging him further, until she panted and moaned his name. Grace had always been a responsive lover, each touch, each kiss an encounter all its own. This was Grace in her rawest form. Open, unguarded. His. No woman turned him on like Grace. It was true back then, and, good lord, it was still true now.

He reached up and stroked her breast, teasing the nipple the way he knew she liked. Again she responded with a blissful whimper, quivering like a tuning fork underneath him. Her excitement fueled his, and he couldn't wait any longer. He needed to be inside her. Now.

After slipping on a condom, he entered her with a force he had not intended, his arousal so intense and so urgent that somehow it didn't seem fast or deep enough. She met him thrust for thrust, lifting herself to him, dragging her nails hungrily down his back. She kissed him, deep and long, and so much without restraint that the knowledge alone was enough to make him come. This was his Grace. The sensitive soul who didn't relinquish control easily, but in his arms she surrendered.

He came hard, his body convulsed with crippling force. He held her tight, taking her with him, giving her everything he had left, and wishing he could offer more.

****

Grace was pleased that her legs still worked when she pushed herself out of the limousine. Her face burned with the friction of Ty's stubble, and a quick glance told her that he now wore more lipstick than she did. Any idiot could tell what they'd been doing behind those tinted windows. Thankfully, there was nobody on the sidewalk willing to make it a Kodak moment.

"You could at least tuck your shirttail in," she grumbled, as they shuffled across the sidewalk to the Waldorf entrance. "Jeez, you've gotten sloppy. Discretion used to be one of our best assets."

"Now it's apathy. For me, anyway." He lowered his head as they came through the door and slipped the room key into her palm. "You head upstairs first, and I'll follow in a few minutes."

"Oh, my God, you're here! Thank you, Lord Jesus." Manny pounced on them from behind the pay phones. His spiked hair and freshly shaven face indicated he was ready for a night out, but the panic in his eyes looked like he wished it was already over.

"Hey, pal." Ty slapped him on the shoulder. "How was the skiing?"

"Don't you people ever answer your cell phones? I've been trying to get hold of you for hours."

Ty looked at Grace, then back at Manny. "Why, is there a problem?"

"You could say that." He turned to Grace. "Your father is here."

"What?" Grace grabbed the two men by the arm and dragged them to the corner near the coatroom. "What do you mean here? Like in New York?"

"No, like here at the Waldorf," Manny said. "Lizzie left me a message at the ski hill. Said your family had a change of plans, and instead of having dinner tomorrow, they came to the city tonight. They left you a message at your hotel. Your father wanted to see you, I guess."

"What the hell are they doing here?" Ty asked. "Her room is at the Plaza."

"I don't know. Lizzie mentioned she was meeting up with some of her old friends."

"Yeah," Grace said. "She used to work here, back when I was still with the Ballet."

"I had a feeling since Ty was staying here, you'd be with him." Manny raised a brow in insinuation. "I didn't think you'd want your father to see you two together."

"I appreciate that." Grace stood on her tiptoes and looked past the men into the lounge. Her sister and Russ stood at the end of the bar, with a small group of people surrounding them. Over their shoulders she could make out the silver tuft of feathered hair. She took a breath when he turned around. Sure enough, it was her father.

"It's almost nine o'clock," Grace said. "They haven't eaten yet?"

"I think they're waiting for you."

That sounded about right. Her father had been uptight about this stint in New York the minute she'd told him she agreed to it. He told Grace he'd treat the family to dinner and keep her company for a night. Of course she couldn't suggest otherwise. It was better just to let Daddy have his way than sit through one of his sermons.

She brushed her hair behind her ear and smoothed her hand over her dress. "Okay, here's the plan," she said. "You two get out of here, and I'll tell them I was late checking in, and I just got the message. I'll see both of you at the interview tomorrow morning."

"Tomorrow?"

The disappointment in Ty's voice made her smile. "It looks like Manny has plans for the two of you. Go out and have fun."

"But Grace Ann..."

"Manny, keep an eye on him." Grace reached up and rubbed a smear of pink lipstick off Ty's cheek. "Stay out of trouble."

She spun on her heel and headed across the lobby to the lounge. If she had a minute to spare, she'd duck into the ladies' room and fix herself up a little. She was sticky in all the wrong places, God only knew if her dress was zipped up all the way, and her hair was unfastened on one side. She brushed it back as best she could on her way into the bar. Thank God, the place was dimly lit. The beard burn she sported would be less obvious.

She raised her chin and approached the group huddled around the baby grand piano. A yuppie crowd, all dressed in trendy black. Not the usual company her family kept. Grace recognized most as Lizzie's former co-workers. She sat among them, sipping fruit juice while Russ stood over her with a hand on her shoulder.

"Grace Ann!" Lizzie waved and motioned her over to the crowd. She hugged and shook hands with the vaguely familiar faces before taking the white wine her brother-in-law handed her.

"Sweetheart, we've been waiting for you."

Grace tensed at the familiar voice. When she turned, her father stood beside her with a martini on the rocks in his hand. "Daddy!" she said with a dutiful smile. "I just got the message you were here. What a surprise."

He hugged her with rigid arms and gave her a tight-lipped once-over. "I'm glad you got our message. I tried you on your cell phone. I told you—when you're in the city, it would make me feel better if I could reach you at all times."

It was more of a scolding than a comment. One the people within earshot would probably pity her for. But she was used to it, and she'd rather just brush it off than act like it bothered her in the first place. "I'm sorry. I was so busy. I must have forgotten to charge it."

"Well, we're all glad you're here now," Lizzie said, raising her glass in toast. "I'm starving. How about we sit down and eat?"

To say she had already eaten would require further explanation. So instead she smiled and raised her glass in an awkward toast. "Sounds good. It's been a while since I've had dinner in New York."

The rest of the group said their goodbyes, and the hostess seated her family in the dining room. Lizzie and Russ pulled out chairs on either side of her, and her father sat directly across. They ordered right away, and Grace made sure it was something substantial. She was too preoccupied with the whereabouts of her underwear to adequately defend a side salad and lemon ice water.

"So, Daddy, I'm so glad you were able to make it home early," Lizzie said, digging into her roast beef. "Dinner at the Waldorf is quite a treat."

He folded his napkin in his lap, as the waitress served him his meal. "I left Father Breen in charge of the Vermont retreat for a few days. It's hard to keep your mind on your work when you're worried about what's going on at home."

"There's nothing to be worried about Daddy." Lizzie took Russ's hand. "We all take care of each other."

"Well, it was ill-timed to go away when I did."

"Don't worry," her sister said, grabbing a roll from the basket in front of her. "Grace is just about ready to open in a week or so, and Russ won't have to travel again until after the baby's born."

"Well we certainly are blessed, aren't we?" The Deacon raised his champagne glass in a toast, then took a small sip. Grace followed with the rest of them but took a bigger gulp. "Grace, dear, not so much now. That stuff goes right to your head. I'm already uneasy about you being in the city by yourself, and I'd rather you have all your wits about you."

She opened her mouth to protest, but Liz kicked her under the table. Grace had come to understand that her father considered The Big Apple a reference to the evil offering in the Garden of Eden and she the weak-willed victim hungry enough to take a bite. Over the past five years, she had only visited twice. Once to see a show with friends and again to Christmas shop with one of the older women from the parish. He called her every hour on the hour to check in. Evidently her survival during the years she actually lived there didn't mean she could fend for herself now.

"Grace Ann, how did your engagements go today? Elizabeth told me you had a few interviews and things. I was going to call you, but she told me I was being over-protective."

Grace eyed Lizzie before she answered him. "Everything went fine. Earl was great company."

"It looks like Earl took you shopping, too," Lizzie said. "You look beautiful all dressed up."

"It looks a little drafty to me." Her father raised a brow. "I suppose you'll tell me this is part of your crazy job this week."

Grace assessed her father and Russ in conservative dinner suits, and Lizzie's plain black maternity dress. She did look a little over the top for her present company. "Yes, well, I guess it comes with the territory."

"And that necklace." Lizzie leaned over to get a better look. "It's gorgeous."

Grace reached up and skimmed her fingers over the cool stones. "It's on loan from one of the jewelers here," she quickly explained. "I wore it in a photo shoot today, and I wasn't ready to part with it yet."

"They let you walk around with that on?" Lizzie asked. "You could feed a small country with what that's worth."

"Grace, you do know self-indulgence like that is a sin, don't you?" The Deacon pulled the napkin from his lap and dabbed the corners of his mouth.

"Which is why I will be returning it in the morning, Daddy." It was nice to know her improvisational skills were still intact. She took a sip of water and nibbled on an ice cube. "I have that big interview with *The Olivia Show* tomorrow." She braced herself for the obvious question.

"Has that Hawthorne character been keeping his distance?"

In unison, Russ reached for his champagne and

Lizzie reached for her juice. Over the rims of their glasses, Grace could tell by their wide eyes that they were as interested in her answer as her father was. "Well actually, it's funny you bring him up." She picked up her fork and pushed the rice around her plate. "Mostly our appearances have been separate, but given what I signed on for, yes, our paths have crossed."

"It makes me sick to even think of you in the same room as him." Her father shook his head in disgust. "Are you sure this whole press thing is a good idea? You can back out if you want."

"Daddy, I gave them my word. And besides, you know I need the money."

"I don't care about the money. What I care about is you being influenced by a man like that."

"He's not an influence on me, good or bad." She glanced at Lizzie beside her, hoping she'd offer a little help. But she was silent, more interested in the leftover mashed potatoes still piled on Russ's plate.

"Grace Ann, I know you're a grown woman, and I've always supported your decisions, even if I didn't approve of them. But I thought you learned your lesson. A woman like you thrives on living a simple life. God has a master plan for you. Your calling is taking care of people. Look at the success you've made of the Inn."

"I know. Thank you, but—"

"That Hawthorne is an operator." He waved his knife in the air, as if making a point. "Just because I don't have access to a television most of the time doesn't mean I'm not aware of his reputation. He took advantage of your goodness."

"That's not how it happened."

"What happened is that letch left you unmarried, pregnant and sick in a hospital a hundred miles from home, and the rest of us had to pick up the pieces. Don't you remember the hell you went through?"

Heads turned from a few tables over. He took a deep breath, and went back to cutting his meat. "I didn't mean to upset you. I'm just glad you won't have to see him anymore. And that's all I have to say about that."

She wanted to tell him that it wasn't Ty who made her sick. It was a lifetime of striving for perfection, and realizing there was no such thing, and the agony of learning that lesson in front of millions of people. "Ty came up to Middle Valley last week. He spent a few days there."

The Deacon dropped his fork to his plate, and Lizzie bit down hard on an ice cube. Russ just shook his head then shoved a bite of steak in his mouth.

"Don't tell me he's badgering you."

"He's not badgering. He came up, and I let him stay."

His mouth dropped open. "Elizabeth, you allowed this? You know how vulnerable your sister is."

"I know, Daddy. She wouldn't listen to reason."

"You don't have to talk about me like I'm not here," Grace yelled, turning the heads of the diners at the next table. "Look, I know that I have a lot to be angry at Ty about, but there is a part of me that needs to forgive him. Isn't that what the Bible says? That the true sign of a person's strength is the capacity to forgive?"

"There's a difference between forgiving and forgetting." The Deacon clenched his teeth, and a vein pulsed in his forehead. Grace had never seen her father truly lose his temper, but the times he came close were directly related to Ty.

"I'm sorry," he finally said. "But I love you too much for you to get hurt again. I only have your best interest at heart."

"I know." She stared at her uneaten food. And

was suddenly reduced to her familiar role as unfortunate victim. The one who always needed to prove herself. The dreamer. The pretty face with the simple mind, who got obligatory smiles and polite headshakes when she shared an idea or opinion. The one who mattered only when the situation was perfect.

When she was perfect.

She dropped her napkin to her plate and shoved the food away.

Lizzie looked at her and picked up her fork. "Grace Ann, you can't possibly be finished. You haven't touched anything."

"I don't suppose you'd believe it, if I said I already ate."

"Come on, don't be like this. We're all just worried about you."

A scan of the table told her it was more like pity. She grabbed her purse and slid out of her seat. "Listen, I'm tired, and I think I'm going to take advantage of my room at the Plaza and get a good night's sleep."

Heads turned as she stormed out of the dining room, in recognition or curiosity she wasn't sure, and at that moment she didn't care. Her things were still in Ty's suite, but she'd figure that out in the morning. Right now, she was much more concerned about getting the heck out of there.

Frozen drizzle whipped around her in a gust when she stepped out to the curb. Not the best night to stand outside in a strapless dress. The seemingly sympathetic doorman rushed over and hailed her a cab, but before she could get in, someone grabbed her by the shoulder.

"Grace, wait!"

Her sister stood with her jacket draped around her, and her purse held in front of her face to guard the wind. "Come back inside," she said. "There's no reason to leave. Dad's just being Dad."

"I'm not going to sit there and let him throw darts at me all night. My relationship with Ty is none of his business." Grace climbed into the cab, but before she closed the door, her sister followed. "What are you doing?"

"I was about to ask you the same thing. What the hell do you mean your relationship?"

"What do you think I mean?"

Lizzie stared at her, her mouth hanging open. "You do realize that this is the man that broke your heart into a million pieces."

"Yes."

"Then what makes you think he won't do it again?"

That was precisely the same question she'd been asking herself, from the moment she agreed to the press event. But she couldn't help her feelings, and every instinct told her to follow them. "Look, do me a favor. Ty is staying here at the Waldorf, and it would be really nice if you got Dad out of here. I don't need the two of them running into each other in the men's room, or something stupid like that."

Lizzie scowled. "Can you at least promise me you'll be careful?"

"I'll be fine." Grace smiled and placed her hand over Lizzie's. "I'll see you at home tomorrow after *The Olivia Show*, okay?"

Grace watched the doorman help Lizzie across the slush to the front doors. She hated upsetting her, but her desire to please others was what got her in trouble in the first place. What would please her right now would be to sneak back inside to Ty's suite. She could spend the night with him, and wake up with him in the morning. But if things were going to be different this time, why bother sneaking around? They should just parade arm in arm right through the lobby for everyone to see, or better yet do it right there on the counter! See how her Dad would like that one!

Yeah, right. She wasn't that brave. Even Lexie Love would think that one through a little more. She sat back in her seat and sent the cabbie back to the Plaza.

## Chapter Eleven

Ty sat on the couch of his suite in a T-shirt and jeans, his eyes fixed on the repeat of the entertainment news. It was close to midnight, and he couldn't remember the last time he had seen the hour sober and alone. Manny was out at the clubs. It would probably be a while before he made his way back. Figured. Ty wanted to send him back to the Plaza with Grace's things. He figured she'd be trapped for the night. Hell, if her family had their way, they'd chaperone her entire stay in New York. He smiled to himself and propped his feet up on the coffee table. Deacon Langley had no reason to worry.

He took a sip on his warm beer. The news was the usual tabloid fare. Brittany Spears' latest parenting blunder, Madonna's religion du jour. And of course the breaking story of Layla's new beach house in Malibu purchased with his money. He turned up the volume when they mentioned the *Undercover Heat* release.

Ty stared at the sexy redhead making fuck-me eyes at him on the wide screen. God, was she beautiful. Even her picture was enough to make him sweat. In less than a week, he had gotten back in the habit of spending time with her. It was just like it had been before. Easy. Natural. And being without her now was just as painful. Like a part of him had been removed.

His heart.

At the next commercial, he snapped off the TV and headed for the bedroom, but a knock at the door interrupted him. Chucking his beer can in the garbage, he headed toward the foyer. He felt like a lovesick schoolboy when he turned the knob and pulled open the door.

The face on the other side was a dousing of cold water. He stared into Langley eyes, but not the Langley Ty wanted to see.

"Hawthorne. We meet again."

The man was shorter than Ty remembered, his salt-and-pepper hair now a silver grey, his face wrinkled and his lips narrow and straight, like he'd never made a habit of wide smiles and they might snap if he ever attempted to.

"Deacon Langley," Ty greeted through clenched teeth. He made a point to look him straight in the eye. "What the hell are you doing here?"

"You mean you weren't expecting me?"

"Should I?"

"I told you if you ever bothered my daughter again you'd hear from me." His dark eyes sharpened in a challenge. "I'm a man of my word, Hawthorne. It would serve you well to remember that."

Ty wasn't Catholic or even religious, but he was sure that when people thought of a man of the cloth, this incarnation was the exact opposite of the gentle, understanding vision one conjured. Colder than ice, and just as rigid. Ty was also aware of his capabilities of deception.

"I thought you and I could have a chat," the Deacon said. "How about a nightcap. I'm sure a man like you has some brandy hanging around, unless you've already gone through it, of course."

"Stone cold sober." Ty leaned against the doorframe, his arms folded against him. "You pay a visit just to get your digs in, or you have something worthwhile to say?"

"Why don't you let me in and find out."

Ty clenched his fists and took a deep breath. He led him into the sitting room and poured two brandies at the bar.

"This place is large for just one person," the Deacon assessed, looking around the sitting room. "You people sure know how to waste money."

"I didn't pay for it." Ty handed him a half-full tumbler. "But I'm sure you didn't come here to discuss economics."

"Grace told me she'd seen you. Says you came up to Middle Valley."

Ty took a sip of his drink, then licked the sweetness from his lips. "Really? When did she tell you that?"

"Dinner this evening. I thought you and I had an understanding, Hawthorne. You're supposed to stay away from her, and I'd holster my shotgun."

"I have."

"Obviously not far enough."

Ty followed him with his eyes, as the Deacon wandered around the room. He looked out the window and spoke to the reflection in the darkened glass. "You know Lizzie almost had me convinced I was overreacting when I cut my retreat in Vermont short. But now I'm glad I did. I see that my daughter is still as naïve and as easily swayed as before. She's weak, Hawthorne. You know that. Traipsing around a heartless city with a renegade like you isn't right for a girl like her."

"You're still playing the same scene, aren't you, Deacon? The do-good, upstanding father. Tell me, do you think Grace would still feel the same about you if she knew the truth?"

He turned, his brow wrinkled in a scowl. "You wouldn't dare."

"Try me."

"She wouldn't believe you."

"Maybe not." Ty leaned against the back of the couch and took a deep breath. "I admit, even I would have a hard time believing it, if someone told me my own father was responsible for my child's death."

Langley scoffed. "I suppose, given the business you're in, you enjoy melodrama. But really, technically speaking—"

"Technically speaking, you don't practice what your church preaches."

"There was a lot more to it than that, and you know it. I had to make a decision."

"What I know is, I brought her to that hospital, and the baby was still alive. They sedated her, and stuck a feeding tube in her, and the baby was still alive. When you and Lizzie showed up the next morning, the baby was still alive."

"Barely, and you know that!"

"I left for an hour," Ty spat, stalking toward him. "I had to go make phone calls, to put out fires at work so no one would find out what was going on. And when I came back, Lizzie told me Grace had gone into labor, and that the baby didn't make it. The next thing I know, Russ is in my face, kicking me out of the hospital."

"Whatever happened, it was for her own good. She fell down stairs. She would have probably lost the baby anyway. And she couldn't even nourish herself, much less a fetus."

"I would have taken care of her."

"And a fine job you had done so far."

Ty lunged at him, fisting his hands but resisting their use. "I had been running interference for months to keep it from affecting work and getting to the press. She was worried about you, and how it would affect your job with the Church. I kept telling her she should worry about herself."

"Then you see, it was for the best."

"So how did you do it?" Ty demanded. "Come on, tell me. What did you do, bribe a doctor? You probably paid him off using Grace's own money!" The anger was as fresh as if it had happened yesterday. Ty stalked around him, his heart racing in his chest. "I kept quiet because I didn't see how knowing the truth would serve her. I kept it from the press to save your family the shame, and you your job. All because Grace would have wanted it that way. Tell me, what exactly did you ever do for her?"

"I saved her life!" Jordan Langley bellowed, with all the fire and damnation that he felt he channeled from the heavens. "I did what I had to do. Protecting my daughter is my first responsibility. Don't question my methods when they're obviously in her best interest." He went to the bar and poured another shot. Ty marveled at his steady hand. "You know, what surprises me is that you're angry about this now. Back then you took off without a fight. All of sudden this matters to you?"

"Don't stand there and judge me, Langley."

"I don't have to. The facts speak for themselves."

Heat rushed to Ty's face. Langley was exactly right. The whole reason he had left Grace in the first place, was because he couldn't bear the guilt of what had happened, and telling her the truth would only hurt her more. He'd made a mess of her life and ultimately drove her to a hospital bed. Leaving her was for the best.

Wasn't it?

"Suppose you did tell her the truth now. What purpose would that serve? She'd hate me, and she'd know you kept it from her all these years and hate you, too."

He closed his eyes. Again, Langley was dead on, and here he was in the same dilemma that had presented itself five years earlier. "You really expect me to just walk away from her all over again?"

"I'm not convinced she means that much to you in the first place." Langley walked back around the couch, a smile snaked across his pencil lips. A white lace bra was draped over the side, and he picked it up with a spindly finger. "And maybe I should stick to my own conclusions."

Ty's throat constricted, and his insides churned like a storm. His first inclination was to tell him the truth. That the bra was Grace's, as was the bag by the door, and the panties on the floor in the bedroom. But what for? It wouldn't change the situation, and it would only cause Grace grief. Instead, he let his silence answer. He took a swig of his brandy and set the empty tumbler back on the bar.

"You son of a bitch." The Deacon seethed. "I suppose you have one waiting in your bed right now."

"I'm sure you were hoping that was the case when you came up here."

"I just sat at dinner and listened to my daughter tell me you were worth her time, and you've got whores waiting in the wings."

"That's not true."

"I guess I shouldn't be surprised, after all the things I've heard about you these days. So not only are you a heartless, selfish bastard who left a poor sick woman defenseless, you're a womanizing degenerate who can't keep it in his pants."

"Now, wait just a fucking minute!"

"Don't you raise your voice to me!" Langley spat, pointing a damning finger in Ty's face. "Grace may have forgiven you for what you did, but I never will. And if you ever had a shred of feeling for my daughter, I'd think you'd never be able to forgive yourself." He gulped the last of his bourbon and slammed his empty glass on the bar on the way to the door.

"How about you, Langley? Have your forgiven yourself?"

He stopped cold, his hand on the knob. His body

heaved with a deep breath before he turned around. "Look, Hawthorne, a piece of garbage like you has no place with a woman like her. She's not a crutch. You used her as one before, and she crumbled under your weight. You were a burden to her then, and you would be now. You're poison, Ty Hawthorne, and you're killing her slowly."

The door slammed behind him, and for a moment Ty thought about going after him. That would have been the right-minded thing to do. But instead, he found himself buying into the Deacon's assessment, and eyeing his wallet and room key lying on the foyer table.

Manny was probably at the Zero club. It was a private party those film producers had told them about. He knew he was expected early at the studio, but somehow it didn't matter. He stuffed his wallet in his jeans pocket before heading out the door.

****

In all his days as Executive Producer of *Undercover Heat*, Earl Simmons had never dreamed things between Grace and Ty were serious. They were close, in a friendly brother-sister kind of way, but never did they act "physical." Reporters drilled them all the time about it. As far as he was concerned, they did their jobs well. Who they shared their beds with didn't concern him.

He didn't mean to overhear what he had. In fact, he wished he hadn't. All he was doing was dropping by to say "hi" to his old friend, Ty Hawthorne, and here he was blindsided by tragedy, hiding behind a plant outside his suite. Grace's father almost ran him over on his way out. Earl had only met him once at a network Christmas party, where he complained about the miniskirts on the waitresses. Yeah, he didn't like that Langley guy very much, and after what he just heard, he had better reasons. Ty, a baby, and lying about everything in between. God, he couldn't write a script more convoluted than that.

Maybe he should have known. Maybe he could have helped. And poor Gracie. She was so young and naïve when he hired her. Ty looked out for her, though, and he always respected that about him. Earl ripped off his glasses and wiped a tear from his nose. They probably would have been pretty good together. God, just like freakin' Romeo and Juliet.

He checked his watch and glanced at the elevator. Ty had been gone for over ten minutes, and he must be out for the night. The coast was clear. He could step out from behind this ficus and forget the last hour ever happened. Besides, he had work to think about. He'd promised a reporter from *It* magazine an interview, and he was expected in the bar in a few minutes.

Pushing the plant leaves aside, he staggered to his feet. He had to pull himself together. These people weren't his children, they were grownups with lives. They made their own decisions. Managed their own problems. He tried to remember that as lumbered down the hall, pulling out his pill bottle as he went.

****

*The Olivia Show* green room was known for its over-the-top morning craft service table. Pastries, bagels, fruits, juices. Anything the heart or stomach desired. Grace fully expected to have to barricade Earl from inhaling the whole thing. But so far he'd done nothing but sit on the couch, every few minutes asking her if she was okay.

"Grace Ann, you're hovering. If it upsets you that I eat the goodies, I won't bother."

"I certainly don't blame you. They look delicious."

"But I just don't want to worry you."

The attitude perplexed her. Never in her wildest dreams had she ever thought she'd be in a position of force-feeding the man. But he looked upset. If anything could cheer him up, she'd bet the house it would be a cream cheese Danish. She picked one from the pile and brought it to him in a napkin.

"Are you sure you don't mind?" he asked. "I promise I'll put a lime in my gin and tonic at lunch."

Grace patted him on the shoulder. "I think I'll get over it."

She wandered to the window and looked out at the city.

"So where's your partner in crime?"

She brushed the crumbs from her fingers and smiled. "I suppose you mean Ty."

"I thought you two would have shown up together."

"What makes you say that?"

"It looks to me like you've been inseparable lately." Earl held out *The Daily News*. The picture on the front page showed them at the restaurant the night before. She scanned the first few lines of the story. Just gossip and speculation and a favorable commentary of her fashion sense. She reminded herself to compliment Ty on his taste in dresses and jewelry.

"You must be pleased," she said, and tossed the paper back. "The free publicity will be good for the release."

"But is it good for you?"

Earl was one of the few people in her life that made her feel like her opinions or feelings mattered. Like her judgment was worth trusting without proof of a past track record. "Ty's a good guy, Earl. You know better than most that he's not the bad boy everyone paints him."

"And I know you're not the worldly vixen you played on TV."

Was he checking on her? Earl wasn't the nosy type. "Self involved" would be a better way to describe him. In a good way, of course. What was with the sudden onslaught of compassion? "Is something wrong, Earl?"

"No, no, no." He dragged his napkin across his forehead. "Look, Grace Ann, I never asked questions about you two during the run of the show. You guys worked well together, and I admit I didn't mind the free publicity. But I don't like to see you two being dragged through the mud for it. Especially you, Grace."

"You're talking about the recent articles about us, aren't you?"

"Look, whatever happened to you at the end of the show…if Ty caused you any anxiety...I'd hate to see it happen again. You know what I mean?"

He raised his brow as if the statement was more of a gentle inquiry. She took the cue and sat down on the couch beside him. "I appreciate your concern, then and now. But Ty is a decent man. And whatever we are to each other, I assure you it's a good thing." She placed her hand over his and squeezed. "It's nice to know you still look out for me after all these years, Earl."

"I just want to see you happy."

"So does Ty."

They both looked up when the green room door opened. Ty trudged through, wearing jeans and a long-sleeved white T-shirt that hugged him in all the right places. He looked like he'd already visited the makeup chair, because his hair was mussed and jelled, and his lips were lightly glossed. It was also obvious they had tried their best to cover a new gash on his cheek, and the red-rimmed eyes that obviously hadn't seen much sleep the night before.

"Well, look what the cat dragged in," Earl teased. "And early, no less."

"Too early if you ask me. " Ty shook his hand and kissed Grace on the cheek before heading for the water pitcher. She watched him pick through the pastries, but in the end he settled on a salt bagel. Her suspicions were confirmed. A salt bagel meant a hellacious hangover.

"Hey, Earl," Grace said, resting her hand on his shoulder. "Do you mind going to see if we're on time, because I promised my sister I'd be home—"

"Whatever you need, sweetheart." Earl ditched his Danish and squeezed her arm on his way out the door.

"What's with him?" Ty asked Grace. "He looks like you shot his dog."

"I was just going to ask you the same thing." She sat down on the arm of the couch. "So it looks like you had quite a night last night."

Ty poured himself a tall glass of ice water and took a gulp. "What makes you say that?"

"The salt bagel, your red eyes. And you need another layer or two of foundation to hide that cut on your face."

"I went out with Manny last night."

"And most of the morning, it looks like." She went for her purse and dug through it. "You want a few aspirin? I'm sure I have some."

"Grace Ann, I'm okay. Really."

His tone sounded strange. The kind he used in front of others. Friendly, but distant. And completely devoid of his southern accent. He stood at the window, staring out at the city. His shoulders rounded, and his free hand buried in his pocket. She came up behind him and slid her arms around his waist. "You want to tell me what's gotten you in this mood?"

"What mood? I'm not in a mood."

"Does it have to do with the bar room brawl you and Manny found last night, or something else?"

"Oh man, don't tell me that made the papers already."

"Not yet, but the day is young."

He rolled his eyes and kissed her on the top of her head. "I'm sorry, maybe I am in a mood. I don't mean to be. I just have a lot on my mind, I guess."

"Anything you want to talk about?"

Grace stepped away when she heard the door behind her open. A stagehand with a frown and a mouthful of the powdered donut made a beeline to the food. "Show's cancelled," he said before swallowing. "Go home."

"What?" She looked at Ty. "What do you mean? We're here and we're ready."

"Emergency plastic surgery in Los Angeles. You've been rescheduled for next week in the west coast studio."

"West coast?" Ty blurted. "What the—"

The stage hand disappeared out the door, leaving Grace with her jaw on the floor. "Did I just hear him right? Spending a week in Los Angeles will be impossible. The Inn opens Thanksgiving weekend, and I can't leave for that long. I could fly out the day of..."

Ty held his hand up in front of her. "Grace, you're staying put. You had prior commitments before you signed on. You're not obligated to go."

"Earl expects me to."

"He has more than enough free publicity for this thing. I'll cover for you, and he'll understand."

"But this is a job. I agreed to do it, and I want to see it through. Lizzie can watch the place for twenty-four hours."

"But why bother if you don't have to?"

He sat down on the couch, his head in his hands. Something was with him, too. Earl wasn't the only one acting strange. "You don't want me to go, do you?"

"Of course I want you to go, but I just want you to be practical. You have commitments here.

Besides, you know LA. You think the paparazzi here are bad—they're relentless there."

"That's true."

"And if I'm out there maybe I can smooth things over with Layla."

She folded her arms against her. "Oh, I see. You don't want me around to provoke her."

"Look, you read those articles. I don't know what she's up to, or what she knows, but maybe it would be easier if you weren't around. Just let me go, and I'll be back for the gala."

She sat down beside him, attempting to look him in the eyes. "And then what, Tyler?"

Again, the door opened, and this time Manny came in. He headed straight for the coffee and grabbed a handful of sugar packets. "So it looks like this party is moving to LA," he said with a smile. "Thank God, because my tan is starting to fade. Earl said he was setting up some appearances out there, so we should catch a flight ASAP. Grace Ann, should I call Lizzie and have her pack a bag?"

Grace stood up and hugged Manny. "Looks like you boys are on your own. I'm sitting this one out."

"Did I miss something?"

"Nope, not at all." Ty rubbed her arm and stiffly moved around her. "She has commitments that she can't get out of, that's all."

Manny frowned. "Okay, well, I guess I'll just make arrangements for the two of us." His eyes shifted suspiciously between the two of them. "Um...maybe I should do that right now."

"That's a good idea." Ty closed the door behind Manny and lingered there with his hand on the knob. The way he gnawed on his bottom lip reminded her of how he used to get into character, and he took an extra long blink in concentration. "So, I guess I should head out with him." His voice sounded slightly higher than his own. "Good luck with your opening, and have a nice Thanksgiving. I'll call you to see how it went."

If this was his interpretation of a heartfelt goodbye, it needed work. Grace stood frozen. For the first time in her life, she realized that, at that moment, she couldn't read him. "So, I guess I'll see you soon," she said for lack of anything else.

"Yeah."

There were a million things she wanted to say, but none seemed appropriate. Instead she just licked her lips and settled on, "I'll miss you."

"Me too." His eyes held a sadness that didn't match the smile. She might have asked him about it if he wasn't already out the door, without so much as a kiss.

## Chapter Twelve

Ty watched the sun set behind the palm trees that passed outside his Hummer's tinted window. He couldn't remember authorizing its purchase, but that didn't mean much. One of his people dropped it off at the airport straight from the dealership, and Manny jumped at the chance to drive it home. That was fine with Ty. He had drunk more than his share of average champagne during the six-hour flight. The last thing he needed was a DUI charge and an unflattering mugshot gracing the cover of *Newsweek*.

"So you want to stop home first, or should we head out for a bite to eat?" Manny asked, adjusting his Oakleys over his eyes. "I could go for a Pink's hot dog right about now. How about you?"

"I'm not hungry," Ty said through a yawn. "I wouldn't mind just going to bed."

"You just sat through a six-hour flight, and now you want to sit some more? God damn, what the hell is wrong with you?"

Ty lifted the cap from his head, and slid his hands through his matted hair. The industrial-strength gel the stylist had used that morning flaked off on his fingers. "Nothing's wrong. I'm just not in the mood to hang out."

"You're still weirded out by Grace's father, aren't you? Why? I mean, I know he's her father and all, but if you want to be with her, and she wants to be with you, you're adults. What's the problem?"

Spoken like a man without a clue.

Ty shook his head and gazed out at the ocean. He'd spent all day listening to the jet engines, trying to figure a way he could make it all work. The easy part was being with her; it was living with the guilt that he couldn't handle. That he was sure of. "The problem is me," Ty said. "I'm the problem, and if she were smart, she'd run the other direction."

"Then it seems to me you're no better than Deacon Langley. You don't give her enough credit."

"Leave it alone, Manny."

"You want to get back together with her, don't you? Come on, man, level with me. You want Grace Ann back."

Why deny it? Talking himself out of it was pointless. "So what if I do? What could I possibly offer a woman like her, anyway?"

"Anything you want. You're one of the highest paid actors in the world."

"That doesn't mean anything to Grace," he said. "Money doesn't impress her. Decency impresses her, and if that were currency, I'd be flat broke."

"Jesus." Manny shook his head. "Remind me to get you some self-esteem for Christmas."

Manny pulled into the circular driveway of Ty's Beverly Hills bungalow. "Cozy" was the word the real estate agent used to describe the place when she sold it to him, evidently because a five-bedroom house was considered small on the west coast. It was also built into the side of the cliff, which was why he never spent much time there. A good hard rain and he'd end up ashes on the Valley floor. That's pretty much how he thought of LA. One minute high and dry, the next, ass end in a mud puddle.

"Ah, shit," Manny mumbled. "That's Layla's car, isn't it?"

Ty looked past the three-tiered water fountain. Sure enough, parked next to the pool house sat Layla's white Maserati. "Looks that way."

"What the hell is she thinking? You two are divorced. She can't just show up at your house unannounced. She's trespassing."

"Right, so I call the police, and tomorrow it's front page news. That's all I need."

"You can't let her get away with this."

"Look, I want to talk to her anyway. See what's up with the whole Grace thing."

Manny shifted the car into park and pushed his sunglasses to the top of his head. "Listen, man, don't take this the wrong way, but Grace was on a hit TV show. Did she really think she'd be immune to the gossip columns? And not to sound totally insensitive, but if she has an eating disorder, or did, is it really that newsworthy? I mean, look at this town, walking skeletons with tits."

"That's really not the point, Manny."

"I know her family would be pissed off if it came out in the press, but for the most part people would sympathize with her. And if Layla was the one who leaked it, she'd be the one who looked bad."

Ty rubbed his temples and stared out the windshield. Manny was a good guy. He could tell him about the baby, and he probably would have, if he wasn't preparing himself for a meeting with his ex-wife. "`I know this doesn't make a lot of sense, but trust me. There's a lot more to the whole thing than you think."

"Layla's a viper, Ty. You know she's not into reason. She's just into money."

"Well, fortunately I have some, and if that's what it takes to cool her down, Grace is worth it." He opened the car door and stepped out before Manny had time to talk him out of it. Grabbing his leather carry-on from the back, he headed across the imported limestone path to the front door.

"Hey. Do you want me to at least wait for you?

"Nah. I'll call your cell if I need you."

The scent of the rose gardens greeted Ty, delivered by a healthy swirl of the Santa Ana winds.

The petals danced in the breeze, and he thought about picking a few and sending them home to Grace. Hell, yeah. He could rent a private plane and fly them back to Middle Valley with a love poem so hokey she'd laugh. Her father would love that.

He tried the knob before bothering with his keys. Like he figured, unlocked, the heavy oak door swung open. But something just inside impeded its path. He heaved a shoulder against it and pushed through. An overstuffed cardboard box skidded across the marble foyer, meeting its counterparts in a pile in front of the stairs.

The place smelled like it had been closed up for a while. Musty. Along with the boxes, the immediate space in front of him held a sea of clothes and linens and other assorted clutter. Most he recognized as his own. He pushed a few aside to deposit his keys on the foyer table, but then realized it wasn't there. In fact, nothing was there. No brass mirror, no sixty-thousand-dollar grandfather clock, the one Layla insisted she have imported from Switzerland. Just empty space and the tiny specks of dust that floated in between.

"What the hell are you doing here?"

Ty froze at the sound. Nails on a chalk board best described her voice. The shrill tone made his body itch from the inside out. He looked to the balcony at the top of the stairs. Layla stood there with a cardboard box balanced under her chin. The words "Layla's Knickknacks" scribbled on the side in purple Sharpie, but he could clearly see the top of his Emmy peeking out of the open flap. "What do you want with my awards?"

She glanced down at the gold statuette. "Oops, my bad." She smiled and dropped the box down the stairs where it landed at Ty's feet.

"Nice to see you, too, dear."

Layla pushed her short blond hair behind her

ears and pranced down the steps. Her flimsy tank top did little to support her enormous breasts, but of course it didn't have to. He'd paid the plastic surgeon enough to ensure they'd support themselves. "So, to what do I owe this warm welcome?" Ty asked, his eyes starting to water from her saturation of Chanel. "I figured a lady like you would have the courtesy to call first. That is, if I still have a phone."

"I didn't know you'd be here. But since you are, I'll take this opportunity to tell you that the Maserati needs some body work, and the boat has barnacles."

"Since when do I have a boat, and what the hell is a barnacle?"

"Since I bought one last month, and it's something that wrecks it if you don't give me money to get rid of it!" She stomped her foot like an angry child. Ty was reminded he was stone cold sober. Life with Layla was much easier at a two-drink minimum.

He stepped into the great room ahead of her. No furniture, no decorative art. Just the imprints of where the furniture used to be on the one-of-a-kind Persian rug. "So, I suppose you're going to tell me you had to sell the furniture to support yourself."

"How else was I going to decorate the beach house? I don't even have enough money to pay the gardener. You screwed me over, Ty!"

"I screwed you! Are you fucking kidding me?" He jammed his hands into his pockets to keep them from wringing her neck. "Listen, sweetheart, I wasn't the one who left you for a woman and sold the exclusive to every paper in town."

"Oh, please, it's not like I broke your heart or anything."

"Why are you here, Layla? The divorce is final. You're free to be whatever you are. And I am free to at least have my locks changed." Ty turned when he heard the pant of a dog on the balcony above him. The burly boxer snarled, then barked when she saw him. "What did you do, convert her, too?"

She folded her arms against her disproportionate chest and scowled. "If you're referring to my lifestyle decision to be in an intimate relationship with a woman, I don't think it's funny."

"Of course not. That would require a sense of humor. So where's Marcy, anyway?"

"Taking a client's poodle to the vet. She has worms."

"Marcy or the dog?"

"Jerk." She picked up a box marked "Ty's computer" from the stack, and pretended to inspect it before dropping it to the floor. It landed with a thud.

He walked around her into the kitchen and surveyed the barren space. The glass-front cupboards were void of dishes. Even the appliances had been removed. He chuckled and peered out the sliding glass door at the empty poolside patio. "So what are you doing here besides robbing me blind, Layla?"

"I told you. I need money."

"I can't help it if you went through twenty million dollars already."

"Hey, I don't intend to live like a pauper, while you're running around buying million-dollar jewelry for your little whore."

It took a moment before he realized what she was talking about. The sapphire necklace he'd given Grace. It had a been a hot topic this morning in the gossip columns, but only a few reports dared to make the leap that he'd given it to her.

"Don't bother denying it, either. A hillbilly farm girl like her doesn't have the scratch to buy things like that."

In his whole life, he had never hit a woman.

He'd never even been tempted until right this moment. But instead, he took a deep breath and a careful step away.

"You know, Ty, I'm just like the rest of the world. I like to keep up on your exploits. What you're doing. Who you're doing." Layla walked around, her freshly collagened lips twisting in an evil sneer. "Looks like you and Grace Ann Langley have been spending quite a lot of time together."

"And it looks like you've been going to great lengths to observe that," he said. "I didn't know you were such a fountain of knowledge when it came to my past history."

"Oh, please, everyone who worked on that show knew you and Grace were sneaking around. I didn't divulge anything that wasn't old news. I was just "reminding" the public that's all."

"And collecting a finder's fee," he added. "Tell me, you haven't taken it upon yourself to have me followed, have you?"

Their eyes locked, and Ty swore he saw a hint of a smile.

"Of course not," she stammered. "What reason would I have to do something like that?"

"Oh, I can think of about twenty million of them."

"Look, I'm the helpless victim here," she yelled. "My wayward husband left me destitute, while he's in the arms of another woman!"

Ty laughed and shook his head. "Please don't stand there and paint yourself as a woman scorned. I was nothing to you except your personal bank."

"That's not true! I love you!"

"You love what I'm worth."

"You broke my heart, Ty Hawthorne. Plain and simple." Tears meandered down her cheeks, leaving long black streaks in their wake. She brushed them away with a freshly manicured finger. "Okay, so maybe I did help out the reporters a little, but how else was I supposed to get your attention? I never meant to hurt you, Ty. I just don't think you realize how much you hurt me."

He stood there a moment, listening to her sniffle and watching her unstick her hair from her cheek. Nothing about Layla was genuine. She was as fake as her silicone breasts and her acrylic nails. But the fact was, he couldn't blame her for everything. He'd had a hand in the mess he made, and who was he to judge one's self preservation. So he sucked it up and went to her, folding his outstretched arms around her.

"Ty, I did love you. I still do. I know our marriage was a drunken impulse, but I tried, I really did."

Her body shook, and he held her tighter. No way could she fake that, or the cold sweat that glazed her skin.

"I don't mean to be unreasonable. I just didn't realize how much I truly loved you until it was already over. And I know that if you love a person you should let him go, and I know I should." She pulled her head from his chest and looked up at his face. "I know you want to be with Grace, and I'm okay with that. I just need one last thing from you."

"What's that?"

She brought her hands to his face and lifted her lips to his. "To say goodbye."

Ty stiffened, and his instinct was to push her away, but if this was what she needed to ease the pain he caused her, he'd allow it. Her lips were hard and forceful. Demanding yet passionless, and completely ineffective in stirring any emotion within him. If this kiss was goodbye, it seemed well-suited. This was what their love life had been like; there was nothing about it to miss.

A sudden bang at the kitchen window drove

them from each other's arms. Ty dragged his sleeve across his mouth and squinted into the dusk. "What the fuck was that?"

"The hell if I know."

Ty threw open the sliding glass door and stepped onto the patio. His vision adjusted just in time to see a man with a camera leap over the wall and disappear into the brush on the other side.

"Chill out," Layla said from the doorway. "It's just the paparazzi."

"No shit. How the hell did he get in here?"

"They have their ways, I suppose."

He eyed his ex-wife in the lamplight. Her tears had dried and her skin had found its color. He took a few steps closer, and he swore he saw her lips fight a smile. "Wait a minute. Aren't you the least bit concerned that a man just snuck onto private property and photographed a moment that was supposed to be just between us?"

"Shit happens." She shrugged. "Look, I should get going. I told Marcy I'd meet her after."

Ty cocked his head at her choice of words. She was already halfway to the front door when he caught up to her. "Hold on, what do you mean 'after'? After what?"

"After meeting you."

"I thought you said you had no idea I'd be here?" Again, she turned toward the door, but he grabbed her by the arm and spun her around. "Hey, listen. You wouldn't be lying to me now, would you?"

"Give Grace Ann my regards." She winked and slung her rhinestone purse over her shoulder before heading out.

The Maserati engine sounded fine to him when she gunned the thing and squealed out of the driveway. The hairs on the back of his neck bristled. Something told him he'd just played a scene in his ex-wife's personal plans.

Harvey hid in the bushes near the curb. He ran the whole half-mile, no small feat for a guy who still smoked a pack a day and was overweight by both Hollywood and Surgeon General standards. He'd been waiting for her at least ten minutes and was still panting. By the itch on his butt cheek he was sure he had planted himself on an ant hill.

At least he wasn't freezing to death like he had been back east. When he got the word that *The Olivia Show* had been rescheduled for the west coast studio, he wasted no time in booking a flight. Thank God, too. Sweating his ass off in paradise was better than freezing to death in hell. Besides, he wanted to give Layla the news about Earl Simmons in person.

The roar of a sports engine filled his ears as it approached the intersection in front of him. It lurched to a stop, and the tinted window rolled down, revealing a pale-faced blonde with pink-tinted shades, expensive enough they allowed vision in the dusk. "Harvey, get in the damn car!" the woman hissed. "Hurry up! The coast is clear."

With his camera still around his neck, he ran around the front of the car and jumped into the passenger side. They were already moving by the time he heaved the heavy door shut.

"Did you get it?" The blonde asked, tapping her claw-like nails on the steering wheel. "God, please tell me you got that."

Harvey glanced at her heaving breasts. Damn, he had forgotten how big they were. They pushed over the top and out the sides of her shirt, and he swore he saw shadows of her nipples under the cotton. It was weird, but usually the sight of jugs like hers made him hard as a rock, but for some reason these didn't do the job. Grace Ann's were smaller. They were perky, and he bet they'd fit in his hand much better than Layla's.

"Hey jackass, eyes up here!"

She snapped her fingers, and he lifted his eyes to her face. Not a bad one. She was cute enough, but if he had to choose, he'd opt for Grace's lips.

"Harvey, the pictures! Did you get them?"

"Yeah," he said, licking his chapped lips. "I'm sure I got it." He held up his camera between them. "I just kept pressing the button until I ran out of film."

She clapped her hands and threw her head back in laughter. "That couldn't have gone any better. I can't believe he bought it."

"So I kept my end of the bargain, and you owe me some money."

"Of course I do." She pulled over to the curb and killed the engine. Her nipples brushed across his legs when she leaned over him to open the glove compartment. His dick rose to the occasion, and he almost forgot to count the wad of twenties she dropped in his lap. "Hey," he said after he thumbed through the stack. "This is half of what we agreed on."

"Well, when you deserve more, you'll get it."

The little whore. He shifted in his seat, leveling his eyes on hers. "Listen, lady, without me you never would have gotten the back-story on Ty and Grace when I followed him and that assistant of his to the diner."

"So what? The girl had an eating disorder. Who doesn't?"

"Well, it ended the show. And when I heard Ty tell the story, it sounded like it would be a big deal to her and her family if it got out. And you damn sure wouldn't know about him buying her prenatal vitamins."

"If you had gotten a clue sooner, maybe I could have prevented my wayward husband from knocking Miss Priss up in the first place." She pushed her bangs out of her face, and blew out a breath. "I wonder why she didn't come out here with Ty, anyway?"

Harvey shrugged. "Isn't there some rule about pregnant women flying?"

"Maybe, but actually that works out for the best. With her out of the way, I can work my magic."

"What are you going to do? Tell Ty you know?"

"Of course not. I'm not laying all my cards out on the table. Not yet, anyway. Obviously, they don't want anyone to know about the impending Hawthorne offspring, so we won't ruin the surprise. At least not until the time is right."

"And when will that be?"

"All in good time." She cocked her head and smiled. "Let's just say we can do a lot more damage if we keep some secrets to ourselves."

He understood the sentiment. Harvey looked her in her blue-tinted contacts and chewed on his lip. If she wasn't going to up the ante, neither was he. What he found out from that producer guy, Earl Simmons, was far too juicy. Yeah, Layla was dead on when she said some things were best kept secrets for a while. He'd save it for when the time was right, like if she ever had a problem finding her checkbook.

"So this plan of yours," he said, stuffing the cash into his pocket. "Do you really think this is going to do the trick? Bullying him hasn't worked so far."

"Maybe not, but scaring the shit out of him might."

Again she laughed in a way that made Harvey think that this woman was a little more off her rocker than he'd initially thought. He scratched his temple and waited for her to speak. "You really think she'd be that easy to get rid off? She's having the guy's kid. She'll probably stick around, at least for the scratch."

"We'll see about that," Layla said. "Grace is

fragile, and believe me, a woman like her won't bother to tangle with a woman like me. I want my man, and the money he comes with. She doesn't have it in her to stand in my way."

Harvey felt himself salivate. Grace was hot, but Layla was here, and Christ, if her mean side wasn't sexy as hell. He imagined tossing her in the back seat and giving it to her good. Make her scream and beg him for more, with her nails digging into his back. "So, where's your friend Marcy?" He winked and slid his hand over her shoulder. "You two busy tonight?"

She raised a brow, in amusement or interest, he wasn't sure. But he didn't care either way when she took his hand and rested it inside her thigh. "Good things come to those who wait, Harvey. And I promise, you won't be disappointed."

He was hoping she'd say that. An image of two sexy women with huge breasts bobbing in the surf of his hot tub flashed through his mind. He closed his eyes and inserted himself into the mental picture.

## Chapter Thirteen

Grace climbed between her flannel sheets and flipped her pillow to the cool side. Opening weekend had passed in such an exhausting blur, she barely had time to miss Ty. Of course she managed to fit it in between loads of laundry and stacking the wood he had graciously cut for her. The first few days he was gone, she expected a barrage of phone calls, and most definitely a Thanksgiving Day chat. But here it was over two weeks since he'd left, and she hadn't gotten so much as a text message. If it wasn't for impersonal updates from the *Entertainment Now* broadcasts, she'd think he'd fallen off the planet.

This was exactly what she had been trying to avoid. The position of letting Ty into her life. At first it was like a dare, to prove to herself how strong she was and how far she'd come from the needful girl five years ago. But now she'd let her guard down, all her old insecurities came rushing back.

So what would the new Grace do? The assertive one, who was at peace with herself and prepared to handle whatever life dealt. The one who missed her boyfriend so badly, he was all she thought about.

She would call him on the phone.

Tossing the covers off, she snapped on the bedside light and reached for her cell phone. She had yet to award him with a spot on her speed dial, so she methodically punched the long string of numbers and waited. Her heart thumped in her chest. Why did she feel like a nervous school girl? It was just a friendly phone call. She folded her legs under her and gnawed on a jagged fingernail.

"Hello?"

Grace checked the display screen when she heard the female voice. "Um, hi," she said slowly. "I'm looking for Ty. Is he around?"

"I think he's out for the evening."

"Really." Grace pulled at the hem of her nightgown and swallowed. "Excuse me, but to whom am I speaking?"

"Well, his wife, of course. This is Layla Hawthorne. And to whom am I speaking?"

Grace pressed her eyes shut and mentally cursed. "Layla. This is Grace Ann Langley."

A gleeful laugh on the other end drove Grace's ear from the receiver. "Oh, my God, it's been so long," she shrieked. "Ty has been telling me how nice it was to catch up with you. And you must have worn him out. I can't get him out of bed."

"Really?"

"Not that I mind, of course. But tonight he said he had a business meeting. I guess he'll just have to make it up to me later."

Grace bit her lip while considering the strategy behind Layla's game. She was lying. Had to be. This woman was a conniving operator who thought Grace was as naïve as Layla was crazy. But what if she wasn't lying? Ty hadn't called her, and the last time she saw him, he was oddly cold. Either way, Grace wouldn't give her apprehensions away. Especially to a woman who was potentially out to get her.

"That's wonderful, Layla," Grace heard herself say. "I was telling Ty that he should give things another chance. So this lesbian thing was all gossip, huh?"

"Yeah, well, you know the tabloids."

"I know the lies and innuendos they print. Makes you wonder where they find their lowlife sources."

"I'll tell him you called, but I doubt if he'll have

time to get back to you. We've decided to take a long weekend at the beach. Sounds like a great place to conceive a baby, doesn't it?"

Grace's fingers cramped around the receiver. " It sure does."

She managed a "goodbye" and flipped her phone shut. How did Layla get Ty's cell? And, God forbid, was anything she said the truth? She pulled the covers back around her and sighed. Ty said they were in this together, and if she were to question his loyalty now, she'd be as gullible as Layla counted on. No, Ty hadn't called because he was busy putting out fires. Protecting her, and to doubt him would be an insult.

The night wind blew against her window, shaking the frame and whistling against the glass. She rested her head on the pillow and closed her eyes. Suddenly the room seemed colder, and a chill settled in between the sheets.

****

Layla hadn't had that much fun on the phone since her days at 976-SLUT. Man, could she still work the charm. She snapped her ex-husband's cell phone shut and tossed it beside her on the couch. Marcy sat on the floor, flipping through the holiday edition of *Canine Life* magazine.

"Was that her?" Marcy rested her chin in her palm.

"Hell, yeah, that was her, and it couldn't have gone any better. You should have heard her voice." Layla rubbed her hands together and smiled. "God damn, am I good."

She lay back against the Corinthian leather pillows and slid her feet underneath her. It was a bold move to swipe Ty's phone. She'd done it on impulse, when she snuck back into his house yesterday. He was in the shower, and at first she contemplated jumping in with him, but scoring his phone and making a getaway seemed way more fun and potentially useful. She didn't know how much until she saw his caller ID flash LEXIELUV.

"So did she buy it?"

"Who cares if she bought it or not," Layla said. "The point is to instill doubt."

"I don't get it."

Could this woman truly be that dense? Layla peered down at her in her army fatigue pants and her mangy green tank, resisting the urge to talk more slowly for her benefit. "Okay, think of this like a court of law. Just as long as she starts to question herself and Ty's feelings for her, she'll cut her losses and run."

"But what if she doesn't? Even if you do leak to the press everything you know about them, what good would that do?"

"Obviously it was important enough to them to keep it secret, and if revealing it to the world can be used against them, I'll do it."

"I don't know." Marcy shrugged. "You hired this Harvey guy, and I don't think he's done that much. All you have so far is that Ty shops for vitamins, and that maybe a long time ago he dated his once-skinny costar. So what?"

Layla scowled. What exactly did she ever see in Marcy? She was negative and boring and smelled like dog poop half the time. But at least she was agreeable, and right now that was exactly what Layla needed. "Look Marcy, this is Hollywood, and in Hollywood everything is drama. Sometimes the material might be weak, but if you get a qualified actress to turn in a great performance..." She stood up as if greeting an imaginary audience. "All of a sudden it's a masterpiece."

Marcy just blinked at her. Sometimes Layla thought Marcy related to dogs better than people. This was one of those times. "Okay, fine," Layla said and grabbed her purse from the coffee table. "I have some business to take care of. The GPS I had installed on Ty's car says he's out on the Strip, and I made sure that a few friends and I meet him there."

"Don't forget to take him his phone."

Layla smiled through clenched teeth and swiped it from the couch. "I won't," she growled as she headed out the door.

****

"Where the hell is my cell phone?" Ty yelled over the Black Eyed Peas blaring from the woofer above him. "I always carry it in my back pocket, and it's not there." He emptied the contents of his jeans pockets onto the bar. Cigarettes, money, wallet. "Fuck, did I give it to you?"

"Your cell phone?" Manny swallowed the last of his Seven and Seven and tossed the bartender another twenty. "What would I want with that?"

Ty put his things back into his pockets and took a long gulp of his bourbon. The hum of the crowd rivaled the base from the speakers, and rainbow-colored lights flashed from the dance floor beyond. "Chic" was the name of the joint, and in Ty's opinion it tried too hard to be that. It was dark and loud and packed to the walls with every echelon of Hollywood. Actors, models, producers, and anyone in between, who liked to be seen. Ty came here for the exact opposite. He was here to disappear, and he was almost there. A few more visits from Mick, the bartender, would do the trick.

"Jeez, man, lighten up. You probably just left it home." Manny turned on his stool and gazed out at the crowd. "Now put a smile on your face and dump the drink down your throat."

"Cut the pep talk, man. I'm not interested."

"No kidding," Manny scoffed. "You haven't been interested in anything since we left New York. You're in bed by ten thirty, you've put most of the gossip mongers on the unemployment line—hell, if it weren't for the *Undercover Heat* promotions, I don't think I could drag you out of the house."

"So I've been a little antisocial lately. So what?"

Manny stared into his drink and shook his head. "I knew having Layla around would cramp your style."

"Layla?" Ty looked at him and chuckled. She was the woman farthest from his mind. "What the hell does Layla have to do with me?"

"Tons, by the looks of it."

"Please."

"Which reminds me. When are you getting your locks changed? She lets herself into your house all hours of the day."

"You don't know that."

"Oh, yeah?" Manny shook his head and leaned closer to his ear. "I showed up yesterday morning and she was sunbathing. Topless, no less."

"Where the hell was I?"

"At the gym. And did you know she wears your clothes? I swear I saw her in one of your T-shirts."

Ty tossed a handful of peanuts in his mouth and chased them with a swig from his tumbler. The image of last week's kiss floated through his mind. He took a long blink in an effort to scatter it. "Yeah, well, I guess she's having a harder time with this divorce than I thought."

"Having a hard time living on a budget."

"No, really," Ty said. "She completely lost it the other day. She told me she still loves me."

"So what if she does? She's making your life a living hell."

"Yeah, well, maybe I deserve it."

Manny set his glass on the bar and spun around on his stool to face Ty. "Okay, I have to ask."

"Ask me what?"

"You slept with her, didn't you?"

Ty almost fell off his barstool. "Are you fucking crazy? How stupid do you think I am?"

"Chill out, man. I was just asking."

Ty picked up his glass and emptied it. He hadn't told Manny about the kiss, or the fact that it was possibly captured on film. It had been a week since it happened, and he figured if it hadn't surfaced by now, it wasn't going to. No paparazzi would hold on to a hot potato like that for this long. Either they scared the guy off in time, or the pictures didn't develop through the glass.

"Fish on the hook at ten o'clock," Manny reported then nodded across the room. "She's heading over."

Reluctantly, Ty followed Manny's nod. Bodies packed shoulder to shoulder moved to the music. Men on the make and girls in huddles drinking drinks as colorful as the lights spinning over them. Fake blondes with even faker tans, and tits the size of their heads.

"See her?" Manny asked. "The one in the tube top."

"They're all in tube tops."

"The one that is making fuck-me eyes at you. I bet she'd make you feel better."

Ty was not a braggart, but it was obvious that most of the women were looking at him. All with the same sleepy, overmedicated stare that screamed one-night-stand. The one Manny was talking about wasn't bad. Tall, dark hair, decent body. He reached around and grabbed his tumbler. Feel better? Hell, he came here to feel worse. "She's all right." Ty shrugged.

"All right? Man, did you see those legs?"

"No."

"Well, here's your chance."

The girl pushed her way through the crowd and slid between them at the bar. She wore a sequined black miniskirt, too much makeup and rhinestones inlaid in her acrylic nails. Using her plump red lips, she dragged a matching cherry from a swizzle stick and struck a pose like a model on the runway. "You're Ty Hawthorne," she purred.

"That's right."

She looked him up and down. "Man, you're even hotter in person."

He looked the girl in her mud-colored eyes and felt nothing. But she had a pulse and was obviously willing, his two major criteria when choosing a casual companion. They could slip on over to the Roosevelt, crawl all over each other all night, and everything would be better in the morning. Hell, screw the hotel, the bathroom would do the trick. "What's your name, honey?"

"Anything you want it to be."

"Well, how about we decide in the VIP lounge."

She winked, weaving her fingers in his. "I thought you'd never ask."

He followed her through the crowd. People stared, mouths flapped, couples made out in darkened corners. All as pathetic as he was. And this was right where he belonged, a step away from hell and a million miles from Grace, away from where all he could do was cause her harm.

She led them past the velvet rope that hung across the VIP entrance. Biff the bouncer greeted her like an old friend, and Ty chuckled. She was a regular. What the guys in Alabama used to call A-Beer-on-the-Wall. One that had been taken down and passed around. He'd probably seen this woman a million times before, hell, maybe even fucked her. God, is that what it had come to? He had been with every woman in Los Angeles, and now he was starting over? Just how low could he possibly sink?

He set his empty glass on the table, his eyes blurred in the white candlelight. The room was empty save for a few people in back, and a guy standing guard in the darkness. The next thing he knew he was in a corner, with her body pressed against his. It was hard and rigid, and it chilled him through his T-shirt. His instinct was to push her away, but instead he dared himself to like it. With misguided purpose, he pushed his hands though her product-stiffened hair, and brought her lips to his.

The sudden movement knocked her off balance, sending her silver pocketbook to the floor. Ty bent down to pick it up along with the money that had fallen out. "Sorry," she breathed, taking the cash from his hand. "I guess sexy men make me jumpy."

"Is that all I make you. Jumpy?"

"Come closer, and we'll see."

Again he brought his mouth to hers. She tasted stale and sour, like the cheap liquor she'd been drinking all night. There was nothing. No passion, no desire, just a physical arousal on the most basic level, where Ty had become used to operating.

"The room's upstairs," the girl hissed in his ear. "Let's go, right now."

With his eyes sealed shut, he buried his face in her neck. The tangy scent of cheap perfume stung his nose and slipped over his tongue like an elixir more poisonous than intoxicating. He was trying like hell to want her. Acting was his profession, after all, and lying to himself was what he did best, but there was no part of him buying it. His insides churned and his head swam. Like his body rejected something foreign. She didn't belong. She didn't fit.

She wasn't Grace.

With a decisive shove, he stepped away from her, and wiped the kiss from his lips. He mumbled something like, "I'm sorry," but it sounded unintelligible even to his own ears. The next thing he knew he was back out on the main floor, the strobe lights stinging his eyes. Manny was still at the bar, a leggy Asian woman beside him who looked like better company than Ty had been earlier.

"Early night?" Manny asked with a smirk. "You sure tired her out fast."

"I'm out of here." Ty grabbed the drink Mick brought without asking and finished it in one gulp. "See you tomorrow."

Manny pulled him back and shoved him down on his stool. "What the hell is with you? Twenty minutes ago, you were making plans for the night. Now you're heading home to bed? Come on, Ty. Something's going on."

"I'm tired, is all."

"Jesus, man, this self loathing thing is getting old. I'm sick of your moping. I liked you better when you were a horny drunk."

"I second that motion."

Two arms slithered under his and clamped down on his chest. He turned his head into Layla's waiting lips, and she kissed him hard before he could pull away. "Hey, hubby, I thought this was where you'd be."

"Layla," Ty groaned. "What the hell are you doing here?"

"Looking for you, of course." She shoved the man off the stool beside Ty and sat down. "You'd think you'd be happier to see someone who was doing you a favor." She reached into her Louis Vuitton clutch and pulled out Ty's cell phone. "You left it by the bed, darling. I thought you'd be looking for it."

Her voice had risen, and Ty noticed that even in a star-studded place known for its discretion, most heads turned in their direction. He also didn't miss the mumbling lips angled to eager ears, and the wry smiles painted on people's faces.

"Keep it down, Layla. People are getting the wrong impression."

She giggled and looked around the bar. "What

impression is that?"

"That you gave up your seat at the lesbian convention," Manny said. "Isn't Marcy looking for you, by the way?"

"Shut up," she spat. "I was talking to your boss, if you don't mind."

Ty painted on a painful smile and eased the phone from her hand. "Okay, so you did your good deed today. Thanks for bringing this to me, but in the future, I'd rather you not snoop around my bedroom."

"Our bedroom, Ty."

"No. Mine, according to the State of California. And how about I have someone bring you the rest of those boxes, so you don't keep dropping in unannounced?"

"Whatever you say, honey." She kissed him on the cheek before heading into the crowd beyond.

"She's up to something, isn't she?" Manny said in his ear.

Ty looked at the glazed eyes surrounding him. "God, I fucking hope not."

"Well, all you have to do is keep on her good side. You have forty-eight hours until *The Olivia Show*, and we don't want her to cause us problems. There are already enough rumors out there for you to shoot down."

Ty groaned in agreement and rubbed his forehead at the thought. His plans were to walk out of the *Olivia* soundstage and jump on a plane. He'd hide out in New York until the launch gala Saturday night.

"So what about Grace?"

Ty started when he heard his own thoughts from Manny's mouth. "What about her?" he stammered.

"Look, man, I hate to see you this way. Why don't you just give the woman a call? It's been over a week since you've seen her, and it would be damn nice of you to see how her opening went. You could game plan a little before the big *Olivia* interview."

"Game plan what? It's just an interview."

"Just call the woman!" Manny blurted. "You know you want to."

Ty looked up at the clock. "It's three in the morning on the east coast. I'll wake up all the guests."

"Call her cell." Manny pulled him from the stool and nudged him toward the door. "Humor me and call her. If she doesn't answer, leave a message."

Ty bit the inside of his lip. Missing Grace was something he had gotten used to over the years, like a chronic illness he tolerated. How many times had he been hunched over on a bar stool in the wee hours of the morning, his double vision blurring the dial pad of his phone. He did want to talk to her, hear her voice. And it was the first time he had ever allowed himself to really consider the option.

"You'd be doing me a favor," Manny said. "If it will make you less miserable to be around..."

"Okay, shut up. I'll do it." He took a gulp of liquid courage and set his glass down on the bar. Pushing through the crowd, he made his way out the front door while punching the numbers on his key pad.

"Tyler?"

"Grace Ann?" He hadn't realized how tense his body was, until he heard her voice. Soft but deepened with sleep, and for the first time in over a week he felt like he could fill his lungs fully with breath. "Gracie, I know it's the middle of the night. And I didn't mean to wake you."

"Why are you screaming? Are you okay?"

The bass spilling through the open door behind him drove him down the sidewalk. He covered the receiver and glanced around before resuming the conversation in a normal voice. "I'm sorry. I'm at a club with Manny. I just wanted to call and ask how your opening was. Did everything go okay?"

"Went fine," she said. "I was a little worried about the Thanksgiving meal. I tried a new dressing, but I think it tasted okay. And before you ask, yes, I had some."

He closed his eyes, picturing her in bed, between the warm sheets, her red hair splayed across the pillows. "I'm glad to hear it."

There was a pause on her end. "I tried calling you earlier but Layla answered."

"Layla?"

"She answered your cell phone. She said she'd give you the message when she met up with you. She made it sound like you two had some big plans."

His fingers twitched around the phone, as he headed back down the sidewalk. There was no accusation in her tone, but it wasn't like her to do so in the first place. Why would he want to spend time with a woman he couldn't stand? Although, maybe if she believed that, it would be for the best. Staying away from her would be easier if she hated him.

He was back in front of the doors when a wave of people burst out to the street, each more obliterated than the next. A woman squealed with laughter and then stumbled to the pavement. She had staggered to her feet when her gaze met Ty's. She was the woman from the VIP lounge.

"Ty? Are you still there?"

The tangy perfume surrounded him like a cloud, and he realized he could smell her on him. He gulped down a gag when she blew him a kiss before scurrying away with the herd she came out with. "Yeah, Grace. I'm here."

"So, anyway, I called earlier and Layla had an earful for me, believe me. How did she get your phone, anyway?"

Man, that voice of hers. The happy little lilt that came to his ears like a song. His chest tightened. "I left it at home, and she brought it to me," he said, not bothering to elaborate.

"Wow, what was she doing at your house?"

Amazing. After everything that had happen, she still trusted him. He could hear it in her voice. Sense it in her words. More proof that he didn't deserve her. He lifted his gaze heavenward and shook his head. He never should have called.

"Ty, you seem weird. Did you just have too much to drink or is something wrong?"

"There you are, sweetheart."

Ty nearly dropped the phone when he heard Layla's voice from behind him. She hooked her fingers on the belt loops of his jeans and hauled him to her for a quick kiss. "Where have you been?" she asked. "I went to mingle, and the next thing I knew you were gone. I wanted to ask you if you had seen my watch. Did I leave it next to the bed? I just looked down to check the time, and I realized that was the last place I saw it."

Her gaze locked on his, and he saw the smile behind them. Layla wasn't looking for an answer. She was calling him to war. He lowered the phone from his ear and covered the mouthpiece with his hand. "Do you mind," he said through clenched teeth. "I'm on the phone."

"Oh, excuse me. I didn't think I was interrupting anything important." She gave his cheek a pinch before turning on her stilettos. The valet was waiting with her Maserati. "Give my regards to Grace."

Ty slipped his hand from the mouthpiece. "I'm sorry I woke you, Grace Ann," he said. "Go back to sleep."

"But Ty—"

"Look, I just called to let you know that the

interview is definitely Thursday and will air that afternoon. I'll be back to New York, of course, for the gala Saturday night."

"But Ty—"

"Good night." He flipped the phone closed and jammed it into his back pocket. He took another lap on the sidewalk before heading back inside to rejoin Manny.

****

"Slow the fuck down!" Harvey yelled, torn between grabbing the back seat "oh-shit" handles and the hot, half-naked woman next to him. "You're gonna kill somebody!"

Layla replied with a scream and a heavy stomp on the gas pedal. "He's been away from her for two weeks, and I can't even get him to look my way," she shrieked, over the roar of the engine. "That's it! I've had it! You people better have done what I paid you for."

"Jesus, you don't have to drive like a fucking maniac!"

"Shut up, Harvey." She tapped her long fingernails on the steering wheel and took a deep breath. "Okay, so tell me the story again. And don't leave anything out."

Harvey rolled down a window, letting the balmy LA air blow through. Jeni sat next to him with her long legs crossed and her tube top dangerously low on her enormous chest. He licked his lips, and she winked back.

"So you said you brought him to the VIP room, and you were seen by the bouncer." Layla eyed them in the rearview mirror.

"Ah, yeah," Jeni said and rolled her eyes. "Like I said, I did it exactly how we planned it. I took him in there, gave him a peek and a grope. I asked him to head upstairs, and he freaked out and bolted." She snapped her bubble gum as if it were a period at the end of the sentence.

"But the point is, the bouncer saw you. So if anyone were to ask him to verify the story, he could. And if Harvey got the picture..?"

"I told you I was standing right there." He slipped his arm around Jeni's body-glittered shoulder and pulled out his mini camera from his breast pocket. "I couldn't have gotten a better angle if they had said 'cheese.'"

"Good. At least something went right tonight," Layla said. "No way am I getting screwed over again."

"Which reminds me." Jeni leaned forward in the seat, giving Harvey a decent flash of her cleavage. "Look, I'm not a back-alley prostitute that you two picked up off the strip. My job title is model-escort, and I was told this was an all-night engagement."

"Oh it is," Harvey breathed, sliding his hand up her sequined skirt. "How about you and me head on over to the Roosevelt and check out the hot tub?"

"God, Harvey!" Layla wailed. "Can you keep it in your pants for five minutes? I'll drop you two off at the hotel, and you give me the film."

"What the hell is with you tonight? The plan went just how you wanted it!"

"He was on the phone with her!"

"He was on the phone with who?"

"Grace!" She gunned the gas, and they surged through a yellow light. Horns blared, and people yelled. A man she narrowly missed on the crosswalk flipped them off.

"Jesus, you don't have to flip out about it." Harvey rubbed the back of his neck from the snap.

"This is it! I'm tired of biding my time. It's all-out war, and I'm ready." Layla glared back at them through the rearview mirror, anger flaring from the whites of her eyes. "Jeni, I'm going to make you the most famous Hollywood hooker the world has ever seen."

"Excuse me, it's escort."

"Whatever. You fuck for money, and I'm the one paying you. I can call you whatever I want."

They pulled into the exit off the Roosevelt, and she skidded to a stop in front of the none-too-pleased valet. No one moved until Layla spun around in her seat. "Well, you two were horny, right?"

Harvey didn't argue the point. He slid out of the car and Jeni followed. Slipping his arms around her waist, he led her up the stairs.

"Is that woman always that crazy?" Jeni asked.

Harvey smiled and answered to her Grand Canyon of cleavage, "Like a fox, baby. Like a fox."

## Chapter Fourteen

"You fucking idiot!"

Ty tumbled to his bedroom floor, bracing himself for the rapid-fire attack of pillows flying at him. Manny stood over him with his arms outstretched, as if he were torn between taking flight and kicking Ty's ass.

"What the hell is going on?" Ty croaked, squinting at the bedside clock. "It's six o'clock in the morning."

"I knew you were going to get into trouble with that woman. I fucking knew it!"

Ty shielded his eyes from the light pouring through the bedroom doorway. "What do you mean? What woman?"

"That bitch ex-wife of yours!"

"Jesus, pal. Calm down!"

"You read this and tell me to calm down!" Manny snagged a wad of newspaper from his back pocket and tossed it in Ty's lap. It was the front page of the *Los Angeles Times*. His heart stopped when he read the headline. "Layla Says 'Ty Must Choose! Me, Grace, or the Hooker!'"

"Christ." He gulped and then dug through the rest. All the stories were the same. Pictures of him and Grace with Layla inserted in the middle. His name next to words like "wild boy" and "sex addict" and Grace's with phrases like "secret lover." He couldn't bring himself to read the actual stories.

Manny launched a pillow out of his path with his foot. "What the hell did you say to Layla last night? What did you do to piss her off?"

"How could I piss her off? I barely saw her."

"Well, she must have some reason to suddenly drop a bomb like this. And since when are you getting hookers?" He kicked the discarded papers, sending them airborne across the room. They floated like snowflakes to the floor, settling in the space around him.

"God, I know I have some bad habits, but even I wouldn't sink that low. She's just making it up."

"Oh, yeah?" Manny pulled another page from his back pocket and flipped it into his lap. "Explain this to me, then."

Ty took a long blink before looking down at the paper. It was the entertainment section of God-Knows-What paper, and front and center was a picture of the girl he had taken to the VIP lounge the night before. The headline screamed "He Paid Me, But He Didn't Have To," and underneath was a still snapshot from what looked like a grainy home video. A circle was superimposed of two hands, dollar bills obviously being passed between them.

"Jesus Christ, she was a hooker?"

"Oh, man!" Manny thrust his hand through his hair and paced across the space in front of him. "So this is real? You and her, and the money."

"No, I must have been set up!" He thought back to the night before. They talked, went into the lounge. "Wait a minute. The girl dropped her purse and money fell out. I helped her pick it up." He looked up at Manny. "Layla must have set me up, and somehow she managed to get it on film."

Manny sat on the edge of the bed and pressed the heels of his hands to his eyes. "You must have done something to set off Layla. Do you have any idea what?"

Ty urged his brain to full function. Last night. He and Layla talked at the bar. Then he saw her when he was outside the club, and she was leaving.

He cursed and shook his head. "She heard me on the phone with Grace."

"You think that's what it was?"

"How the hell do I know? The woman's crazy." Ty pushed himself off the floor and pulled on his jeans before storming out the bedroom door. "This can't be that big a deal, can it? I mean, this is Hollywood."

"What do you mean? It's the front page of the fucking *Times*! That means you've trumped the President and the Lakers as far as public interest."

He bounded downstairs and glanced out the front window. The gate at the end of the driveway was already crowded with photographers. Even a few news vans had parked haphazardly on the curb. "How far has this gotten, anyway?"

Manny stared at him at the top of the stairs with a look Ty had never seen before. Pity, fear, disgust. Any or all seemed to fit. He brought his hands to his hips and shrugged. "You mean, do I think Grace has seen it? I don't know, man."

Ty jogged into the great room and grabbed the remote from the top of the TV. He'd refurnished the house in the few weeks he'd been back to LA. Not totally, but just enough that they could follow his own downfall on CNN, and have some place to sit other than the cold marble floor.

"If it's on CNN, you can bet it's a top story everywhere," Manny told him.

"I got it." The big screen blinked to life, revealing an old publicity shot of him and Grace. In the background a man identified as a specialist in psychological disorders recited the characteristics of a person with sex addiction. "Oh, my God. I can't watch this." He handed Manny the remote and buried his face in his hands.

"I don't know, man. Maybe you should."

Manny changed the channel, this time to a

blonde talking head. She gave a spiel on the life and times of Ty Hawthorne and highlighted her monologue with a picture of him and Layla mid-kiss in their own kitchen. His body seized with realization.

"Jesus Christ, tell me that's an old picture, man!"

Ty just shook his head and let the TV explain. When the overly excited voice signed off for commercial break, he braced himself for his friend's reaction.

"You kissed her, and she took a picture of it?"

"It wasn't like that."

"Well everyone else thinks it is." Manny rubbed his temples. "This is just the tip of the iceberg, isn't it?"

"Can you cut the lectures?"

"Look, man, I don't even know where to begin anymore. It's not that I have a problem with the publicity. You're a movie star. It comes with the territory. But your ex-wife is an extortionist. She's trying to take you down, Ty. A hooker scandal could ruin your career."

"Oh, come on. It's not like I killed someone. And besides, it's not true."

"You know as well as I do that for some reason Hollywood takes sex scandals pretty seriously. Remember Pee Wee Herman?"

Ty fell back on the pillows and groaned. "Okay, you're right. You win."

"Look, if you want to get back together with that witch, that's cool. But from what I can see, she's using the press to manipulate you. She wants money."

"I don't want to be with her! She was upset, and I was comforting her."

"She snowed you, and you bought it." Manny pressed the "mute" button on the remote and peered down at him. “Listen, man, she’s out for blood. Money is a big part of it, but she’s also after your dignity and your career, and I don’t think she cares who she destroys in the process.”

Ty nodded. He had known it all along, but he didn’t want to believe that the woman he once shared a bed with could be capable of that kind of vengeance. “I got to go talk to Layla,” he mumbled. “Who knows how far she’ll go now.”

“What about Grace?”

The thought of her seeing the news made his head spin, and he couldn’t let her weather this alone. Suddenly filled with purpose, he pushed himself off the couch. “I’ve got to get to Gracie before Layla does.”

“Wait a minute, I thought you said that her father was right, and you were keeping your distance.”

“I just want to make sure she knows I’m on her side in case this all explodes.” Ty paused at the top step and checked his watch. “It’s already noon in the east. I’m probably too late.”

“Not necessarily. The news broke too late to make the papers, and she doesn’t strike me as the type who cares about cable news. Now might be a good time to use your clout and use your agent’s private plane. We could probably get there by dinner.”

“Do what you have to.”

“And what about Layla?”

Ty grabbed the cell phone from the nightstand and started dialing. “I think it’s time she and I had a chat.”

****

Layla adjusted the jet inside her thigh and eased down further into the water. Her poolside hot tub seemed the perfect place to watch the news coverage, and she was glad Harvey had hung around so he could move the HD set out on the patio. Having people at her beck and call was nice, she'd decided, and as long as the jerk was around scoring dirt like he just told her, she'd have enough money to pay for the extras.

"So where's Marcy today?" Harvey peeled off his leisure suit jacket and sat down in a lounge chair beside her. "I thought she was going to be around."

"I told her she should lie low for a few days," she said. "People are supposed to believe Ty and I are reconciling. If Marcy is hanging around, it might screw that up."

He was looking at her again. With the wide eyes and the coffee-stained teeth and the greasy hair that stuck to the skin behind his ear. It was a bold move this morning to actually pay him money. But thank God she did, because her ten-thousand-dollar payout was rewarded with a mother lode of information straight from the executive producer of *Undercover Heat* himself.

Talk about juicy gossip.

Harvey watched her closely; his chin practically glistened with drool. Money obviously wasn't the only thing he was looking for. He wanted action, something neither she nor Marcy would consider on his best day. But that didn't mean she couldn't have fun teasing him. She pretended to stretch and slid herself higher in the water. Just high enough for the cool air to harden her bare nipples before his eager eyes.

"Wh-what about the stuff I told you about Grace Ann?" he stammered, with his eyes fixed on her breasts.

"A little at a time, Harvey. You don't want to shoot your wad all at once. There has to be foreplay. You know what I mean?"

He grunted. "So what do we do now?"

"We wait. If I know my hubby, he'll be hopping a

plane as we speak, to try to console the love of his life. Believe me, it won't work out." She pulled the shades over her eyes and rested her head on the leather cushion behind her. "Grace Ann made it impossible for Tyler to ever love me. My broken heart deserves to be vindicated."

She was almost asleep when her cell phone jumped to life beside her. She grabbed it just before the vibration pushed it over the edge of the tub.

"Hello?"

"You planned this, didn't you?"

She nodded to Harvey, who sat up in his seat. "Ty, I'm so glad you called."

"Who took those pictures?"

"Damned if I know." She winked at Harvey, and he winked back. "I'm just as appalled as you are, you know. And a hooker, Ty? Why buy the cow when you can get the milk for free?"

"What are you doing, Layla? What do you want?"

Even his acting talents couldn't hide the fear she sensed in his tone. She might have even felt bad about it, if it wasn't Grace he was worried about. "What I want," she seethed, "is for you to realize that you owe me. I'm sorry that those stupid pictures have you so riled up, but I'm more concerned with mending my broken heart."

"I'm on to you, and if you think you can blackmail me..."

"Blackmail! Tell me how I'm gaining anything from this?"

"This has to do with Grace Ann, doesn't it?"

She bit her lip, trying to hide the smile from her voice.

"Why would Grace Ann have anything to do with ending our marriage?"

"Look, I don't know what game you're playing, but if it involves exploiting Grace, think twice."

"I never thought of it in the first place. And besides, I won't have to. The truth will speak for itself." She dragged her finger around the thick layer of bubbles and listened to Ty curse on the other end. Man, it was great to be the puppet master, and she was good at it, too. She bit her lip to swallow her laughter before she leveled her cheap, yet potent shot. "You know, *I* would have been happy to have a baby with you, Ty. And you and I both know *I* have a healthy appetite. Food or otherwise."

"You son of a bitch!"

"Have fun in New York!" She snapped her cell phone shut and clapped her hands together. And they said she'd never make it as an actress.

"I take it that went well," Harvey said, shading the sun with his hand.

"Better than I expected." She slipped herself back under the water and smiled. "By the way, book us on the next flight to New York."

"New York?"

"That's right. I'm in the mood for a little vacation."

****

Grace scooped the last of the snow from the walk then scattered the bag of salt onto the stones. Thanksgiving weekend had been unseasonably warm and sunny, but now it seemed winter was making up for lost time with a fresh dump of snow. This morning, the task had taken more time than usual, given the icy drizzle they'd had overnight. Lizzie hovered in the doorway, a cup of something steaming in her hand. "You need help with that?" she asked.

Grace smiled at her sister. Her socked feet and lack of a jacket told her Lizzie had no intention of helping. Nor should she, in her condition. This was her attempt at conversation. The last few days Lizzie had been the poster child for nosiness, following her around, asking open-ended questions that reminded her of a Barbara Walters interview. So far Grace had done a pretty good job of keeping her mouth shut. And that's the way she wanted it, at least until she knew a few things for sure.

Lizzie disappeared and then re-emerged in a jacket and boots. Dragging a blanket from the mud room, she perched herself on the porch swing. "I'll keep you company while you do the stairs, if you like."

"That's not necessary," Grace told her.

"I know, but I thought we could chat and pass the time." Lizzie took a sip from her cup and kicked an ice chip with her boot. "So, how are things?"

"Fine."

"Thanksgiving weekend went well, don't you think? The guests really liked that new dressing you put together."

"I guess so."

"So have you heard from Ty at all?"

"I knew it." Grace stabbed the ice on the bottom step with the shovel. "Remind me to give you some acting lessons. Your 'being subtle' needs work."

"What? A woman can't ask her sister about her boyfriend?"

"Can we talk about this later?"

"Has he called? And you haven't answered, or he hasn't called, period, or are you secretly talking on the phone with him every night and not telling me?"

"Why all the questions, Lizzie? Do you want him to call?"

"Do you?"

"Okay, fine! I give up!" Grace jammed the shovel into the snowbank. "What do you want me to say?"

"That you'll sit down and fill me in."

Grace sighed. In the past when she and Lizzie had discussed Ty, Lizzie's tone had reeked of skepticism. Like a mother pumping info about

Saturday night plans from a teenager. But her attitude today didn't convey that at all. Taking a chance, she climbed the steps and sat down in the wicker chair across from her sister.

"Look, I know I'm annoying, but I guess I just realized in the past few weeks that Ty's been gone, you actually do miss the guy, and from what I can see he makes you happy." Lizzie pulled at the ends of her blanket and slid it over her knees. "You guys smoothed everything over when you were in New York, didn't you?"

Had they? Grace leaned back in her chair, remembering the drive back to the hotel in the limo. The things they'd said to each other, making love. She had to admit it seemed to erase a lot of heartache between them. But the phone call with Layla, combined with his lack of contact, made her wonder.

And then there was the other problem.

Lizzie reached out and patted her knee. "Look, if you think I'm going to lecture you about him and your past, relax. You're an adult, and you can do what you want. But I just miss talking like sisters. You know, about boys and clothes."

Grace couldn't help laughing in her face. "Boys and clothes, huh? Don't you think we're a little past that?"

"You know what I mean. Remember our marathon late-night chats when we lived together in New York? Come on. I'm like everyone else in the world. What's up with Grace and Ty?"

"If you put it that way, I'm definitely not talking."

"Oh, please." Lizzie rolled her eyes and batted her hand. "You've been preoccupied about something for three weeks. It has to be him, and I just want to know. And before you ask, Dad hasn't said a word to me. I'm being nosy on my own behalf."

Grace smiled and tucked a hair back behind her ear. "Okay fine. What do you want to know?"

"How was the sex?"

"Lizzie!"

"Well, it's an important question!"

Grace pulled off her gloves and tossed them at her. "I'm not going to get into the details, but it was great. Not that I have that much of a frame of reference."

Lizzie looked around the porch before motioning for her sister to come closer. "I know Dad may hold grudges, but I, on the other hand, try to practice what he preaches and not judge. If you have forgiven Ty for what happened, than I can, too."

The smile on her sister's face meant more than any words. This was Lizzie telling her she had faith in her judgment. That not only could Grace have an opinion, but she'd impressed Lizzie enough to think they might be the correct ones. "Thanks," Grace said, and took Lizzie's hand. "It means a lot to know you're there for me."

"Do you think being with Ty will make you happy, though? I mean, think about it. Your life sure would be different. He's an international movie star who jet-sets all over the world, and you shovel snow in Middle Valley."

"I honestly don't know what to think."

"Well, consider it. You don't have to rush into anything."

Grace's throat tightened. No, there wasn't a reason they couldn't take it slow. Unless, of course... "Lizzie, I think I'm pregnant." Grace closed her eyes and waited for the bomb to detonate.

"What?"

"You said you wouldn't judge me," Grace said with her hands in front of her face. "And before you ask, no, this was not planned, and yes, we used protection. I have no idea what happened. All I know is that I'm two days late, and I'm never late."

"You're pregnant?" she repeated in a whisper. "You're sure?"

"No, I'm not sure. I just have this feeling."

"Maybe you just counted wrong, or your body could be out of whack. Remember, you didn't have your period at all when you were sick. Maybe all the stress from seeing Ty, and your eating recently has been a little questionable."

"My weight has been totally stable," Grace corrected. "I just feel like I am, is all."

Lizzie leaned back in the swing and rested her arms on her bulging belly. "I don't suppose Ty knows."

"No. There's nothing to know. Not yet, anyway." Tears welled in her eyes. She wasn't sure what for. Fear, happiness. Heck, maybe her hormones could wreak havoc just as much as Lizzie's could.

"Hey, don't cry about it," Lizzie soothed, taking Grace's hand in hers. "Children are blessings, remember that. You're healthy, and you always have your family and friends to help and support you."

"Yeah, why don't you tell that to Daddy?"

"Tell me what?"

Grace turned to the door to see her father pulling on his jacket. He was in a suit, and his briefcase leaned against his leg. "Hi, Daddy." She pushed herself up off the chair. "I didn't hear you. I thought you had already left for the church."

"No, my lunch meeting with Bishop Kling was pushed back an hour." He adjusted the collar of his jacket and slipped on his driving gloves. "You girls look like you were having a nice chat."

"Yes!" Lizzie said. "We were talking about Christmas plans."

"And our new addition, of course."

Grace gulped. "What do you mean?"

"Your new nephew or niece." Her father

chuckled and pinched her cheek. "What did you think I meant?"

Grace looked at her sister and back to her father. "You know, I need to go to the barn and get another bag of rock salt. Have a good day at work, Daddy." She planted a kiss on his cheek and headed down the porch steps.

****

Ty peered out the windshield at the graying horizon and the swirling clouds gathering over head. He'd managed to get to New York and beat the rush hour traffic out of town, but if the building storm creeping over the western hills moved in too fast, he'd never get to Middle Valley by nightfall.

"Can you keep your eye on the road," Manny grumbled from the passenger seat. "We're going ninety. I would at least like to know you're watching where you're going."

"Give me my cell phone. I'm going to call her again."

"You've called her a million times. She's not answering."

"So, I'll call a million more. Give me the fucking phone." Ty glanced at his friend beside him and rolled his eyes. "I'm sorry, man. I don't mean to yell."

"Look, I'm on your side. I just want to see you get there in one piece." Manny leaned forward, gazing heavenward out the spattered glass. "Does the sun ever shine in this part of the country?"

"It's the Catskills. It snows here. What do you want?"

"To not die in a ditch." Manny shifted in his seat, and the leather whined underneath him. "So what's going to happen once you get there?"

A great question. The whole flight, Ty had watched cable news feeds about the "Undercover Scandal" as it was now dubbed. He didn't bother with the radio stations on the car ride. Instead, he checked his watch every three minutes and rehearsed his scene as he drummed his fingers on the steering wheel.

Ty wanted to be with her, to protect her from the whole thing. The press would be after her for her side of the story, and if he could take the brunt of that storm for her, he would. "All I know is that I have to talk to her."

"What are you going to say?"

"I figure 'I'm sorry' is a good place to start." Ty ran his hand through his hair. "Look, I filled you in on most of what happened between us. I told you about us and about her being sick, but there was other stuff, too."

"Okay," Manny said slowly. "I don't suppose you want to clue me in."

"Hell, no. It's personal."

"I understand, but as your personal assistant I feel I should know about anything that might be used as ammunition against you."

Ty groaned. Manny did have a point.

"You know I like Grace. And I know I work for you, but when it comes down to it, it's like you guys are a package deal right now. If I can help protect her, you know I will."

A lump formed in his throat. The image of his baby daughter wrapped in her tiny pink blanket drifted through his mind. "She was pregnant, Manny."

"Huh?"

"Remember when I told you about taking her to the hospital after she fell down the stairs?"

"Yeah, you said that she had an eating issue, and you felt like if you stuck around it would make it harder on her and her family."

"That was most of it." His hands tightened around the steering wheel. "When she fell down the stairs, she lost the baby and her parents freaked out.

They didn't know she was pregnant. We weren't married, and we were trying to keep it from the show. Her father is a Deacon, and he was in the process of being awarded a big job with the Catholic Church."

"Wow, he must have flipped."

Ty inhaled deeply. It was safe to tell Manny the story that Lizzie, Russ and even Gracie knew, but what had happened between him and her father was something he'd never divulge. Better off taking his chances with Layla, on that one. "The particulars aren't important. What is, is that I stayed the hell away from her. I just need to make sure she knows the truth about these rumors, and I want her to hear it in person."

Manny chuckled. "Yeah, right. You just want to see her."

Ty turned back to the road and pressed his foot harder on the pedal. He did. He couldn't help it.

## Chapter Fifteen

Sally Hartman's voice filtered into the kitchen from the great room's big-screen TV. Grace tried to ignore it, instead focusing on the gigantic tossed salad she was about to serve to the sixteen guests waiting in the dining room.

No matter how many times Grace tried to steer her patrons to local news or even *Friends* reruns for dinnertime TV, their choice was always the tabloid news shows. Normally she wouldn't mind, but *Entertainment Now* had been advertising a sneak preview of the *Undercover Heat* interview on *The Olivia Show*. She wondered if she could get away with changing the channel, or better yet turning the TV off altogether.

"Hiding out with the baked ziti, huh?" Lizzie teased, snagging the garlic bread heel from the stove. "Don't worry. Maybe Jessica Simpson has a new hairdo or something. I don't think you're headline news today."

Grace closed the oven door and tossed the mitt on the counter. "Tomorrow is the big interview."

"And all they're going to talk about is the show. Ty won't let the subject wander."

Grace took the piece of bread crust her sister offered and took a bite. "Admit it," she said. "You like Ty now, don't you?"

"I told you. I respect the fact that you do."

"That's not what I mean."

Lizzie took another bite and chewed thoughtfully. "Look, I do like Ty. I don't think he's the awful guy Dad thinks he is. But do I think he's good for you? That's a whole different thing."

Both their heads turned when they heard Sally Hartman's voice mention *Undercover Heat*. "I guess Jessica Simpson's hair isn't so interesting after all," Grace muttered.

They both stared at the screen with the rest of the crowd in the room. An old publicity photo of her and Ty mid-kiss made heads turn and mouths shut. Some even applauded.

"Good Lord," Grace mumbled. "Couldn't they have chosen another picture?"

"Shh. I want to hear!"

Lizzie pushed the button on the remote, and Sally Hartman's voice drowned out the surrounding chatter. "Breaking news on the ever-eventful private life of Ty Hawthorne. The latest? Ty is caught with a hooker at the Los Angeles nightclub Chic."

Lizzie grabbed her shoulder. "Did she just say 'hooker'?"

"Shhh!"

"Ty is shown here passing money to a lanky brunette in the VIP lounge. Patrons confirmed it, and the whole town is buzzing."

Grace blinked twice, unable to believe what she saw. Ty in a darkened room, handing a half-naked woman money. When their mouths joined she covered her eyes with her hand. "That can't be Ty," she said out loud. "No way would he ever do that."

"Will this affect the rumored reconciliation with his once-lesbian wife, Layla? This picture was taken just a few days ago in the Beverly Hills bungalow they once shared." Sally Hartman's face was replaced by a candid snapshot of Ty and Layla in each other's arms, kissing, framed by a sliding glass door.

"Oh, my God." Lizzie put her hand over her mouth.

"And what about Grace Ann Langley?" Sally's

voice asked. "In a related story, *Entertainment Now* has just learned that it was a bout of anorexia that drove her from the show *Undercover Heat*, along with the stress of dealing with her then-boyfriend Ty Hawthorne's sex addiction. Ty was scheduled to appear on the *Olivia Godfrey Show* this afternoon but abruptly cancelled when the news broke. No word on if he's seeking treatment."

"Ty's a sex addict?" Lizzie asked.

"Of course not." Although, given the "evidence" Sally presented, it was hard not to think he was. A slew of "eyewitnesses" were paraded across the screen. Some "expert" bald guy discussed the habits of addicts with a world famous psychic, handicapping which woman Ty might choose.

Every eye in the room was on her, waiting for a reaction. If she were a weaker woman, she would cry like she wanted, or scream like she needed, but she wouldn't give them the satisfaction. Instead, she drummed her fingers against her leg, and raised her chin in forced bravery.

"Anyone want some salad?"

Mercifully, Lizzie pulled her by the sleeve and up the back stairs to her bedroom. She stood in front of the bed with her arms folded, waiting for her sister's assault.

"What the hell was that all about?" Lizzie asked.

"I don't know," she said simply. "I'd like to wait and hear Ty's side of things."

"What other side is there? He's gone to hell, and he's taking you with him...again."

"That's not what's happening. You don't know Ty like I do."

"Don't you at least care that the whole world knows about your health situation?"

Grace sat down on the bed and pulled a pillow into her lap. "Of course I care, but I can't control that, can I?" The sound of her own words impressed her. A far cry from the manic micromanager who five years ago hid in her bed and skipped dinner. "It's unfortunate that this got out when it did. But right now I'm more worried about Ty."

"Worried about Ty!" Lizzie's face turned strawberry red, as she rubbed her belly through her sweater. "The guy is running around Los Angeles, is with his wife..."

"Ex-wife."

"Caught with a hooker?" Lizzie threw her hands in the air. "I can't believe this is happening."

"His ex-wife, Layla, has it in for him," Grace said. "She has to have something to do with this."

"What about the prostitute?"

Over Lizzie's shoulder, she saw her father in the doorway. Grace pressed her mouth shut and nodded for her sister to turn around.

"So it looks like Ty has been busy on his trip out west."

"Daddy, those are rumors." Grace said.

"Are you sure?" Lizzie asked. "I mean, those photos, Grace. He was kissing them."

"Maybe it was an old picture. Maybe it was doctored. God, they do that all the time in the gossip magazines. Haven't you ever heard of Photoshop?"

"So, you're going to defend him?" Lizzie asked.

"Yes, until he gives me a reason not to."

Her father groaned and cast his gaze to the ceiling. She could tell by the way he rocked back and forth in his boots that an angry outburst, in the form of a sermon, was obviously not far way.

"And how did they find out you were sick?" Lizzie asked. "And what else do they know, for that matter?"

"I'm not sure."

"Damn it, Grace Ann, I warned you about that man!"

Grace winced as her father's voice echoed like

thunder inside her. She stared at the floor, then back at her sister before getting up and walking around to the opposite side of the bed. "I told you I'm not jumping to any conclusions before I talk to Ty myself."

"Why, so he can lie to you?" The Deacon spat. "Why would you give the man so much consideration when it's obvious he doesn't care a thing about you? His only concern is for himself. He is a greedy, heartless letch, and if you believe for a minute that you're the only woman in his life you're blinder than I thought."

"Daddy, you can't be so harsh on Grace," Lizzie said. "She can't help how she feels."

"The man was videotaped with a prostitute hours after being with his wife, who, by the sounds of it, has been victimized by the man the same way you have."

"Believe me, Daddy, Layla is no victim. And neither am I, for that matter." Grace hoped the volume in her voice hid the slight tremor. What was it about this man that could reduce her to a child, to someone incapable of making her own decisions and possessing decent judge of character? Well, that may have been true in the past, but not anymore. If anyone was making her a victim, it was him. Her own father.

Lizzie walked around the bed and put her hand on her shoulder. "Gracie, we're just worried about you. Daddy and I just want to make sure you're thinking clearly about this whole thing."

"And obviously she isn't," Langley roared. "That man is a womanizer. He's got a tramp in every port. Hell, he had one in his hotel room the other night when I saw him!"

Grace lifted her gaze to meet his. "What do you mean? When were you in his hotel room?"

The Deacon looked at Lizzie and then back at

her. He cleared his throat and raised his chin, as if what he was about to say was gospel. "I went to see him the night we had dinner in the city. When I got there he had a woman in his bed."

Grace glared at Lizzie beside her. Her sister had always been in her corner when it came to battling her father. She couldn't imagine why that had suddenly changed. "You told him Ty was at the Waldorf, didn't you?"

Lizzie stepped away and bit her lip. "I'm sorry, Grace but I was worried about you."

She felt trapped, like armies with guns blazing assaulted her from every side. Deacon Langley was many things. Controlling, rigid, but he was never dishonest. Even to serve his purpose, he wouldn't make up something that wasn't true. "Daddy, are you sure there was a woman there? How do you know it wasn't a business associate?"

"I know what I saw, and I can also tell a deceitful rat when I meet one. I just feel sorry for that wife of his."

Grace wasn't sure what hurt more. Her father's unfavorable assessment of her, or the feeling that he was absolutely right. Maybe she had let her guard down too easily. Her stomach churned as she lowered herself on the bed. All of a sudden it was five years earlier, and she was stuck defending the father of her child and her belief that somehow, some way, he still cared about her.

"So now I suppose you have to speak to these rumors during this ridiculous press tour of yours." Her father stared down at her with his hands on his hips. "And what about our parish? Do you know what this will look like to them? My perfect daughter, who suffers from some sort of curse of self-mutilation and destruction. Never mind if they find out she conceived some bastard child. Do you realize that you have disgraced the family?"

"Now wait just a God-damned minute."

Grace looked past her sister and into the halo of the hallway light. Ty stood in the doorway with his arms folded, his forehead creased in anger.

"Tyler?"

His boots fell hard as he strode across the hardwood and pushed in front of her father. "Just because she's your daughter doesn't mean you can talk to her like that."

"You're a fine one to lecture on right and wrong. Why don't you save it for the reporters? They seem to have an interest in what you have to say, more than I do."

Lizzie scurried around the bed and stepped between the two men, taking her father by the sleeve. "Daddy, how about we leave them alone a minute."

"I'm not leaving Grace here with this manipulator."

"Daddy, please." Grace's voice cracked. "I understand your concern, but I'd appreciate a few minutes with Ty."

Langley groaned and took a step toward the door with her sister. "We'll be out in the hall if you need us."

Ty kept his distance, with the bed between them, his eyes running over her in a quick study. "Are you okay? I heard your father screaming from outside."

"Great. I bet the guests loved that."

"Look, I can see that you're angry and hurt and probably scared, but I got here as fast as I could. I even used my agent's private plane." He glanced behind him at the closed door before making his way to her side of the bed. "I wanted to get to you before the news did. I tried calling your cell phone, and I got the voice mail here at the house. This must have been hard for you to see. I'm sorry."

He reached down to touch her cheek.

"Don't."

"Gracie, I..."

"I said, 'Don't.'"

His hand fell with a thud against his side. She concentrated on the lace fringe of the comforter, weaving her fingers in the fabric.

"Can you at least look at me?"

She waited a beat for drama's sake before she flipped her hair over her shoulder. He looked as tired as he sounded. His eyes were red, his pale skin obvious despite the blush of his California tan. There was a good few days' growth on his chin and cheeks, and his clothes were wrinkled from the long trip. "So where's Layla?"

"What?"

"Your wife," she said with a hint of venom. "You two seem pretty chummy these days. Congratulations on your reconciliation, by the way."

"Wait a minute. Don't tell me you actually believe those rumors."

The picture of him and the tall blonde in a steamy embrace floated through her mind. "Why not?"

"Gracie, that picture...it wasn't what it looked like."

"I suppose you're going to say the same thing about the hooker."

He winced, as if he'd been slapped in the face, and a weird satisfaction swept over her. If this was what it was like to stand up for herself, she liked it. And if he felt bad, maybe he deserved to.

He rubbed his temples and paced. "Okay, I admit I screwed up. But I didn't sleep with her. And I damn sure didn't know she was a prostitute."

"If you thought I was implying that you needed to justify yourself to me, you're wrong. We never said we had an exclusive relationship."

"Come on, Gracie. This goes way beyond a verbal agreement between two people, and you know that."

She jumped up from the bed and, finding nothing more adequate to do, chucked a pillow at him. "God, what's with you, Ty? You come up here three weeks ago, sweep me off my feet, make me believe that there was something between us that was actually worth salvaging. Then what? You suddenly have this epiphany that I can't hack the pressure of being with you, so you take off. God, where have I played this scene before?"

He cocked his head, as if he hadn't heard her right. "Wait a minute. You actually think these stories are true? Layla? the hooker? And you think I am standing here lying about it now?"

Her father's accusation drifted through her head. The woman in the suite with him. Her father wouldn't lie.

Ty buried his face in his hands and cursed. "Good Lord, Grace Ann, have I really fallen that far in your eyes? In all the years we were together, did I ever lie to you? Did I ever give you a reason to believe I wasn't true to you?"

"Does it matter?"

"It matters to me."

"Then you tell me what am I supposed to make of this? In two weeks I have spoken to you once, and the one time I dare to call you, I get your ex-wife on the phone, who tells me what a wonderful time you two are having together. The next thing I know, I see pictures of you and her together. And then, to top it off, you're caught in some back room with a prostitute? Never mind the whole world now thinks you're a sex addict who caused me a nervous breakdown."

Ty shut his eyes and stuck his hands in his pockets. His chest heaved with a deep breath before he opened his mouth. "Layla stole my cell phone," he finally said. "Hell, she probably figured you'd call and she could plant the seed in your head. I'm telling you, she's on a mission. She hired some dumpster diver to dig up dirt, and then she hired a prostitute to seduce me."

"And you couldn't help yourself."

"I told you nothing happened!" He cursed and pressed his fingers to his temples. "Damn it, Gracie, I hate fighting with you."

"So don't do it." She plopped back down on the bed again, and Ty looked at her a moment before walking around and gesturing to the space beside her.

"May I?"

Grace scooted over to give him more than enough room. He sat down with his elbows on his knees and scrubbed his face in his hands. "Look, I'm not going to bother giving you lines, because I think you and I are way past that. The truth is, I put myself in some stupid situations that I have no excuse for. But that's not why I'm here. I'm here because I thought I should warn you."

Grace heard the tremble in his voice. She hated that she wanted to reach out and touch him. Instead she folded her hands and held them in her lap. "Warn me about what?"

"Layla knows about the baby."

Grace let the words settle around her. The blood rushed to her face, and her lungs tightened in her chest. "Are you sure?"

"Yeah, I'm sure. I think her plan is to play this whole thing out in the press so she looks like a victim."

"She's trying to blackmail you. She wants your money."

"That's part of it. But now I'm beginning to think she's out to get you. She's jealous, Gracie. She wants to scare you off." He slid his hand over her knee and squeezed. "I came back because I wanted to talk to you about this face to face."

"You know, this is why I left this business in the first place. All the deceit and underhandedness. That's not me."

"I know, and I hate that I exposed you to all this." He looked back at the closed bedroom door. "I shouldn't have come up here in the first place. But when I saw you at the studio..."

She slid off the bed and stood over him with folded arms. "Oh, I get it. This is you letting me down easy."

He looked up at her and shook his head. "Jeez, darlin', what the hell is that supposed to mean?"

This was it. It was happening all over again. She allowed herself to go where her feelings took her, and this was where she ended up. It was the same mistake she'd made five years ago, and she would be damned if she made it twice. "Get out, Ty."

"What?"

"Get out!" she repeated, pulling him off the bed. "If you think I'm going to let you play the hero, you have another think coming. I'm not letting you say goodbye this time, because I am saying it first."

"Gracie I—"

"I want you to go," she said on the wave of a breath. "I want you to leave."

He stared at her a moment, as if waiting for her to change her mind, but when she didn't, he turned back for the door. "Listen, Earl has been calling my cell phone. I think this whole thing has him freaked out. But if he or anyone else tries to contact you, you let me handle it. This is my problem, so I'll deal with it. Okay?"

He didn't wait for an answer. By the time she opened her mouth, he was out the door, his footsteps echoing in her ears.

****

In the three days since he left Middle Valley, Ty hadn't left his New York hotel. He wouldn't have bothered today except that Manny told him Earl needed to see him pronto at Hoggins Diner. So here Ty was, wiping the sleep from his eyes at three in the afternoon, eyeing a breakfast that miraculously included nothing from a vending machine. Across from him, Earl hadn't touched the cheeseburger and chili fries. Maybe this wasn't just his usual melodrama.

"I think I may have done a bad thing."

Ty took a gulp of his coffee and studied his former boss. The pudgy cheeks were flushed and the man's upper lip trembled. "When you say you did something bad," Manny said, "is this a personal thing, or something that has to do with Ty?"

Earl wiped his brow with his napkin and stared into his coffee. "Well..."

Ty pulled his cap over his eyes and slumped down in the booth. He didn't think he could handle any more bad news. "Come on, Earl, just spill it. Places to see, things to do."

"I know all about Grace."

Suddenly engaged, Ty lifted the bill of his cap. "What the hell do you mean, 'you know all about Grace'?"

Earl squeezed his eyes shut, like suddenly struck with pain. "I had this interview with this guy from *It* magazine," he said. "And he asked me some questions, and I answered them, but I'm not sure I said the right things."

"What kinds of things did you say?" Manny asked.

"Well, he asked me about the gossip about Grace Ann. Said the magazine was about to break a story about your love child."

Ty blinked. "What?"

Earl made a pass across his forehead with a napkin. "I felt bad. I know how rough the tabloids have been on you two, and I wanted to make sure the stories in the magazines were at least the right ones."

"Wait a minute," Ty lowered his voice, and leaned further over the table. "Earl, how would you even know there was a right story to begin with?"

His eyes closed again. "Because I overheard it."

"Overheard what?"

"The night you left for LA, I went to visit you at the hotel, just to be nice, and I sort of overheard you and Grace's father yelling at each other inside. I mean, I had an idea you two were messing around, but I didn't know." He picked up a piece of cold bacon and chucked it back on his plate. "Poor thing, how could she just not eat?"

"Wait a minute," Manny said. "This guy who interviewed you. What was his name?"

"That's the thing." Earl dug into his pockets, and after producing a stray button and a petrified stick of Trident gum he found a tattered business card. He looked at it and slid it across the table to Ty. "Harvey Tillman is what it says on the card, but when I called the number, it didn't exist."

Ty wracked his brain, thinking of every word passed between him and the Deacon, and what spin Earl could have possibly applied. He lifted his cap and ran his hand through his hair before replacing it. "Listen Earl, you didn't spill everything, did you?"

Earl pushed the heels of his hands to his eyes, and groaned. "I'm sorry. I thought I was doing you a favor."

Ty felt the grease shift in his gut. If Earl was any other person, Ty would have wrung his neck. But instead he felt sorry for the poor guy. He cared about Grace almost as much as Ty did. "Look, Boss, I know you didn't mean any harm," Ty said. "I just don't want to make things worse for Gracie."

"Anybody want more coffee?" Stacey looked at Manny when she asked the question and snapped her gum at Ty with a scowl. It made him like the girl even more to know she was mad at him on Grace's behalf.

"I suppose I should be glad you didn't spit in mine, huh, Stacey," Ty kidded.

"I'm not talking to you."

"I can see that."

"And I hope Grace Ann Langley isn't, either. Jerk." She left the pot on the table and marched back to the counter.

"She a huge fan of Grace's," Ty said. He nodded in her direction, just in time to catch her nasty look. "I knew Stacey was a nice girl when I met her. She's got good taste."

"And not a bad judge of character, either," Manny said through a mouthful of bagel.

"I just feel terrible for Grace," Earl said. "At least this is good publicity for the show. She'll benefit from the sales."

"Is that all you care about?" Ty asked. "The money?"

"No, but she does," Earl said. "She made it pretty clear when she first signed on to do this that she needed the money for that bed and breakfast of hers. Otherwise, I don't think she would have gone through with it. From what it sounds like to me, she wasn't wild to see you again."

"Yeah, she still isn't."

Manny dumped a pack of sugar in his coffee. "She still hasn't answered your calls, huh?"

"Christ, can you blame her? This is all my fault."

"How? You can't control what Layla does."

"Well, now that the mess has been made, I want to be the one who cleans it up as best I can. Maybe we should talk about the gala."

Earl's eyes widened as a glob of ketchup fell from his burger to his lap. "Oh, man, no. Don't tell me you're backing out."

"Not me. But Grace should, and I want to make sure she won't catch any grief about it."

"What do you mean? It's a closed party," Earl said. "Sure, the press will be outside, but once she's in the hotel, it'll be fine. Besides, in the message she left me last night—"

"Wait a minute." Ty looked at Manny, then back at Earl. "Grace called you? What the hell did she say?"

"Not much." He shrugged. "Just that she was looking forward to the gala, and that she'd be bringing her sister and father as her escorts. I made sure her wishes were granted, of course. I'm just hoping this *It* magazine thing doesn't turn into a fiasco."

"Hold on," Manny said, his eyebrows raised. "If Grace is going to be there, you want to make sure the attention is off her, right? Well maybe the best way to do that is to make sure it's all on you."

"It's on both of us."

"Well maybe it doesn't have to be."

Ty watched as Manny motioned for Stacey.

"Don't tell me you want me to bring a date?"

"Why not?" Manny asked. "Right now the public is drooling over Ty Hawthorne's love life. Maybe if people think there's a new woman in the picture, they'll leave the old one alone. You can suck up the limelight, and Grace can lurk in the shadows. "

Earl rubbed his hands together and laughed with a snort. "This will be great. They'll leave little Gracie alone, and you'll be on the front page of every rag in this town."

Stacey stopped at the table and tossed her long brown ponytail over her shoulder. "What can I do for you guys?"

"What are you doing Saturday night?"

She looked at Ty, then back at Manny. "Why?"

"Ty here was just saying that you two are old friends. And he was wondering if you wouldn't mind doing him a favor." Manny gestured for her to sit down.

Ty listened as words flew around him. He topped off his coffee and leaned back in his seat while Manny cleared his throat and presented a pad of paper and pen. "Okay, people," he said. "This is the plan."

****

"They're whispering!" Layla hissed, then kicked Harvey under the table. He spit out his coffee and uttered a curse, torn between kicking her back and throwing her on the table and giving it to her like he'd been meaning to.

"Can you see what they're saying?"

"I'm not a fucking lip reader," he told her. "But if you would shut up, maybe I could hear them."

"Don't talk to me like that, you little weasel. You work for me, remember?"

He wanted to punch her in that hot little mouth of hers. Even smothered in that cheap pink lipstick, it made his cock twitch. He didn't even mind the new red hair of hers, or the bag lady clothes she wore as a disguise. Hell, he'd still do her. He'd do her good. So hard and fast she'd be senseless, and that little pink mouth of hers would beg him for more.

"God damn it, Harvey! Pay attention!"

The foursome huddled in the booth behind him. They talked softly through the sides of their mouths, and eyes darted in every direction. They were up to something. Making plans. And damn it, she was going to find out what.

"How dare that man slap me with a lawsuit," Layla grumbled, drumming her long red nails against her arm. "Libel and slander. Do you know he's asking for an amount more than the damn settlement itself?"

"You wanted to play dirty."

"He can't sue me for selling stories that are true. At least, I don't think he can."

"He's Ty-fucking-Hawthorne. He can do whatever he wants."

"Well, now it's about what I want." She snagged his tie and dragged him halfway across the table, meeting him nose to nose. "Look, money or not, I can still have the satisfaction of wrecking his life. And you're going to do everything in your power to help me."

Harvey eyed her in her purple irises. As much as he wanted her, he was beginning to regret working for her. He'd only seen half the money he had coming, he hadn't gotten laid, and he was sick of waiting around just so he'd have a chance with this macadamia nut. This lean, blonde, tanned, hot macadamia nut. "Okay," he croaked and freed himself from her grasp. "So what do you wanna do?"

"Now is the time we use the trump card." She glanced over her shoulder, then back at Harvey. "You have to get us into that gala."

"What? How am I supposed to do that?"

"I have faith in you." Harvey gulped when he felt her foot wedge itself right in his crotch. Whatever she was doing with her toes made him way more motivated about the situation. "You game, Harvey?"

"Huh?" he stammered. "Um, what, well, yeah."

"Perfect." She gave him a wicked wink. "Then it's time for a dramatic conclusion, don't you think?"

## Chapter Sixteen

"How hard can it be to pick out a blue dress?" Grace mumbled to herself. She jumped up on the bed in her Plaza suite. Even from this vantage point, the situation looked hopeless. Discarded dresses in various shades of blue covered every available space, and matching shoes had been kicked off in elimination. The bed was the last place she could stand without trampling priceless fabric.

An aquamarine number lay neatly across the pillow, still on the hanger. Grace almost felt sorry for it. It looked short and drafty and not at all her style. It would probably meet the same fate as the rest of them, scattered on the bedroom floor. Pulling the dress over her head, she waded through the mess to the full-length mirror. She rolled her eyes before peeling it off and tossing it on top of the pile.

Nothing like waiting until the last minute. It had been three hours since she locked herself in here with a rack full of wardrobe choices for the big gala, now only half that amount of time away. At least her search was limited to just one color. In every event since the show's inception she had worn blue, or at least a variation. Earl said it symbolized cosmic intervention and fate, which inspired him to write *Undercover Heat* in the first place. Secretly, she thought he just had a fetish for the color on her. Either way, it didn't bother her. At this moment, it wasn't the color that was the problem, anyway.

She went back to the rack and pulled out a midnight blue gown that had more fabric than the others put together. Rhinestones adorned the bodice and speckled the full-length flowing skirt. She checked the tag and smiled. Oscar de la Renta had always been her favorite designer. She should have tried it on in the first place.

Her skin chilled with cool friction as the elegant fabric slipped over her. It felt light and sexy, and it hugged her in all the right places. Even the zipper cooperated. She breathed a sigh of relief and stepped in front of the mirror.

She turned sideways and studied her profile. For days she had ping-ponged between incredible delight in a second chance at being a mother and fear of the repercussions. Keeping it to herself made it seem almost hypothetical. But now she'd see Ty for the first time since finding out, and the world would be watching. Anxiety over the news won out over her elation. A knock on the bedroom door startled her. "Come in," she called, and smiled when she saw her father gazing at her in the doorway.

"Darling," he said with a chuckle in his voice. "You look like a princess."

"You think so? I was worried that you'd have a problem with it being strapless."

"If you had something to cover you, I'd like it even more. But tonight I'll give you the benefit of the doubt. After all, you are the leading lady."

Grace turned and looked her father in the eyes. They held a softness that normally wasn't there, a sense of compassion or understanding that compelled Grace to take his hand. "Is something wrong?" she asked. "You look like you want to tell me something."

He looked at her a moment before sitting on the bed. His gaze fixed on the floor as he sat quietly, his hands folded in his lap. "Look, Grace Ann, I know how much you've been through, and how much you've dealt with over the years. I mean—your illness, and your mother, and of course, him," he said with a growl. "I just want you to know that I am proud of how you've pulled through it."

"Thank you, Daddy."

He took a deep breath and lifted his eyes to hers. "I'm proud of you. And it will be a privilege to be by your side tonight."

Grace sat down next to him and rested her hand on his shoulder. It was times like this that reminded her how much her father loved her. He had a knack for speaking to his congregation, but to his daughters it had always been a struggle, and just the attempt itself was enough to move her to tears. "It means a lot to me to have you there. Really."

"I can't tell you how happy I am that after tonight this whole nightmare will be over, and we can all go back to our lives."

"Yes well—"

"And we'll never have to lay eyes on Ty Hawthorne again."

"Excuse me?" Lizzie knocked on the doorframe and then stepped into the room with a small briefcase in her hand. "Am I interrupting something?"

"No!" Grace said, pushing herself off the bed. "Dad and I were just chatting."

"Wow what a dress!" Lizzie came closer to touch the fabric. "This is beautiful. I love the color. It's so...blue."

"That's supposed to be the point, I think."

"God, and with your hair." She put her hand over her heart and bit her lip. "I wish Mom could see you right now."

"Well, I guess I should go get into my tuxedo." The Deacon kissed them each on the cheek and headed for the door. "You girls have fun playing dress-up."

Lizzie frowned. "Looks like I missed the best part."

"Not really." Grace said. "Most of the zippers wouldn't even go halfway up." She went back to the mirror and wound her hair around her fingers. Up was definitely the way to go. She turned left and then right, pulling soft tendrils down her cheek. Out of the corner of her eye, she caught Lizzie still staring over her shoulder. "What? Why are you looking at me like that?"

"I don't know." Her sister shrugged. "I guess I'm just impressed by you. I mean, here you are, off to a ball where literally the whole world will be watching your every move. I remember a time when a stubborn zipper sent you on a month-long fast. Or to bed for a week. But here you are. Solid as a rock."

"I wouldn't go that far." Grace slid her hand over her gown. Her sister was right. This was a high pressure situation that would have crushed her like bramble had it been five years ago.

"So, you're going to talk to him?"

Grace moved around Lizzie and grabbed the robe off the bed. If this was another not-so-subtle attempt to pump her for info about Ty, she wasn't interested. Especially when she had to deal with the rest of the world's nosiness in a few short hours. "Talk to him about what?'

"Oh, please," Lizzie scoffed. "Are you really going to try and pretend our conversation the other day didn't happen? Are you pregnant or not?"

"Well…"

"And don't bother lying about it, because I can already tell."

"There's no way you can tell this early!"

"Of course not. That is, unless her sister drags it out of her." Lizzie propped the pillows against the headboard and plopped down on the bed. "So congratulations are in order?"

The calm in her sister's eyes made her all the more agitated. Now was not the time or the place.

Later, after tonight, she would have this conversation. At this moment, however, she was happy to keep the secret where it was safe. To herself. "Look, Lizzie, the woman who's doing my hair and makeup will be here in a few minutes. I don't have time for all of this."

"Fine," Lizzie frowned, then maneuvered off the bed. "I should go get ready myself. But first, aren't you going to open the box?"

"What box?"

"This one." Lizzie brought the briefcase from the dresser and set it on the bed. "Some guy just delivered it. I think the man with him was a police officer."

Grace set the box on the dresser and took a closer look. There were no markings, but she knew from experience that was for safety's sake. "It's probably from Earl. Usually the network arranges to loan expensive jewelry for big-time events."

"Really?" Lizzie's eyes opened wide. "Well, in that case, open it."

Grace unfastened the latch and popped the top open. Inside lay a pair of sapphire-and-diamond earrings and a matching bracelet.

"Wow!" Lizzie put a hand over her mouth. "I've never seen diamonds that big. And all of them put together on two earrings. No wonder they sent a sniper to deliver it."

Grace pushed around the velvet fabric looking for an accompanying note. "Earl probably made an arrangement with Harry Winston or something. Was there a card with it?"

"No," Lizzie said. "Why? Should there be?"

She bit her lip. Unless things had changed in the half decade she'd been out of the loop, the stores always supplied at least a note of appreciation. Not that she needed the gesture, but knowing who to thank would be nice. "Well, it doesn't matter.

Whoever's gems I'm wearing will step forward and claim them sooner or later."

"Let's hope later." Lizzie held an earring to the lamplight. "I have to admit, this is like Cinderella getting dressed up and heading to the ball."

Grace waited until Lizzie left before stepping into the dressing room to retrieve her suitcase. Inside, tucked under her shoes, was a small velvet bag tightly bound with a drawstring. In one hand she held the bracelet, while she freed the necklace from the pouch with the other. A perfect match.

Maybe Earl wasn't the one she should be thanking.

****

"Wow, look at all those photographers."

Ty took one last gulp of his bourbon and glanced out the tinted window of the stretch limousine. Stacey leaned across him with her boobs in his lap and her eyes squinted against the constant camera flashes.

"I told you this would be a circus," Manny mumbled, adjusting the lapels of his tuxedo. "I guess that makes you the ringleader."

"God, I hope I look okay," Stacey said. "I told my mom to look for me on the entertainment news." She sat up straight in her seat and smoothed her crimson dress over her. "What do you think, guys? Do I look okay?"

Ty glanced at the brunette bombshell next to him. The dress looked like someone had run a red paint brush over her rather than her wearing an actual garment. It barely covered her ass when she sat down. Normally, he wouldn't mind a woman who did a little advertising, but tonight it only reminded him of how uninterested he really was. "You look great," he said and winked.

"And you smell incredible," Manny added over his martini glass.

"Well if you like this, you should see what I have on underneath."

Ty raised his brow and glanced at his friend. Stacey was on board with the whole platonic arrangement with him, but that hadn't stopped her from hitting on Manny since the moment they picked her up. He wasn't sure if it was an attempt to make him jealous or if she was genuinely interested in Manny. Either way, it was highly amusing to watch, and Manny didn't seem to have any complaints, either.

"So what's the plan when we get out?" Stacey said when they pulled up to the curb. "Pose for the paparazzi? Wave at the fans?"

"And keep moving," Manny warned. "The faster we get inside, the faster we're out of camera range."

The driver opened the car door, unleashing a fury of cheers from the crowd. People screamed and clamored, leaning over the velvet ropes, reaching out with pens and papers and cell phones, waiting to get their pictures.

"Ty, over here!"

"Just one picture!"

"Marry me, Jax Sinclair!"

Flashbulbs lit up the night sky like midday, so much so that Ty was tempted to pull out his tinted Oakleys. The December chill was replaced by July warmth, thanks to gigantic space heaters so high-end fashion wouldn't be hidden by pesky winter jackets. People screamed, and some even cried. Chanting, running, jumping. Ty had been on a million red carpets, but this was sheer madness. This was fandom at its most fevered pitch.

"God damn!" Manny yelled over the hiss of camera shutters. "It's like the fucking Academy Awards. It's crazy!"

"Smile and wave, pal," Ty said. "Just smile and wave." He took Stacey's hand and guided her between the clumps of guests that had formed along the way. He patted backs and kissed cheeks, the whole time with one eye on the arrivals.

Odds were Earl had put her in a blue dress. He had some sort of weird fetish about it, which Ty tried like hell not to think about. He loved the color on her. There was nothing like peeling it off her, with her looking at him with eyes the same color.

"I think they think we make a good couple," Stacy murmured in his ear. She slid her arm around him and gave him a little hug.

"We certainly look the part, don't we?"

"Hey, Ty," Manny yelled over his shoulder. "Keep moving up the line. Grace's limo just pulled up."

Ty turned toward the white stretch limousine that idled at the curb. The driver walked around and opened the door while the crowd waited with cameras poised. First Lizzie emerged with her father and Earl, followed by a tall burly man Ty assumed was there for security's sake. Finally the driver reached back inside, and Grace stepped out onto the carpet.

Just as Ty suspected. A knockout in midnight blue.

The crowd seemed to agree, given the sudden barrage of catcalls. A few over-zealous men lurched forward, pushing the rope to its limits. It took all of Ty's nerve not to barrel down there and throttle them.

"Jesus, she looks incredible," Manny said, with wide eyes. "The fans are crazy about her."

"Join the club," he said to himself, as he watched the pandemonium. It took every bit of his acting abilities not to react to her. Even yards away the woman appealed to his every sense, either because of memory or maybe because of desire. He could smell her, his fingers twitched with the need to touch her and brush her copper hair from those bedroom eyes.

The Deacon and Lizzie hovered on either side of her. He was glad she had their support, and maybe somehow they'd buffer the madness if he couldn't. But as far as he could tell, she was doing fine on her own. With her shoulders back and chin held high, she stepped out to the middle of the carpet. Her smile was easy. She laughed and shook hands. She was exactly what her name implied. Grace.

"Wow, I love that dress," Stacy said. "And where did she get the jewelry?"

Ty smiled. "Beats me." He licked his lips, watching the light reflect from diamonds and sapphires hanging from her earlobes. They were more beautiful on her than he'd imagined. The hell with the rules. He had to talk to her, just once. And maybe get her alone, kiss her.

"Hey, Ty! You look great!" Earl shook his hand and let it linger for photo op's sake. "I'm pretty pleased with the turnout."

Ty could tell by his smirk that he meant the press more than the party's guest list. "Yeah, well, you're the hostess with the mostess. How about we head inside and send all these people home? "

"Now, Ty, remember this is a press event. Which means you and your costar need to say 'cheese' first."

"Grace, over here!"

"Lexie Love! Show us a smile."

"Turn around, Grace Ann!"

The crowd grew louder as Grace came closer. Most chanted her name and urged her to pose with him. Lizzie hung in the shadows with the body guard and her father. Ty tried to catch her attention but caught her father's daggers instead.

"Come on, Ty," Earl said. "Get your costar and strike a pose."

And in that instant, the carpet seemed to clear, the distance between them only feet instead of yards. An energy surged within him, weakening his legs and stealing his breath.

"Get together!" The crowd shouted, using both their real names and their characters' names to coax them. Ty took a chance and held out his hand, but she surprised him by pulling him close and wrapping her arms around his waist.

The shock of her touch almost knocked him to his knees. Her eyes twinkled like stars, and her skin glistened in the spotlights. Sliding her hand over his arm, she laid her head on his chest.

"Over here, you two!

"Grace Ann, this way!"

"Kiss her, Jax! Kiss her!"

Photographers, at least ten deep, collected in front of them. The ropes bulged as they heaved forward in a wave, and then gave way in a snap. People fell forward in excited shock before the burly armed guards herded them back behind the barrier.

"It's like a riot," he heard Grace say, with the slightest tremble in her voice. His reflexes responded by pulling her closer, and he hadn't realized he did so until she subtly resisted. Grabbing his hand, she stepped out to arm's length, doing a full three-sixty to show off her dress.

"You look beautiful," he said when she spun back into his arms. "Earl is right about you and blue."

"Thank you. I like it myself." Her tone was all business. Not something he was at all used to, and something he discovered he disliked when directed at himself. Even her body felt foreign against him. Stiff, rigid. He was a prop in her scene, and when she wrapped her hands around his neck and smiled up at him with fake adoration, he felt more like screaming than smiling.

"You know how much this is killing me," he croaked through his best showbiz smile. "Not being able to talk to you. Or touch you."

"Hmm, interesting thing to say to your costar when your date is a few feet away."

"She's here as a favor. I thought she'd deflect the attention from us a bit."

Grace placed her hands on his chest and adjusted her pose. "It doesn't look like its working."

"I need to talk to you, Gracie."

"Really?" she muttered, through a smile. "I have a few things to say myself."

"Just one kiss!"

"Come on, you two!"

"Hey, Jax and Lexie, give us a smooch!"

He looked down at her. Her eyes reflected the bright city lights and the flashbulbs that continued to pop. She smelled like lilacs and night air, a combination so incredibly arousing that he was sure if he wasn't careful his smile wouldn't be the only giveaway about how happy he was to be with her.

Suddenly she wrapped her arms around him, bringing her lips to his. It took all the willpower he possessed not to really kiss her, taste her with his tongue, run his hands all over her. He hated how lifeless she felt. Guarded. Indifferent. When she slipped away, a puff of cold air swirled around him. Her fingers traced over his, as she moved around him toward the door, disappearing up the red carpet and inside the hotel.

"Wow, you really are a good actor." Manny slapped his back on the way by. Ty cursed, following him and Stacy through the entrance.

****

Grace hadn't seen such extravagance in a long time, and she hated to admit she liked it. It amazed her that her father hadn't said one thing derogatory all night, even engaging in polite conversation. Things were going smoothly. Almost too smoothly. But the night was young, and there was no sense expending energy questioning it, given the extended performance the occasion required.

"My goodness this place is beautiful." Lizzie pulled her black silk wrap around her. "I did a lot of parties in my days at the Waldorf, but this tops them all." She studied a gigantic ice sculpture in the shape of a flame of fire. Spouting from the top ran a stream of champagne.

"It looks like they pulled out all the stops," Grace said. The entire place was lit by candlelight, either with large candelabras or small votives in elaborate, blue rose centerpieces. Along the wall hung gigantic posters of her and Ty from various photo shoots and episode stills, with spotlights attached at the bottom.

"So what do you think?" Earl asked, handing Grace a chardonnay and Lizzie what looked like a ginger ale. "We went all out."

"I can see that," Grace said. "There certainly are a lot of people here.

"You bet. Network executives, press people." He took a step closer and glanced around the room. "There's also a bunch of film producers here. They're clamoring for a big screen reunion."

The excitement was evident on Earl's face, and she hated to be the one to squelch it. But there was no way on God's green earth she would costar with Ty doing anything. Scripted or otherwise. "Good luck with that." Grace raised her glass.

"Hey, listen, what do you think it would take to get Ty to tickle the ivories a little? That would impress the hell out of everyone."

"Ty plays the piano?" Lizzie asked. "Huh, he doesn't seem the type."

"Not for people," Grace corrected. "That's more of a personal thing."

"I was thinking after dinner, when people are milling around again and drinks are flowing. Hell, you could make a quick getaway if you needed to."

"That's not necessary, Earl."

"I'll see what I can do." He jammed the last of his stuffed mushroom into his mouth. "Well, holler if you need anything. I think I'll drop in on your partner in crime and see how he's doing."

Grace scanned the room. Ty stood at the bar with a drink in one hand and his date in the other. As usual, he was surrounded by a sea of penguin suits and well-dressed women, all with eyes focused on him. She could tell by his posture and the way he gestured that his party demeanor had kicked into high gear. When he laughed, they did, and when he raised his glass the rest of them did, too.

Earl descended the stairs in front of her, and suddenly her head began to swim. It had started that morning, and despite her best efforts to keep at least crackers in her stomach at all times, she realized that once again her morning sickness would be more of an any-time-of-day kind of deal.

"Grace, you okay?"

Again she glanced down at the bar to where Ty stood. As if sensing her, his gaze locked on hers. "I'm fine," she finally said. "I think I just need something to drink."

"And eat," her sister emphasized as they made their way down the stairs.

She looked at Lizzie and back at Ty, who pretended to do anything but look back. Again, her focus seemed to swim, and she shook her head to right it. "Maybe you're right. Let's go find something to eat."

****

"God, quit staring, Harvey. She's just a woman."

Harvey leaned on the bar and wiped the syrupy liquor from his fake moustache. The thing felt like a caterpillar crawling across his face, but he couldn't take the chance of the Simmons guy recognizing him. Getting past security was enough of a pain in the ass, but now that he had, he was happy just to sit and enjoy the top-shelf bourbon. It would probably taste even better if he didn't have Layla yammering in his ear.

"Hey, dip shit, are you listening to me?"

Man, tonight was his golden opportunity. One he had waited far too long for. If he played his cards right, he would leave this soirée with pictures and a story he could retire on. He could give up this stint as a paparazzi. He missed his old hobbies. Ones where payment was guaranteed. He sipped his drink and pictured a Brazilian beach with topless companions smearing him with cocoa butter. After putting up with a whack-job all this time, that's exactly what he deserved.

"I don't get what's so great about Grace," Layla said. "She's short; she has red hair. But look at those men; they're falling all over her."

Harvey turned on his stool. Grace stood at the foot of the stairs with a guy having a conversation with her cleavage.

"I thought men preferred tall blondes," she grumbled.

Harvey looked back at Layla. Tonight she'd opted for the long brunette wig and conservative black dress that covered all the good parts. She also wore glasses and a shit-eating grin that Harvey couldn't help feeling good about. Tonight was the night he'd score. He'd snap his pictures, get his story, and give Layla the boot. Tall blondes, hell. Broads like her weren't worth the trouble.

"Hello, are you deaf? I'm talking here."

Harvey signaled to the bartender. "Why don't you have another drink and chill out for a while. After dinner is when we'll make our move."

"Why not now? How do I know I won't be recognized?"

"You won't be. Relax."

She grabbed his arm and squeezed. "You know, I thought you'd be a little better company, considering tonight's the big payoff."

"Which reminds me. When am I seeing my money?"

"After tonight, lover," she cooed, then licked her lips with a seductive wink. "Besides, I thought you were more interested in the benefits than the salary."

He groaned, more out of frustration than lust. Once again he'd let his small head dictate instead of his big one, and now he was getting screwed in a way he hadn't bargained for. He glanced across the bar at Grace Ann, smiling and laughing with a herd of guys gawking at her. Tonight he'd get what he deserved, one way or the other. This time he wasn't walking away empty-handed.

"Looks like it's time for dinner," Layla purred in his ear. "Perfect. Plotting makes me hungry."

"I have a serious appetite myself," he mumbled before tearing his gaze away from Grace and making his way to the press dining room.

## Chapter Seventeen

Grace sat at the bar, sipping ice water, her stomach bubbling in her throat. She'd struggled to eat at dinner, a fact that drew a few concerned eyes, including Ty's. Her sister and father just leered, a normal occurrence when it came to her appetite. She'd probably be drilled about it later by one or both of them. Biting down on an ice cube, she smiled. Now that was one conversation she wasn't looking forward to.

"You okay?" her father asked, resting his hand on her shoulder. "You look a little pale."

"I'm just tired, I guess."

"You should be, holding up a front like this." He brushed a hair away from her face, and nodded toward the crowd behind him. "Look at this debauchery. The drinking, the carousing. Watching that half-naked girl climb all over Ty is turning my stomach."

Grace sucked in an ice cube and took a bite. Of course she noticed the way Ty and his date had carried on all night, especially in front of the invited press. If she was there as a favor, watching her jam her tongue down his throat didn't do much to invoke her gratitude. "She's here as a screen, Daddy."

"Who?"

"That girl." She turned in her seat and nodded toward Ty's entourage at the far end of the bar. "Her name is Stacey, I think. She and Ty are friends, but I think she's here as more of a favor to me than anything else."

Grace watched the girl nuzzle Ty's neck and run

her fingers down the lapel of his tux. He was smiling, but in a guarded way. The smile he used when he was in front of the camera. "I know it's hard to explain, but Earl probably arranged it to get the spotlight off me. Studios in old Hollywood used to arrange dates all the time for the press's sake."

She could tell by the snarl on her father's face that he wasn't buying it. She probably wouldn't either, if she were him. But right now staying on her father's good side wasn't a top concern. There were other things to worry about. Like keeping down the few bites of prime rib she'd forced down at dinner.

"Daddy, I think the band is starting up again, and Lizzie told me how she looked forward to dancing. How about you go find her?"

"Are you sure?"

Over his shoulder, Grace saw a man hovering. He had been doing that all night, in a creepy kind of way, and in any other situation, where the security wasn't so tight, she'd avoid him. But he wore a press identification tag, and given what the event was for, she was obligated to talk to him. Tonight was a business engagement plain and simple, and she had a job to do. "Go ahead and dance." Grace urged her father. "Lizzie will love it. I should talk to a few people, anyway."

"Fine, one song." He kissed her on the cheek and disappeared into the crowd. She mentally cringed when the seedy man sauntered up and slid onto the bar stool next to her. "Excuse me, Grace Ann Langley?" He set his scotch down on the bar, and extended his hand. "You have no idea how long I've waited for an opportunity like this."

"Good to meet you, Mr...."

"Tills. Hank Tills. I'm a reporter for *It* magazine."

"Well," she said, accepting his hand shake. "A pleasure to meet you."

He smiled, his yellow teeth showing between his chapped lips. "No, believe me Miss Langley, the pleasure is all mine."

Grace waited while he took a noisy slurp of his drink. He eyed her over his glass, and a shiver passed through her body. She knew the look. The lustful one some men had at parties like these, where women were expected to be as fast as the scene implied. Usually Ty was around to police a situation like this. She wasn't used to fending for herself.

"So, your costar has a pretty hot date," he said. "Why didn't you come with one?"

"Oh, well, I came with my family, instead."

"Really, what's the problem? No boyfriend?"

Grace thought that over. Saying 'no' would give him hope and a 'yes' would probably require proof, or at least an explanation. At that moment she didn't have the mind or the stomach to summon her improvisational skills, so she opted for the generic no-comment angle. "Maybe we should talk about the show," she said sweetly. "That's what we're here for anyway, right?"

"That dress is sexy as hell on you," he said with a voice too low for her comfort. "And, man, do I love redheads. You're staying here at the Ritz, Miss Langley?"

She resisted her urge to gag. "Well—"

"How about you answer that after we share a drink?" He winked and patted her knee before signaling a bartender at the far end of the bar.

****

"Who's the jerk-off with Grace?" Ty grumbled, craning his head over the crowd. "He's had her cornered at the bar for," he checked his watch, "thirteen minutes."

"Her father was just with her a second ago," Manny said. "How much trouble can she get into with that guy standing guard?"

From where Ty stood at the opposite end of the bar, he could see the Deacon with Lizzie on the dance floor. Figures. Langley hadn't left Grace alone all night, and he chose now to do a cha-cha with her sister. "I've got a bad feeling," Ty said. "I'm going to talk to Grace."

"No!" Manny pulled him back by the arm. "Look, man, you've avoided a scene this long; don't mess it up now. If you want to talk to her, you can do it later. Catch her on the way out or something."

"Is everything okay?" Stacey wrapped her arm around Ty's neck. "You guys look a little tense."

"Nothing to worry about, honey." Ty kissed her quickly for show and looked back at Grace. The jerk was admiring her earrings. Ty ground his teeth, when he saw his fingers brush her skin. The guy sported a press tag, but there was nothing businesslike about his smile. Horny. Like the only thing holding him back was a room full of people, and even that didn't seem like much of a deterrent.

Ty's fingers constricted around his tumbler as if choking the guy's neck. The glass shattered in a million pieces, sticking to his clammy hand. "Damn it!" He shook the shards to the floor. His palm stung with blood. Snagging his handkerchief from his pocket, he wrapped it around the wound.

"Are you okay?" Stacey asked.

"He's fine," Manny said more to the concerned onlookers than to her. "Go to the bathroom and take care of that before the press reports a near fatal injury."

With his eyes still fixed on the two at the bar, Ty pushed through the crowd to the hallway. He'd just turned the corner to the restrooms when a hand snaked around his arm.

"Need a little help, baby?"

The voice almost knocked him from his feet. He

spied the red nails gripping his sleeve before his gaze slowly lifted to hers. The long brown hair was unfamiliar, but the narrow eyes were unmistakable. "Layla, how the hell did you get in here?"

"Wasn't hard," she cooed. "You'd be surprised how many people out there sympathize with a woman scorned." She kissed his cheek and took a step back, leaning low to flash him her cleavage. "The bathroom is empty, by the way, if you have a minute."

"What happened? Marcy drive you straight?"

She smiled. "Go ahead and take your cheap shots. But I'm the one who'll have the last laugh."

Ty's stomach churned, and his hands clenched at his sides. "So you did set us up, huh? You had us followed, dug up dirt, spread rumors." His heart pounded in his chest. "Why, Layla? What do you want from me?"

"Everything."

Ty stole a glance at the bar, but Layla gripped his chin and dragged his eyes back to her. "You know, I didn't want things to go this far. But Harvey can be very persuasive."

"Harvey, huh?" Ty chuckled. "Who's Harvey?"

"He's a big fan of *Undercover Heat*—well, of Grace's, anyway. That's how we met. Through a fansite." She shook her head and frowned. "It's shocking how they let sex offenders chat on line, especially to make plans to do something a lot like what got them tossed in jail in the first place."

"So what are you telling me? That you hooked up with some pervert and decided to come after Grace and me for kicks? Is that it?"

She shrugged. "I admit I have my own agenda and he has his."

Ty took a deep breath to steady himself before jamming his hands in his pockets. "If you think you can get away with hurting her..."

“Not me, Ty. Harvey. And if you have a bone to pick, he’s right over there.”

He followed Layla’s blood-red finger to Grace and the seedy man still chatting to her at the bar.

The bartender delivered a round of drinks, and they lifted their glasses in toast. In the instant they knocked glasses, Ty realized where he had seen the guy before. He was the creep who had been hanging around that day in New York.

And he was the guy who took the picture of him and Layla.

Ty pulled free from Layla’s grasp, and pushed his way through the crowd. He had them in his sights when he saw the guy lean over and dump a hint of white powder in her drink.

****

“Son of a bitch!”

Grace almost fell from her stool when she heard Ty’s voice. She turned just in time to see him pounce on the man beside her, and wedge his head against the bar.

“Grace, put the glass down!”

“What are you doing?”

“Put it down!” Ty knocked it from her hand and smashed it against the bar. Flying shards drove Grace’s head around, and when she turned back, Ty held the jagged neck to Harvey’s jugular. “Answer me, you fucking bastard! What the hell kind of game are you playing?”

“Jesus, what’s going on over here?” Manny yelled over Ty’s shoulder.

“This guy just slipped something into her drink.”

“What?” Grace wiped the moistness from her lips.

“We were just talking!” Harvey said, with his hands in the air. “I’m a reporter, for Chrissake.”

“You’re a thug and you work for my ex-wife!” Ty yelled. “Your name’s Harvey and Layla’s paying you with my money, isn't she?"

"Hey, wait a minute!" Earl pushed through the crowd of people, and ripped off his glasses "You're him! You're the reporter for *It* magazine! The one who interviewed me! The guy who doesn't exist."

"You son of a bitch!" Again Ty rammed Harvey's head against the bar, just as security swarmed. Two burly guards wrestled the man out of Ty's grasp and held him by the arms.

"Grace Ann, you didn't drink any of that, did you," Ty asked.

"No!"

"Are you sure? Not even a drop?"

Now wasn't the time to inform him of the real reason she wasn't drinking wine. So she left it at that. "I said, no!"

"What's going on over here?" Deacon Langley demanded. "Honey, are you all right?"

"This asshole just tried to slip something in her drink." Ty took her by the hand and pulled her off her stool. "Come on, Grace Ann. I want you out of here."

"No one is going anywhere, until we all set a few things straight!"

Grace gulped when she heard the familiar feminine voice. When she turned around, two hundred sets of eyes settled along with hers on the long-haired brunette, striking a pose at the top of the stairs. "Surprise!" she said, with a bottle of champagne held high in a toast. "Happy gala, everyone. Consider yourself crashed!"

She pulled off her wig and tossed it like a Frisbee. It hit a waiter in the face, sending him to the floor with his tray full of brandies. "First of all, I'm not one who usually does this kind of thing. I don't have to. I'm Layla Hawthorne, after all." She nodded in Ty's direction. "My invitation must have gotten lost in the mail. Right, sweetheart?"

She took a gulp from the bottle, then descended the three steps to the landing, right in front of the bar. The crowd scurried out of her way, as if making room for a street fight, until all that occupied the ring was Ty, Grace, and her.

"I've never hit a woman," Ty seethed, "but for you I might make an exception."

"Ty, leave her alone," Manny said. "Let security take care of her."

"You'd love that, wouldn't you, Ty," Layla taunted. "Let security sweep me under the rug, so you all could have your little party. Well, you can't just cast me aside like a broken toy. The crash-and-burn way you live your life has consequences, and I deserve some consideration." Her narrowed eyes locked on Grace's, and she smiled. "And now I'm here to collect."

****

Security pushed through the onlookers and grabbed Layla by the arms. She kicked and bit until one took aim with pepper spray. Grace gasped and stepped in between them. "Wait!" she heard herself say. "Let her talk. I want to hear what she has to say."

"Grace, are you crazy?" Her father grabbed her by the shoulder. "Let security take care of this."

"No, if she has a problem with me, I want to hear it, here and now." Grace took a breath and brushed the stray hair from her face. Photographers hovered around her with cameras in their hands, and people stood frozen, their mouths as wide as their eyes. She didn't care. Let the world see. If this was what she had to do to finally rid herself of this drama, she'd do it.

"I'm beginning to see that your issue with Ty has more to do with me than anything else anyway," Grace said, taking a step toward her adversary. "So, no more tabloids, and no more paparazzi. How about we settle this once and for all?" She drummed her fingers against her leg, the habit she used when getting into character. In that moment, she realized that maybe drawing on a little of Lexie Love's strength wouldn't be that bad. She needed all the help she could get.

Layla towered over her in her three-inch heels, and the over-abundance of designer perfume did nothing to hide the liquor on her breath. Grace must have winced when the woman exhaled in her face, because it drew a few "oohs" and "ahhs" from the crowd.

"You know, Grace Ann. I used to be an admirer of yours. But then I realized how much happier I'd be if you never existed."

"Believe me, I can relate to your sentiments."

Ty's hand appeared in front of her. "Grace, come on. You're done here."

"No, I say let her stay." Layla handed her champagne bottle to a stunned waiter beside her and took a step toward Grace. "Well, here you are. The object of everyone's affection. You look wonderful, by the way. Starving your unborn child to death must have taught you a lesson."

Grace blinked. She wouldn't let Layla's low blow do more than graze her. Not in front of all these people. "Funny you say that. I was just thinking it's about time someone taught you one."

"Now, wait just a damn minute!" Deacon Langley jumped to Grace's side. "How dare you sling mud at my daughter?"

"Oh, and this must be Daddy, the Jesus freak!" Layla giggled and made the sign of the cross. "You must be shitting in your pants right now, huh, Deacon. I mean, that would probably be pretty bad, if the Archbishop caught wind of how your good little girl almost killed herself because she was so freaked out that the world might catch wind that her costar had knocked her up."

"Shut your fucking mouth!" Ty screamed. 'Shut it, or I'll shut it for you!"

"Tell me, Deacon," Layla said. "Has the Catholic Church changed its policy on murder? Because you don't look much like a rule breaker to me."

"How dare you?" the Deacon seethed. "How dare you?"

A group of security guards descended the stairs behind her, so she scrambled to the bar and hopped up on the counter. "Did you think I wouldn't find out, Grace Ann? The trips to buy prenatal vitamins, and shopping sprees at New York baby boutiques? You want everyone—including me—to be stupid enough to believe your love affair was over long ago? Well, it isn't, and now I'm the one breaking the story."

"Get off the bar," Ty demanded.

"Grace Ann Langley is pregnant again, folks. And my dear husband, Ty Hawthorne, is the father."

Stunned mumbles hummed around them, and Grace swallowed hard when Ty grasped her shoulder. A flashbulb blinked beside them. Harvey, still bookended with a guard on each arm, lowered his camera from his face. "Do you guys think you could push together? I only got one more picture and I don't want to waste it."

"You son of a bitch!" Ty roared and pounced on him, leveling him with a fury-filled right hook that sent him to the floor in a lifeless heap.

"Set him up!" Ty demanded when the security swarmed. "Set him up, damn it! I'll knock every God damn tooth out of his fucking mouth. I want to teach him a lesson for messing with people's lives!"

The room spun around Grace. She shook it off, and raised her chin in fight. She had never seen Ty lose his cool in a crisis. She was usually the one who unraveled and he the one left to clean up the mess.

It suddenly occurred to her that if there was ever a time to return the favor, this would be it.

"Tyler, stop!" She slipped herself under his arm, while he held Harvey by the collar. "It's not worth it."

"Grace, step away from them," her father ordered. "You're going to get hurt."

She tightened her grip on Ty's shirt and then calmly tried again. "Tyler, listen to me. I want you to let it go."

"This guy is spreading lies about us, Gracie. He can't do that. The two of them are selling stories that aren't true. He's breaking laws and ruining our lives."

"But he's not lying."

He looked at her and shook his head. "What are you telling me, Grace?

With strength, she had no idea she possessed, she pried Ty's hands free and led him up the stairs to the landing. Gazing around the ballroom, she saw every wide eye in the place. The wait staff, security, the network suits still nursing watered down drinks. Lizzie, her father, even Manny and Earl with hands in their pockets and cheeks so red they looked feverish.

It had all come down to this.

Grace realized it was five years' worth of idleness that had gotten her to this point in the first place. Maybe if she hadn't been so concerned about hiding, as well as protecting everyone else, this situation wouldn't have spun so far out of control. In the few weeks since Ty had shown back up in Middle Valley, she had found a new resolve. Facing things head-on allowed more control than hiding from them, and perhaps this situation was the perfect test for her new attitude.

"So, if you want to know the end of the story, listen up," she said to the crowd, with a conviction in her voice that made her glad for her acting background. "And if the press people are still here, get your pens ready." She locked her knees, cleared the lump in her throat, and took Ty's hands in hers. "She's right, I am pregnant, and Ty is definitely the father."

A collective gasp from the crowd confirmed that her news had registered. She closed her eyes and braced herself—for what she wasn't sure. Fire, a bolt of lightning, a plague of locusts, maybe. But nothing came. Suddenly she felt lighter. Like a weight had been ceremoniously removed. She looked up at Ty, and the rest of the room fell away. Any misgivings she had about her announcement were erased when she saw the stunned smile pull at his parted lips. "What the hell are you doing?" he mumbled. The room hummed with chatter around them. "You're not pregnant."

"Don't break character," she whispered back. "Just trust me, and stay with me in the scene." She grabbed Ty by the back of his head and clamped her lips on hers. It was a stage kiss in every sense. Dry, dramatic, and executed in order to highlight a point. She pulled away and smiled, then offered a wave to Layla, who was now corralled by a group of armed guards. "Excuse us, everyone, but Ty and I have decided we would like to celebrate the happy news in a private party."

She took Ty's hand and led him down the stairs. The crowd parted, and Grace made a point to paint on the happiest face she could muster. From the bottom step, she saw her escape route clearly. To the elevators and beyond. But before she reached the hall, someone stepped in front of her. Her nose crashed right into the broad, unyielding chest of Jordon Langley.

"Not so fast." He seethed, his eyes fixed on Ty beside her. "You're not going anywhere with this man."

Ty slipped his arm around her shoulder. "Come on, Grace," he said. "Let's get the hell out of here."

"Over my dead body!"

"Both of you, stop it," Grace ordered, with a hand on each of their chests. "Look, I know you both think you have good reasons to dislike each other, but if you're looking to blame someone, blame me."

"Oh, Grace Ann, no one is blaming you for anything," the Deacon scoffed. "See the trouble you cause, Hawthorne?"

"The only reason you two bump heads is because you both want what's best for me, and I admit there was a time when I was truly my worst enemy. But that's over. I can make my own decisions." She turned to her father and slipped her hand over his. "Daddy, I'd like to think that you instilled me with a good sense of faith. I know in my heart that Ty's a good man, and as my father who loves me, you should give me the benefit of the doubt."

Grace stepped away from her father and grabbed Ty by the lapel. The path was still clear to the elevator. It was tempting to break into a full sprint, but she settled on a prideful strut.

"Well, that was a scene if I ever saw one," Ty muttered.

"Just keep walking, Hawthorne. Just keep walking."

## Chapter Eighteen

Ty's feet barely carried him over the threshold of his Waldorf suite. It was like they'd just played a scene from an *Undercover Heat* episode, the way they snuck through security and hid in stairwells, even hijacked a network limo to make the getaway. They were laughing about it when they pulled away from the curb, but now they were back here it didn't seem that funny anymore.

Grace sat at his feet, unstrapping her shoes. The job would probably be easier with the help of light, but she didn't ask, and he didn't offer. The darkness seemed oddly comfortable at the moment.

She stood, chucked her shoes into the closet, and strode to the long wall of windows. The glare of the city lights cast a silver glow across her, and the mass of diamonds around her neck reflected like prisms against her skin. He mentally cursed. If he wasn't so damn taken by her beauty, he would have tried harder to remember he was angry.

"There are flashing lights going in the direction of the Ritz," she said. "You think that's where they're going?"

"Grace, I think we need to talk about a few things."

She didn't answer, but he could tell by the way she pursed her lip that she heard him. He took a few steps toward her but stopped short, hiding himself in the shadows. "Look, I know there were a lot of words and accusations tossed around tonight, and I think we should get to the truth about them..."

"I forgive you for leaving me, Ty." He heard her

suck in a breath and sigh. "After what my father did, I shouldn't blame you, but I did anyway, and I'm sorry."

The words hit like a well-placed punch. One he would have braced for, had he seen it coming. "Grace," he croaked. "We don't have to talk about this."

"Yes we do, because I'm tired," she blurted. "I'm sick of the secrecy and lies..."

"But Grace—"

"You left the hospital, or at least I thought you had. I was pretty out of it, but I heard my father discussing my options with the doctors. Something about cardiac arrest, or a stroke, and me being pregnant risking my life. I was only what, twenty weeks along, and everybody knew there was no way the baby would live, but they delivered her anyway."

Ty scrubbed his face with his hands and paced across the room. After all this time. She knew. She fucking knew.

"So I had the baby," she told his reflection in the window. "A little girl, and she lived for five minutes. I didn't know if you knew, and at first I thought you left because I had disappointed you. I know how much you were looking forward to being a father, and I hated that I took the opportunity from you. From both of us."

"Darlin', I never blamed you for anything."

"Well, I blamed myself. I still do. If I had been stronger and more present, I would have fought the decision. But my father was adamant." She turned from the window and wiped the tears from her cheek. "I'm sorry. I didn't know how to tell you."

His legs unsteady, he leaned against the baby grand piano in the corner. The moonlight spilled around her like a spotlight, glistening on her pale skin. "Grace, what's in the past is one thing, but what about tonight? How could you tell the world you're pregnant?"

He couldn't see her face. But he heard her take a breath before she came toward him. "What, is that something you feel angry about?"

"Angry isn't the issue," he snapped. "I just don't get it. It's enough that now the whole world knows about our past. Did you think you being pregnant would put Layla off and she'd give up? Or was it just something that sounded good at the time?"

"Tyler, you're yelling."

"Yes, I'm yelling. And what about your father? What do you think is going on in his head right now? Why would you say something like that?"

"Would me being pregnant be that bad? Would it cramp the Ty Hawthorne style or something?" She stopped in front of him and thrust her hand to his chest. Her eyes were on him wide and clear, and his breath hitched in response. "Tell me, would you run the other direction?"

He wasn't sure he understood the question. Layla's scene alone would thrust Grace onto the front page of every gossip magazine in the country. Stories that would display their dirty laundry for everyone to see. And what about her family? How would she square things with them? That was a nightmare all its own. But she didn't seem concerned about that. There had to be something else.

She strolled around him and sat down on the piano bench. "Your girlfriend, Stace, looked like she was having a good time tonight."

"Oh Grace, she was just there for show. It was Manny and Earl's idea."

She stared down at the keyboard, pressing a few keys before slipping her hand back in her lap. "You know, when I saw those pictures on the news of you with Layla and with that girl in the bar, I was really hurt. Not that I had a right to be."

"Grace, those pictures... I know what it looked

like, and I admit I made some wrong decisions."

"And the woman in your hotel suite?"

"The woman in my hotel suite?" He shook his head. "What are you talking about?"

"My father said there was a woman in your hotel suite the night he went to see you."

"He told you about that?"

She flinched as if she had been struck. "Wow, so it's true? So you mean after what happened in that limousine and everything that we said..."

"No, I mean I didn't know he told you that he came to see me," he said. "There was no woman. He saw your things lying around, and he came to his own conclusions."

"And you didn't correct him?"

"Why, so he could give you a hard time?" Again, Ty paced the room. He stopped at the window and glanced in the direction of the Ritz. No flashing lights, and he wasn't sure if that was a good thing or a bad one. "Man, tonight was a big disaster. I'm sorry. I thought I had safeguarded against a scene like that."

"You may not know it, but you and I are a lot alike. If we aren't in control, we lose control."

He stared out at the city and smiled. "I think that's what made me crazy all these years. I couldn't control what was happening to you and with the baby. I thought if I could keep all the balls in the air with the network, and with Earl and your family, I could see you through it. I wanted to be the hero and save you. And if I couldn't do that, I figured that it was just better if I left." It was enough truth for now, he decided. When the time was right he'd tell her the rest.

"By the way, I'd like to thank you for the jewelry," she said. "They're beautiful."

"You're on to me, huh?"

"Yeah, and I think they're quite appropriate."

"Appropriate?" He came back over to her. "How so?'

"Well, sapphire is the birthstone for the month of September, and if the baby is a few weeks late..."

In that instant, his gaze locked on hers. All of a sudden it was five years ago, and he was standing in the kitchen at the farmhouse. With the same hopeful eyes, wide smile, and her cheeks glazed in a cherry blush. He gulped and slid his hand to her face. His palm heated against her skin and her eyelashes brushed his fingertips. "What?"

She stood, taking his hands in hers. "I'm pregnant, Tyler. For real."

His legs turned to rubber bands and his mouth went bone dry. Never in his wildest dreams did he think this moment would ever happen to him again. And now that it had, he didn't think he could want anything more.

He pulled her close, burying his head in her hair. The condoms. Angie's condoms. That's how it must have happened. But right now the logistics weren't what concerned him. He laughed, holding her tight against his chest.

"This is good news, right?"

He looked down at her and laughed some more. "The best. But I thought that whole thing was for show?"

"Haven't you heard? I'm one hell of an actress." She tweaked his lapel and dragged him to her for a kiss. It was deep and long and so incredibly powerful that it drove the breath straight from him. She took a step away and took him by the hand with a smile. "So, since I'm having your child, I think I'm allowed a favor."

"Anything."

"Will you play the piano for me?" Grace flipped her dress dramatically behind her and slid onto the bench. He sat down beside her. The black and white keys stared up at him in the shadows. The last time he had played was for Gracie. And, if he remembered correctly, she was sitting next to him just like she was now. With her legs bumping his, and her head resting on his shoulder. He'd considered the talent a characteristic of the Ty he no longer knew, but he realized now it wasn't that he didn't know him. He just belonged to Grace.

He slipped his hands over the keyboard, his fingers finding their places in the darkness. It was the old Elton John tune that reminded him of everything he loved about her. Her strength, her compassion, and how much she was willing to risk by loving him back.

His body moved with the sound, and as it echoed in his chest, he felt renewed. Like a snake shedding his skin. He was reminded of what Grace had told him. That they, together, were something bigger than each alone. But whatever it was he brought to the union, he wanted it to be the best incarnation of himself he could conjure.

"I love you, Tyler," she whispered. "I always have."

The admission crippled his fingers, and he dragged them off the keys. Words he had heard only in his dreams, but when her eyes met his, he realized how real they were. He scooped her up and sat her on the keys, making an out-of-tune sound that distracted neither of them. Her long hair fell loose around her, and tears shone in her deep blue eyes. "Baby, I've loved you from the minute I saw you step into Earl's office a decade ago. Everything about you." He ran his hands over her—her shoulders, her arms, and more—until they rested on her belly. "About us."

He couldn't say anymore. Tears spilled down his cheeks; he would have been embarrassed if it hadn't felt so right. He rested his head in his lap, and held her for dear life. This was his second chance and, God help him, he was going to take it.

"It's okay," she breathed, stroking her hand through his hair. "It's just me. I'm right here."

Damn right she was. And that was where she was going to stay.

After a moment, he reached up, slipping his hands over her hair. Soft like silk, with golden highlights that glistened in the light. His insides hummed with electricity so potent his body shivered. God, if this was what he had to look forward to for the rest of his life, he'd die a happy man. No longer able to hold himself back, he stood and kicked away the piano bench behind him.

He brought his mouth to hers, running his hands over her bare back. He tore at the zipper and pulled off the dress, tossing it into the darkness. And then, there she was, in all her naked splendor, save for the necklace and earrings that danced in the silver shadows. She didn't move to cover herself, and that alone made him want to look at her more.

"Remember when you were kidding me about my cravings?"

He ran his hand over her breast and smiled. "Yeah."

"Well I'm having one really bad right now," she teased, unfastening the fly of his pants. "You up to helping me out?"

His instinct was just to take her. An animalistic need to stake his claim. His woman, his child. Not just to satisfy the nagging desire to spill his seed inside of her. Clothes were stripped off and discarded like rags before he pushed her legs open and captured her in a kiss. "I love you so much," he gasped with his lips on hers. "It would kill me if I lost you twice."

"Well, then, take me, if you want me."

He lifted her around his hips, and when their

eyes locked, he eased himself inside her. It felt so right, with no barriers between them. Flesh to flesh. An intimacy he hadn't shared since being with her. He watched her in the moonlight. Her head thrown back, her hair fanned out around her, her lips parted as soft moans escaped from between them. She looked like one of those paintings he'd seen in Italy. A woman in rapture in every sense. Raw. Beautiful. His.

Splaying one hand on her stomach, his fingers on the other traveled over her. Between her cleavage and over her neck, cupping her face in his hand. He pulled her down on him, on the piano keys, driving himself further into her. He couldn't get deep enough but tried anyway, each thrust like a purging of his soul. "Things are going to be different this time. I promise," he said, and repeated it to make sure she believed him.

Her taut ballerina legs wrapped around him like a vine, and her breasts flattened against his chest. The soft round flesh of her buttocks warmed in his palms, and he pulled her harder down onto him. This was where he belonged. With the love of his life. The mother of his child. She was his. Always had been, always would be. Proximity and circumstance wouldn't change that.

"I need you, Grace," he said, with the last of his breath. "I need this."

When she smiled, he knew she understood, and in that moment he quickened his pace. Pressing harder, thrusting faster. He closed his eyes and let himself go, eagerly following her wherever she wanted to take him.

And then they came, hard and fast, both gasping for the breath that had been driven from them. He was paralyzed. Energized. Completely claimed by the tiny waif trembling in his arms.

****

Grace pulled the pillow over her eyes in an effort to block the glare of the TV. Her stomach churned like a violent storm and her body shivered with beaded sweat. A half hour ago she'd felt great. The interlude on the piano with Ty had a lot to do with that, but now she felt like she'd been run over by a truck.

"You okay, Gracie?"

She groaned. "I can't sleep with the room spinning."

"Yeah, been there, done that."

A wave of nausea washed over her, and she tossed the covers aside. Grabbing Ty's shirt from the nightstand, she sprinted to the bathroom. She made it just in time to bury her head in the toilet.

When she caught her breath, she leaned against the cool tile wall. Ty stood over her in his gray sweat pants, a cup of water in his hand. "I forgot how much fun early pregnancy can be," she said through chattering teeth. "Go back to bed. We have a long day ahead of us."

"I can't sleep, knowing you're in here sick."

"I'm not sick. I'm pregnant."

"I know." He smirked. "I was just reading all about it on the crawl on CNN before you ran in here." He sat down on the floor and pulled her into his lap. "Just relax," he whispered, kissing her head and stroking her hair. "Take it easy, it'll pass."

"I can't believe we haven't heard from anyone. I thought for sure Lizzie would have called at least ten times by now."

"She did."

She sat up and looked at him. "What?"

"Look before you get mad, I sent her a text message back. I told her that you were okay, and that we would catch up with them after the interview tomorrow."

"Oh, God, the big *Olivia Show* is in the

morning." Just as she finished the sentence, her stomach pushed through her throat. She dove to the toilet and hung on for dear life. "I'm sorry," she croaked when she finished, then thanked God out loud when Ty placed a cool wet cloth against her cheek.

"Don't be sorry. I've held your head praying to the porcelain god before. Remember that network party where you decided you loved spiced rum?"

"Ugh." She held her stomach. "Please, I don't want to talk about it."

"I took you back to my room and took care of you all night. You puked all over me twice."

"You should thank me, then, for making it to the bathroom this time."

"Hey, are you people here?"

Ty covered her ear with his hand. "Manny? We're in here, buddy."

Manny barreled through the bathroom doorway with his bowtie dangling, his shirt shredded, and his jacket missing all together. His lip was swollen, and his face crimson red. He held his hand up while he caught his breath before stepping inside the bathroom.

"Wow, Manny," Grace said. "What the heck happened to you?"

"I want a raise." Manny glanced at himself in the mirror and cringed. He wet a washcloth, ran it over his face, and sat down on the edge of the bathtub.

Ty laughed. "Don't tell me Layla kicked your ass."

"No, but she's a lunatic, by the way. After you left, she escaped from the security and got in Earl's face about ruining her career. She hit him over the head with a barstool."

"Oh, my goodness," Grace said. "Is he okay?"

"Are you kidding? He's thrilled. He already

called *The Post* to make sure it makes the morning edition police blotter."

"What about that Harvey guy?" Ty asked. "What happened to him?"

"He's in city lockup with Layla. They both might be there a while, too. Turns out the guy is a serious sex offender. Done time twice for spiking women's drinks and assaulting them." He patted Grace on the shoulder. "Good thing you didn't drink that stuff. Who knows what he had planned for you."

Grace smiled at Ty in a silent "thank you" before turning back to Manny. "I don't suppose you saw my family?"

Manny took the cup of water from Ty's hand and helped himself to a sip. "Lizzie ushered your Dad out of there pretty quickly. They were long gone by the time the cops showed up. I got to tell you, you two really know how to drop a bomb." He shook his head and wiped his mouth on his soiled sleeve. "So why are we sitting in the bathroom, anyway?"

Again Grace looked up at Ty. He smiled wide, his dimples plain through his heavy stubble. "Grace wasn't feeling very well."

"Wow, Grace, I didn't know you were a big drinker."

"She's pregnant, asshole." Ty took the washcloth and smacked Manny in the head with it. "What the hell is wrong with you?"

"Oh, my God! You were serious?" Manny slid to the floor. "I thought you were just razzing Layla. Congratulations. Wait—congratulations are in order, right?"

Ty pulled her close and kissed the top of her head. "Damn straight."

"Then you should be excited that you have the chance to share the happy news with the millions of people tuning in the *The Olivia Show* tomorrow." He pushed himself back to his feet and handed Ty the cup. "After tonight, the whole world will be watching."

Grace swallowed, bracing herself as her stomach again churned. Ty must have sensed her distress, because he shoved the water under her nose and massaged the nape of her neck.

"Manny, I'm sorry about all of this," Grace said when the spell passed. "I know this puts a lot of pressure on you, and I didn't mean to make a scene." She pulled on the leg of his wrinkled pants. "If you look like this because of a scuffle I caused..."

"Who says I was in a scuffle?" He winked and smoothed his hand down his rumpled shirt. "Look, Stacey is waiting for me in my suite. I'll see you guys at seven a.m. sharp."

Manny reached down and shook Ty's hand before making his way toward the door. "I don't know, guys. If this is what it's going to be like to babysit both of you, I'm not sure I can handle it."

"Soon there will be three." Grace slipped her arms around Ty's neck. "I hope you know how to change a diaper."

The door to the suite slammed, and Ty eased himself back against the bathtub. She snuggled in close and let her eyes close, eternally grateful that the revolving room had come to a stop. "I think I'm okay now," she said. "Let's go back to bed."

"If you're comfortable here, stay here. I'll take you back when you fall asleep."

"I don't want to stay here. I want to get in bed with you." Grace ran her hand down the crease of his bare chest. "And if I don't fall asleep right away, that's okay, too."

"Well, there's an *Undercover Heat* marathon on one of the cable networks. Earl arranged it for promotion. We could watch that, if you like."

"TV wasn't what I had in mind."

He lifted his head and peered down at her with

one eye. "Good Lord, darlin', mighty strange time to have a craving." He scooped her up in his arms and kissed her hard. "I better hurry before it wears off."

****

"Three minutes to air!" A production assistant announced from somewhere in the dark depths behind an *Olivia Show* camera. "Mr. Hawthorne, take your seat, please?"

Grace watched him from the soundstage couch while Ty spoke in a huddle with Earl, Manny, and the legendary Olivia herself. No doubt, after last night's spectacle, Ty was concerned about the direction of the interview. If Grace weren't more worried about keeping down the two saltines she'd had before leaving the hotel room, she would be over there, too. But it was easier just to let Ty handle it. And if he wanted to, she'd allow him.

The meeting broke up, and Ty jumped up onto the sound stage. "You ready for this?" he asked, sitting down on the couch beside her.

"I hope so." She looked out at the sea of staring eyes. "God, these people see movie stars all the time. You'd think they'd be used to it."

"People are people, Gracie. And we're pretty juicy at the moment."

"Looks like Earl isn't even trying to hide his happiness about the whole thing." She looked out at the smiling, chubby man, who waved at her like a five-year-old. "Although I'd have thought less of him if he had only fake concern."

"Oh, come on. The guy is worried sick about you. We all are."

She hated the implication that she required special consideration. The scene last night was like ripping a Band-Aid off a wound. It had been quick and probably a lot less painful than if the whole thing had been drawn out. Now that everything was in the open, she could rest easier, but judging by Ty's bloodshot eyes, he didn't share the sentiment. "What about you?" she asked. "How are you doing with all this?"

"As long as I can get you through it, I'll be great." He winced and bit his lip. "I didn't mean it that way. What I meant to say was..."

"No, you're right," she said. "You're better at handling these things than I am. You've never lied to me before. Don't start now."

"I just meant that, given your condition, I don't want you upset," he said. "You didn't sleep well last night, and you're feeling a little woozy this morning. I'm just looking after you, is all."

Her stomach lurched as if reminded to do so by his suggestion. Without being asked, he handed her the mug of water beside him. "You know, you can still back out. In fact, I think Earl's impressed you showed up at all."

Another assumption she resented, even more so because it was so logical. Five years ago, heck, five days ago, she'd have backed out. But something had changed. A fighting spirit had risen inside her. A resolve that hadn't been there before last night's scene at the gala. "I don't want to back out." Her gaze met Ty's. "I'm actually looking forward to this. I have to set things straight."

"With who? Olivia?"

"No, with myself." She took a deep breath and stood to slide off her blazer. She had purposely chosen a black tank blouse and matching short skirt. If she was going to go through with this, she wouldn't hold back. The hell with her fleshy arms and fat legs. It just didn't seem important anymore. She tossed the jacket over the couch and sat back down. By the smile on Ty's face, she knew he understood the gesture.

"You look beautiful," he whispered, brushing her hair over her bare shoulder. "Everything about you,

Gracie. Beautiful."

Maybe it was the timing of his words, or the tenderness with which he said them. Heck, maybe it was the hormones, but something inside her was inclined to believe him.

Olivia Godfrey stepped up on the soundstage and extended her hand to Grace. The woman was gorgeous on TV, but in person she was all the more stunning, tall and slender, with long dark hair and bright, wise eyes that seemed to house a knowledge that went beyond her forty years. She sat next to Grace and placed a gentle hand on her knee. "First of all, Grace, it's wonderful to see you after all these years. Second, I want to offer my congratulations to both of you. A baby is quite a blessing."

"We both feel that way," Ty said with his eyes on Grace. "It's just a little overwhelming right now."

"We're fine," she blurted. "And really, I'm okay to talk about it."

"Grace Ann, Olivia and I agreed that I would talk mostly about the show, and that any personal questions would be better directed at me. How does that sound?"

"Tyler, will you change seats with me?"

His forehead wrinkled. "Why? This is how we always sit. Me between you and whoever is interviewing us, so I can do the talking."

"We'll both do the talking," she said, and squeezed her way between Ty and the arm of the couch.

"Are you sure about this?"

Before she could reply, the countdown began and the light in the camera flashed on. They straightened their seats and shared a quick glance before the director gave the cue.

Olivia offered a spirited read from the teleprompter, introducing Ty and Grace as the First Couple of Television. First they aired a montage of clips from years ago. Some from the show and others from interviews and trips down various red carpets. Then a quick rundown of the questions surrounding them. Were they secretly involved? Why did the show end? Had she been sick? And what was going on between them now?

Grace felt like a dying woman watching her life flash before her eyes. All these years of keeping secrets and self-scrutiny suddenly seemed senseless and stupid. The man she loved sat by her side, and his child was in her womb. She had been reborn. This was an opportunity to share her triumphs and her happiness. There was nothing left to hide.

"How do you two feel, watching that piece?" Olivia looked at Ty. "There's a lot to speak to, isn't there?"

"Yes, there is," Grace heard herself say. "And I'd like to."

When she was done, the camera snapped off and people milled about on the sound stage. Olivia thanked her and hugged them both before disappearing stage right. The next thing Grace knew, she was in Ty's arms, enjoying the soft circles he made on her back. She closed her eyes and let herself relax, and for the first time in her whole life she could truly say she was relaxed.

"You have no idea how great it feels to hold you like this and not give a rat's ass who sees it."

"I can imagine it."

"Let's go back to the hotel," he whispered.

"Why?"

"Because there are some things that aren't meant for anyone else's eyes."

"Hey, you two!" Manny jumped up onto the sound stage, and flipped his razor phone shut. "Break it up, because I have big news. Lizzie is in labor as we speak. You're expected at the North Country Medical Center."

Grace clapped her hands. “Oh, my God! Is Russ there? And what about my Dad?”

“I don’t know. But I have a limo waiting—”

“You can take the limo, Manny,” Ty said. “I’ll take Grace myself in the Hummer.” He grabbed her by the hand and maneuvered around the camera stand. “Let’s go have a baby,” he mumbled and kissed her on the cheek.

## Chapter Nineteen

Grace leaned out the window of the idling Hummer and stared at the parking lot gridlock in front of her. "Jeez, did every pregnant woman in upstate New York go into labor today? This place is packed."

"Can you get back in the car, please? You hanging out the window like that makes me nervous."

"You know, if this car wasn't so huge we could drive up on the sidewalk and sneak around to the parking garage."

"Even if I was driving a golf cart, it wouldn't make a difference," Ty growled, checking his watch. "It's going to take me longer to dump the car than it did to get here in the first place."

"Well, in that case, let me off here." Grace pointed to a snow-decorated Labor and Delivery sign in front of them. "I'll jump over the snowbank to the door."

"Are you crazy? No way. Not in your condition."

"How much coordination does it require to put one foot in front of the other over a little pile of snow?"

"I'd rather not have you in a position to find out."

"I'll be careful." She shoved the door open with her foot and slid down to the wet pavement. With a few careful steps, and one or two curses, she made her way through the snow and into the delivery ward entrance.

"Grace Ann! We're down here!"

Russ stood at the other end of the hall. He met her halfway and scooped her up in a hug. "Oh, man, Grace, we're so glad you made it!" He giggled like a child as he swung her around in a circle. "You have to see her!"

"Lizzie?"

"No, the baby."

Grace planted her hands on his shoulders and looked him in the eyes. "Wait a minute. Her? You mean it's a girl?"

"And she's beautiful," he said. "It was incredible. I can't believe I'm a father."

"And I can't believe I missed it. When did it happen?"

"About a half hour ago."

Grace spied the closed door at the end of the hall and broke into a jog. She slowed to a walk when she was close enough to read the sign on the door. Written in pink calligraphy were the words "Baby Girl Haines." It also listed her size and time of birth. Grace ran her hand over it and swallowed. "Oh, my God. I have a niece."

"You sure do," Russ gushed.

"I have to go in and see them."

"Grace, wait a minute." He gestured for her to take a step back. "I just want to warn you. Your father is lurking somewhere around here. I know you guys had an awful night last night." Russ stared at his feet and shrugged. "I think he's in trouble with the Archbishop."

"There you guys are!" Ty called, from behind her. "I dumped the car about a mile from here. Did I miss the main event?"

Grace shrugged. "Actually, it looks like we both did."

He slipped one hand over her shoulder and extended the other to a scowling Russ. "So I guess congratulations are in order."

"I suppose I should say the same to you."

"They have a little girl, Ty," Grace said quickly. "Isn't that wonderful?"

"It is wonderful. I just wish we could have gotten here sooner."

"Yeah, I'm sure you were keeping my sister-in-law very busy."

Ty bristled against her as she stood between the two men. It would be easy to rely on old habits and let Ty do the fast talking for both of them, but she wasn't interested in that anymore. Cleaning up her own messes was the ultimate form of control, she discovered. And mending fences between Ty and her brother-in-law was a good place to start. "Listen, you two, I know you guys have had run-ins in the past, but can we cut the male posturing and get over it?"

"You got her fighting your battles now, huh, Hawthorne?"

"There is no battle, Russ!" She pushed away from Ty and took Russ by the hand. "Look, I appreciate how you and Lizzie both have looked after me. But the best thing you can do for me now is to call a truce. If I can move past everything that's happened, you can, too." Her fingers slipped over Russ's as she stepped back towards the door. "Now, why don't you two get a cup of coffee or something?"

Grace knocked softly on the door before slipping inside. She waited a moment, then barreled in without waiting longer for an answer. She was surprised to see her sister out of bed and hovering over a bassinette.

"You up for a visitor?"

Lizzie smiled. "If it's any consolation, I tried to hold her in until you got here."

Grace covered her mouth as she approached the bassinette. "Oh, my gosh. She's so small."

"She didn't feel so small when I was pushing her out."

"I'm sorry I missed this," Grace said, hugging her sister. "I know we planned on me being here."

"I know, but I'm glad Russ was."

"That's nice. You all were together as a family." Grace looked up at her sister, who looked remarkably well for having just given birth. She was still in a hospital nightgown, but her hair was brushed and neatly pulled back, and she even had applied a little lip gloss. She reached in the bassinette and touched her fingertip to the baby's cheek. "I can't believe I have a niece. I'm so excited!"

"I bet. And just think—in nine months maybe you'll return the favor." Lizzie brushed a hair from Grace's face. "I didn't get to see you after what happened last night. Congratulations."

"Thanks."

"How's Ty handling it?"

"He's thrilled. But he's not actually the man I'm worried about." Grace glanced behind her, making sure the door was shut. "Listen, I know you've all been a little preoccupied, and I hate to focus on my drama, but I don't suppose Dad has said anything to you?"

Lizzie pulled the hat down over the baby's ears and sat down on the bed. "He saw the interview, Grace."

She bit her lip. "The whole thing?"

"Yeah. We all did. Along with the rest of the world. You really spilled your guts."

"I know. But it was something I needed to do. I can't help it if Dad is angry."

Lizzie patted the mattress beside her, and Grace took the cue to sit. "Look, Gracie, you know how much I love you, and I know the struggles you've gone through. After last night, Dad was pretty worried about you."

"It looked to me like he was pretty angry."

Lizzie shrugged. "Okay, maybe a little of both. I

know Dad's tough. But after the interview today, he seemed different. Softer."

"Maybe becoming a grandparent has mellowed him."

"Maybe. But I speak for all of us when I say that we only want the best for you. Dad loves you."

The baby whimpered in her bassinette, and little arms and legs freed themselves from the tight wrap. Lizzie moved to go to her, but Grace beat her to the punch. "No way! Auntie wants a chance to hold her niece."

"Great. While you're at it, you can change her diaper."

"No problem. I could use the practice."

"Do you think your old Dad could help you, Gracie?" The two girls looked up at the man in the doorway. He held a pink teddy bear and a bouquet of flowers. "I brought a few things. I hope you don't mind." Planting a kiss on Lizzie's cheek, he placed his goodies on the bedside table. "So, I see your sister made it. You must have hightailed it from the city. You were just on television an hour and a half ago."

"I'm sorry I missed the birth. We got here as fast as we could."

"We," he said, like a declaration. "You must mean Hawthorne."

"I think I feel like brushing my teeth," Lizzie said and slid off the bed. "Why don't you two chat?" The door closed behind Lizzie, and Grace scooped up the whimpering child, more for comforting herself than the baby.

Langley paced across the room and stopped in front of the window. "So, you had a pretty dramatic night last night. And you pulled yourself together today for an interview on national television." He turned around to face her. "That's impressive."

"Thank you."

"You know your mother used to watch *The Olivia Show* all the time. She called her the Hollywood Mother Teresa. I guess she helps a lot of people through charity and what not."

"She's big into that."

"I was thinking that maybe today you might have helped some people. I mean, by telling your story and about your faith, and your capacity to forgive."

Grace smiled at the thought. "You think?"

"Well, you helped me." He sat down beside her on the bed. "You reminded me of the importance of forgiveness, and how a person like me is better off leaving the judging in God's hands." He lowered his gaze to the floor. "I didn't know you knew I told the doctors to deliver the baby. And I never told you because I didn't want you to blame me."

"I know, Daddy, and I do understand." Grace looked at her father. He didn't seem the rigid, emotionless man she was used to. He was gentler, his voice deeper, and when he looked at her he almost smiled.

"If I've been hard on you, Gracie, it's because I love you, and I worry about you. And I had good reason to worry. You were very sick for a long time."

"But I'm better now. And I know you think Ty is to blame for a lot of things."

"I blamed him because he was convenient. I realize that now. And when I watched that interview, I was prepared to hate him. But God help me, all I could see was love in his eyes."

"He does love me. And I love him, and I know that me being pregnant and not married embarrasses you."

"I already talked to the Archdiocese. They're reviewing the situation, but given my history of service, I think they might work around it. They even mentioned a new project in Mexico. I know it's more travel, but we go where God takes us." He reached for the baby and brought her against him. "The most important thing to me, though, is that you're okay. A chance to bring a new life into the world is the biggest gift the Lord can bestow."

She watched her father cuddle the child, planting a kiss on her hat-covered head. At that moment she did feel blessed. A second chance at love, at happiness, at motherhood. She ran her hand over her belly and rested her head on her father's shoulder. "Thank you, Daddy."

****

"So what are you going to say to him?"

Ty brought the plastic cup of black sludge to his lips. He'd been rehearsing a bunch of monologues in the half hour he'd been sitting outside Lizzie's room. None were working for him. "I don't know," he said with a groan. "Whatever it takes, I guess."

"I suppose this is as good a time as any to invoke your acting talents."

"Nothing to act, man. I love the girl."

Russ patted him on the shoulder. "Right answer."

Ty stood up when the door in front of them opened. Deacon Langley emerged with a smile, but when he saw Ty, it slowly faded. "There you are, Russ," Langley said. "I was wondering where you went."

"I thought I'd get a cup of coffee and let you visit with the girls."

Langley nodded, then glanced at Ty. "Well how about you get another one, while Ty and I chat."

The two men stared at each other under the fluorescent lights. Buzzers and bells sounded in Ty's ears, and his nose stung with the scent of antiseptic. He had played this scene before. In a hospital like this, in a hall like this, a half a decade ago. This time, however, he'd play it differently, with different words and different direction. This time it would turn out right. "Look, Deacon, I wanted to apologize about last night. I know that was quite a scene."

"Hold it, Hawthorne." Langley held out his hand. "I have a few things I'd like to say to you, too."

Langley nodded to the door next to Lizzie's, and Ty followed him into the empty room. Dusk had settled and the place was dark, but neither made a move to turn on a light. Ty took a deep breath. The sweat pooled on the small of his back, and the hair stood up on his neck.

"I think I owe you a 'thank you,'" Langley said.

"For what? Getting your daughter pregnant?"

The man chuckled and shook his head. "That's not what I meant, but in a way I guess I'm grateful for that. Being a grandfather is a wonderful thing. As is being a father. You don't strike me as someone who would know anything about that. "

Ty folded his arms against him and raised his chin. If this was the Deacon's way to urge him to bow out, it wasn't working. "If you think you can come between Grace and me again, that's not going to happen. I'm not leaving her. Not this time."

"And I don't want you to." He took a step toward him, straightening the cuffs on his raincoat. "I saw that interview today, and I realized that maybe I never gave you enough credit."

"You don't give your daughter enough credit."

"Maybe so, but you can't blame me for trying to protect her. That's why I'd like to offer you my gratitude. You seem to share the same concern for her as I do, and I appreciate that."

Ty swallowed, letting the words settle around him before he opened his own mouth. "Jordan, you need to know a few things, too. First of all, I'm not saying that I'm a saint, but there was no woman in my hotel suite the night you came to see me. Those things you found were Grace's."

Langley cringed. “I realize that now.”

“And second, I don’t plan on going anywhere. I don’t know if she’ll have me, but I’m asking Grace to marry me.”

Ty braced himself for protest, but none came. Langley simply nodded and pulled his gloves from his jacket pocket.

“Then you have to understand something, too, Hawthorne. The decision I made when Grace was in the hospital was made out of love, not hate. If someone told you that your child would certainly die, but you could somehow prevent that, well, there really wasn’t anything to decide in the first place, was there?”

Ty nodded. He did understand. He also knew that this time things would be different. “Look, I can’t guarantee she’ll have a quiet life, but I’ll make sure it will be a happy one.”

“Don’t tell me. It’s her decision.” He slipped his glove on his left hand, but stopped short with the right. He extended it to Ty. “Peace?”

Ty looked at it a moment before looking Langley in the face. Slowly he unfolded his arms and placed his hand in his. “Peace,” he mumbled, with a small but solid shake.

“Well, I have to head home,” Jordan said. “The Inn employs a small staff of parishioners to help in a pinch, but they could use an extra set of hands. Give my best to Grace?”

“Of course.” Ty stood stunned as the Deacon headed out the door. He’d expected a showdown or at least a long-winded scene in which he would have to bite his tongue and plead his case all at once. But instead he was offered an olive branch. Maybe the Deacon practiced what he preached after all.

He opened the door and shuffled into the hall. It was deserted now, and the artificial lights had softened for night time. The only sounds were the hum of chatter from the nurse's station and the muffled cries of newborn babies echoing from the nursery at the other end of the hall.

The door to Lizzie's room stood open a crack, just enough to see inside. Lizzie slept, while Grace sat in the rocking chair by the window. The baby was in her arms, and, if he had to guess, he'd say she'd probably been there for a while.

He stood there a moment, marveling at the love in Grace's eyes as she gazed at the tiny child. She was a natural mother. Caring, selfless. A woman who was exactly what her name implied. He realized she was never the one who needed him. Her illness, her travails—she would have come through just fine if he had never been there. She was the one who rescued him, all one hundred and two pounds of her. From the uncertainty of his life, and the hollowness of his existence. Without her, he'd be nothing.

She was his Grace.

"How long have you been standing there?"

Ty pushed himself off the doorframe and came into the room. "Not long. I didn't want to wake Lizzie or the baby."

"I don't think you have to worry about either one. They both sleep like rocks."

He crossed the shadowed room and slipped his hand over her shoulder. The baby breathed deeply, her little pink lips parted. The paleness of her skin against the newborn blush reminded him of peaches and cream.

"She has red hair, you know."

"Hmm?"

"Red hair," Grace repeated, and gently pushed the tiny hat aside to show him. "She's beautiful, isn't she?

"She's your niece. I guess she'd have to be."

For the first time, Grace turned away from the baby and smiled at Ty. "Where have you been?"

"I went to get a cup of coffee, and I had a talk with your father."

"God, he didn't make a scene, did he?"

"No," Ty said and chuckled. "But I sort of did."

"Goodness, Tyler, do I have to hear this, or can I just read the account in tomorrow's Page Six of *The Times*?"

"No, it's not like that. We talked about a few things, and I think everything is going to work out okay." He ran his hands over her hair. "I was proud of you this morning in the interview, by the way. That took a lot of guts."

"I want things to be different this time. I want us to be happy and have a healthy baby. The stress of hiding everything was too much."

He understood exactly what she meant. He pulled up a chair and sat down in front of her. "May I?" He held out his hands for the baby.

"Tyler, she's sleeping."

"It's not fair to hog her. Besides I need the practice, right? Let me hold the baby, Grace."

She rolled her eyes then eased the blanket into his arms. "Be careful of her head."

The baby stirred, then relaxed with a deep breath. Ty smiled. Man, did he want this more than anything. Grace was right about keeping secrets and holding back. It was time to tell her the whole truth.

"I knew what your father did, Gracie." The sound of his own voice echoed in his ears. He bit his lip and stared down at the sleeping child, too afraid to look anywhere else.

"What?"

His heart pounded, and his throat constricted to a lump. "I didn't tell you I knew you had the baby, because I thought you'd be angry at me for letting it happen."

"I don't understand," she said. "What are you telling me?"

Afraid his limbs would no longer be trustworthy, he stood up and eased the baby into the bassinette.

This was it.

The last secret.

The last obstacle that stood between them and the truth.

"I know you thought I left because I was angry or disappointed in you, and at the time I thought it was better that way. You would hate me, and I was okay with that because I figured I had caused you enough grief. You had your family to take care of you."

He looked down at the sleeping child and tucked the blanket tighter around her. Tears pooled in his eyes. Five years before, he had stood in a room much like this one, staring down at a little creature who looked a lot like the one he stared down at now. "Jamie had red hair, too," he whispered. "Just like her mother."

In the light from the hospital hallway, he saw the tears reflected in her eyes. She covered her mouth with a trembling hand. "Oh, my God, you saw her."

"I bribed a nurse." He dragged a finger across his damp cheek. "She gave me a slip of paper with her name and a piece of her hair in an envelope. I've carried it with me ever since."

He pulled his wallet from his back pocket and pulled out the yellowed paper. Carefully, he unfolded it in front of her. It read "Jamie Grace Hawthorne, April 10" and stuck in between the wrinkles were the finest strands of red hair.

"Oh, my God."

"Baby, in my heart I never left you. I knew it, Layla knew it, and now you do, too."

"Your tattoo." She pulled up the sleeve on his arm. "That's not from some movie. That's us."

"I didn't mean to lie to you about it. I just

figured you'd never see it." He brought her in close, resting his cheek on the top of her head.

"I never gave up on you, Tyler. There were times I wanted to and needed to. But I couldn't."

It occurred to him that he was the one who had given up on himself. No one, not fame, money, or material trappings could pull him from the grips of despair. It was the Herculean strength of this tiny woman's love that had redeemed him.

"I told your father I wanted to marry you."

"You did?" She raised her brows and looked at him. "That was gutsy."

"Safest place to do it. I figured if he came after me with a shotgun, the emergency room was close by."

"Maybe it was good to catch him now. He's so excited about being a grandfather. What about you?"

Ty looked down at her. "What about me what?"

"Are you excited? I know this came out of nowhere. And if this affects your career—"

"Who cares about my career, Grace Ann?" He brushed his hand over her cheek. "If there was ever a role I wanted to play, this is it."

"I was hoping you'd say that."

"I want to get married right away. I was thinking Christmas, if you aren't too busy."

"Tyler, if this is a proposal, the one we scripted in front of a camera was better than this."

"Okay, then, how about I start over and begin by telling you how much I love you?"

"That's better."

"And what if I told you, I can't wait for you to have our baby, and I intend to take care of you and our family for as long as I live."

"Keep going."

"And I want to marry you as soon as possible."

She nodded her head, as if assessing his performance.

"Very nice, Hawthorne. Well paced, very heartfelt. I especially like the little tremor in your voice and the tears in your eyes."

"So what's it going to be, Lexie Love? Yes or no?"

"Yes!" she blurted and wrapped her hands around his neck. "Now hurry up and kiss me."

## Epilogue

Ty awoke to the muffled sound of his newborn son's cry and the shift of the mattress as his wife attempted to answer it. "Hey, what are you doing?" he whispered. "You promised me you'd let the nurse take care of the baby overnight."

"But he's crying."

"If you were in the hospital like you should be, the baby would be in the nursery, and you wouldn't even know he was crying in the first place. Now come on, you gave birth an hour ago, and the nurses have to check him out before they let you have him back, anyway." He wrapped his arms gently around her and eased her back onto the pillow. "You know, you promised me if you had the baby here at the farmhouse you'd rest more."

"I feel fine. I'm just a little sore. Pushing out your nine-pound son was a lot more painful than I bargained for."

"I noticed. I think you fractured my hand."

"Sorry about that." She looked up at Ty and smiled. "I also find it fitting that your namesake chose to make his debut in the wee small hours of the morning. He must be a night person like his dad."

"We can only hope. Can I get anything for you? Something to drink, eat?"

"No, just you." She pulled his arm around her, but when he grazed her breast she winced.

"They hurt, huh?"

"They're just full already."

"You want me to ask the nurse for some pain

relievers?"

"No!" she said. "I don't want anything to get in the milk for the baby."

He felt helpless and hated it. "Are you sure there isn't anything I can do?"

After a moment she rolled over and brought her hand to his cheek. "Honey, I know you want to help, and believe me I want you to. But at this moment I'm perfectly content with being right here in your arms. That's all I ask."

When she lay back down, she moaned. He could tell the pain was a lot worse than she let on. "How about a shower?" he asked.

"I'm too tired to take a shower."

"Who says you have to do anything?" Gently he slipped his arms under her and scooped her off the bed. Instead of protesting, she snuggled against him, letting him carry her to the bathroom.

"You know, I'm not sure I'm comfortable with you as my nurse."

"Hey, let me remind you I have played a doctor twice in my illustrious career."

She looked up at him with a wrinkled brow. "A coroner and a veterinarian."

"Oh, and I thought you didn't watch my movies." He maneuvered the shower knobs until the water felt suitably warmed. He set her down on the tile, her feet adjusting like a newborn doe.

He loved how she felt against him. The fullness of her body and the pride he felt for the duty it had performed. Grace Ann was the mother of his child, and that alone made him want to worship her. "You feel better?"

"Uh-huh," she muttered, and he felt the tension ease. He took the bar of soap and stroked it over her, then went for the bottle of lilac shampoo. "So, the doctor said six weeks, right?"

He felt her smile against his chest. "Yes, and I

trust you'll behave for that long."

"I'm not worried about me. It might drive you crazy, though."

She punched him playfully, and he kissed the top of her wet head.

"You know," Ty said, "I meant to tell you. Now that the baby is born, I was thinking that I should probably think about getting back to work. I was talking with a few people about a new project."

"Oh, yeah?"

"Yes, well, it's sort of a sequel, or I guess a new movie with old characters. Problem is, I'm not sure if the other actor wants to reprise the role."

"What's the problem? They have other commitments?"

He rinsed the conditioner from her hair and wiped the remnants from her cheeks. "You could say that. Anyway, the producer thinks maybe the other actor could be talked into doing it, and suggested I take a shot."

"Well, I suppose if it's a good role, and the script is acceptable. You can be very persuasive."

"I was hoping you'd say that." He took her face in his hands. "What do you say, Lexie Love? Wanna be my costar?"

Spray from the shower stuck to her lashes. She was pale, but her eyes were bright and her pink lips formed a smile. "Honey, I don't know. I just had a baby, and I have this place to run."

"Four-month shoot right here in New York. No travel. The baby stays here, and so do we. I already talked to Lizzie. She's willing to help with babysitting."

"Ty, Lizzie already has Emily to worry about."

"And Manny is also really excited about it. I think he thinks that a small baby is much easier to look after than a big one."

"I'm curious about that myself."

"Gracie, everything is all worked out. Just say the word."

When she stumbled, he caught her and swung her back into his arms. "Maybe we should get you back to bed, darlin'." He turned off the water and wrapped her in a towel. With patient hands, he dressed her and dried her hair before tucking her back under the sheets.

"You spoil me," she mumbled.

"That's the idea."

He slid in next to her, stroking her arm to relax them both. "I'm right here," he whispered in her ear, but realized the words were meant more for himself. He laced his fingers in her damp hair as if anchoring himself to what was his. "I'm not going anywhere, Grace Ann. Never."

As he drifted, he realized he never really had. He had always been there, hidden in her heart, belonging to her, and only her. And now he was finally home.

**Other Champagne titles you might enjoy:**

HOW MUCH YOU WANT TO BET? by Melissa Blue. Neil never thought a game of pool could change the course of her life, but against Gib she may lose both the game and her heart.

CATASTROPHE by Sharon Buchbinder. Cats! Twenty-three! Being evicted! Their handsome neighbor doesn't want to lose their curly-haired, curvaceous owner. So what's the rescue plan?

HIBISCUS BAY by Debby Allen. Picture love on a sun-drenched white sand beach surrounded by hibiscus-covered cliffs, with your yacht anchored in a blue Mediterranean Sea.

TASMANIAN RAINBOW by Pinkie Paranya. A concert violinist grapples with remote ranch life, intrigue and the mystery of a missing diary, the peril of a flood in which all could be lost, and the undeniable attraction of the man who would do anything to protect his son.

THREE'S THE CHARM by Ellen Dye. Rachel vowed never to speak to her ex-husb[illegible] again. When her beloved horse needs a vet and Hea[illegible] the only one within three counties of West Virgini[illegible]untains, some vows need to be broken.

SEE MEGAN RUN by Melissa Blue. City-succes[illegible] Megan goes home to the boonies to save her childhood home but finds she must not only agree to stay for her mother's wedding but also deal with the man she left when she hitchhiked out 12 years ago.

A MOTHER'S HEART by Misty Simon. Carrie wants a simple life. Helping Gran with the animal shelter is complication enough. When the new neighbor and his two kids come in to adopt a dog, Carrie's life goes out of control.

SECRETS OF SEBASTIAN BEAUMONT by Pinkie Paranya. Love and suspense on an exotic South American vanilla plantation.

Breinigsville, PA USA
30 September 2010
246427BV00002B/10/P